Queens Ransom

The latest Sofie Metropolis mystery . . .
Christmas. A kidnapping, Jake Porter
and a stray reindeer, oh my!

Sofie's mother tells her it is the season for miracles, but Sofie's convinced it's more of a season for whackos and flashing Santas. After nearly losing a battle with the local strange vampire a month ago, she regrets ever having bitched about boring cheating spouse cases and process serving. She's ready for a quiet spell doing nothing but finding people's lost pets. But Sofie's life will probably never be boring again. After all, kidnapping is never boring. Especially when it's Sofie who's being kidnapped.

Queens Ransom

A Sofie Metropolis Novel

Tori Carrington

Severn House Large Print
London & New York

This first large print edition published 2013
in Great Britain and the USA by
SEVERN HOUSE PUBLISHERS LTD of
19 Cedar Road, Sutton, Surrey, England, SM2 5DA.
First world regular print edition published 2012 by
Severn House Publishers Ltd., London and New York.

British Library Cataloguing in Publication Data

Carrington, Tori author.
  Queens ransom. -- Large print edition. -- (A Sofie
Metropolis mystery ; 6)
  1. Metropolis, Sofie (Fictitious character)--Fiction.
  2. Women private investigators--Fiction. 3. Detective and
mystery stories. 4. Large type books.
  I. Title II. Series
  813.6-dc23

ISBN-13: 978-0-7278-9634-6

Severn House Publishers support The Forest Stewardship Council
[FSC], the leading international forest certification organisation. All
our titles that are printed on Greenpeace-approved FSC-certified paper
carry the FSC logo.

MIX
Paper from
responsible sources
FSC® C018575
www.fsc.org

Printed and bound in Great Britain by the
MPG Books Group, Bodmin, Cornwall.

As always, for Tony and Tim.

Acknowledgements

'It ain't easy being Greek.' Yes, I admit shamelessly borrowing this quote from Kermit the Frog and editing it for my purposes; it helps keep certain aspects of real life and fiction in focus, especially when it comes to this sixth installment of Sofie Metropolis' adventures. Tradition plays such a large role in life, and is especially true in Greek-American households. There are nice traditions ... and not so nice ones. In the case of the former, dancing and plate breaking come to mind. The latter? Well, let's just say in *Queens Ransom*, Sofie doesn't get much opportunity to indulge in yummy Greek food. Well, unless you consider boiled potatoes, lentils and fava beans yummy. Gasp! I know, right? Curious why? Turn the page!

Of course, sons Tony and Tim are lucky they really haven't had to endure Sofie's dietary trials. But they are an endless source for love and laughter, both very American but incapable of denying their Greek heritage, often much to their own exasperation. And with the birth of lovely Layla, Tony's first child with lovely Raegan Searing, life's cycle and family tradition continues. Looking forward to spoiling her rotten in all ways Greek and American!

Agent extraordinaire Robert Gottlieb has been by Sofie's side since the beginning and deserves a special nod. Along with everyone else who works behind the scenes at Trident Media Group, including Adrienne Lombardo and Mark Gottlieb: thank you for covering the business angle with brilliant aplomb so the creative end might flourish.

Publishers Edwin Buckhalter, Rachel Simpson Hutchens and Michelle Duff of Severn House are wonderfully supportive partners-in-crime and deserving of utmost appreciation.

To Patricia Longenberger, Sabrina Schlachter, Charlie and Jaelynn for turning up the music when it goes silent, understanding that deadline isn't just a word in a book, and for providing copious amounts of 'zombie' love!

And last, but by no means least, heartfelt gratitude goes to the entire Sobczak family – including little Cameron – for bringing warmth and sunshine on cloudy days and reigniting life's pilot light. And special friends Noreen Fitch, Alexandera Guerrero, Kenneth Guerrero, Angela Zink, Xenios and all the gang at Good Times Restaurant & Grill.

Here's to honoring old traditions ... and creating new!

One

Tis the season to be jolly, fa-la-la-la-la-la, la-la-la...

Fuck.

Yeah, that about summed up my feelings on the matter.

Whoever penned the annual holiday ditty? I guess they hated winter as much as I did. Probably the writer was trying to make himself feel better through the power of suggestion. Me...? Well, I find absolutely nothing jolly about two feet of heavy snow, wind that stretched spiny fingers under umpteen layers of clothing to squeeze the air out of my lungs, and store sales that might result in the loss of a limb if you happened to be interested in an item an animalistic fellow shopper also happened to have her eye on.

Of course, it didn't help that I hadn't had a decent meal in two weeks.

It's a Greek thing.

Oh, I know most if not all Christian religions observe advent. It's just ... well, let's just say the Greeks aren't known as the birthers of drama for nothing. Pre-holiday fasting was not merely a religious tradition; it was an all out experience.

And my mom, Thalia, adhered to it as tightly as hot wax applied to certain delicate areas come bikini time. Which meant instead of tucking away plastic containers of yummy Greek food whenever I visited my parents' a couple of blocks up from my Astoria, Queens apartment, I instead was presented with a plate bearing nothing more than a boiled potato sparsely drizzled with olive oil and sprinkled with salt and pepper.

'Woman cannot live on tasteless potatoes alone,' I'd muttered yesterday, and received a Thalia cuff to the back of the head for my efforts.

Now I stood in front of my bedroom mirror admiring my new shoulder holster and distracting myself from the simple fact that I could easily remedy my limited menu by going to the grocery store. But as much as I bitched and moaned ... well, traditions were traditions and even I followed them. For the most part. If I'd stopped at the Chirping Chicken last night on my way home for some much-needed comfort food, then that was between me and the chatty Asian cashier.

Of course, it didn't help Thalia somehow always knew when I cheated. Revoke my bad girl card, but I, Sofie Metropolis – PI by trade, good Greek daughter by life – was utterly incapable of lying to my mother, even when I did lie.

Well, most of the time.

I withdrew my 9mm Glock and waved it at my

reflection in the bedroom mirror.

'You talking to me...? You...? Me...? You...?' My pathetic Robert De Niro *Taxi Driver* imitation was doing nothing to boost my own idea of bad girl me.

Probably because no matter how much I'd like to think of myself as bad, I really was a good Greek girl at heart and probably always would be.

Which absolutely sucked dead canaries.

As for the gun itself and my handling of it, let's just say my recent wielding experiences wouldn't exactly be landing me on any Marksman Today magazine covers anytime soon. While I now made a point of carrying it everywhere – including my parents', which resulted in my having to fish it out of the trash can draped in spinach on more than one occasion – my last scary encounter ... well, I'm sorry to say the firearm helped me not at all. Not because it hadn't been loaded or I hadn't been prepared to use it. No. Rather, bullets were completely useless when it came to certain blood-draining creatures of the night.

And I wasn't talking bats. Not entirely, anyway.

Still, despite my midnight standoff with the neighborhood vampire Ivan Romanoff's creepy nephew, Vladimir, I was determined to return to my stance that there was no such thing as vampires.

A side note: I wasn't having much luck.

Muffy the Mutt came into the bedroom and

plopped his furry bottom on the floor next to my feet. I looked down at the Jack Russell terrier; he whined and tilted his head to the side, his tongue lolling out of the side of his mouth.

'What?' I asked. 'There aren't any such thing as vampires.'

My response indicated that the dog – that had been my first-found pet of what had become a now regular pet-detecting part of my job – could read my mind. Which, of course, he could not.

He gave a sneeze and stared up at me as if to say, 'Yeah, right.'

'By the way, just so you know, you're not coming with me tonight.'

He gave a low growl.

I growled back.

OK, so I was coming to understand he felt the same about winter as I did. Probably more so because I didn't have to go outside in the snow in my bare feet the way he had to. I also didn't have to climb the slippery fire escape to the roof to do my business in the icy wind coming off the East River, either. The same wind that found the window I usually left open for him closed most of the time, Thalia's words ringing in my ears: 'What, are you trying to heat the whole of New York? Or will Astoria do?'

Astoria. Manhattan's less sophisticated younger sister that had onetime been referred to as the bedroom of New York City, but was now more about young couples raising their young families. I'd grown up here, and liked that the borough maintained much of its ethnic Greek flavor even though most of the Greeks themselves had already used the money they'd made and moved to the Long Island suburbs.

I asked my father why he and my mother hadn't fled. He'd merely looked at me and wondered aloud, 'And do what? Grow flowers? You can get plenty from the corner fruit stand.'

He had a point. One of my many uncles had relocated and had begun flower growing as a summer pastime, and then erected a greenhouse so he could do it in the winter, too.

He and my father had nothing in common anymore and within five minutes of finding themselves anywhere near each other, they both catapulted in the opposite direction.

The fact that my dad was still actively involved in the steakhouse he owned on Broadway might also have something to do with it. My mother once remarked that despite all intentions to the contrary, she'd ended up marrying her own father and that *my* father would probably never retire.

I would strongly advise no one tell my maternal grandfather how similar he was to my father. Grandpa Kosmos – or, the more affectionate Greek, *Pappou* – and my father had long ago agreed to disagree and if they had any speaking to each other to do, they usually did so through my mother. And if she didn't happen to be handy? Any available family member would do.

Family member? I'd seen them do it with the mail carrier, so let me revise that to say 'human'.

If there wasn't anyone else around? They didn't speak. Period.

Conversations around the dinner table usually included this:

'Tell what's-his-face to pass the potatoes, would you?'

'Ask the old man on the other side of the table if he plans to do anything with that newspaper he stole from me this morning.'

That was usually the extent of their interaction. Well, beyond my grandfather emptying the contents of whatever food platter happened to be in front of him and my mother silently taking most of it back on and handing the platter to my father, who sometimes passed as if the food had been somehow contaminated, resulting in a triumphant smirk from my grandfather.

Thalia didn't complain too much about their juvenile behavior. I guessed because she was glad they were sitting at the same table at all.

My younger sister, Efi, on the other hand, usually ignored them both when they tried to enlist her as intermediary while my younger brother – also Kosmos – had an uncanny way of anticipating what either of them wanted and gave it to them before they had a chance to finish the first smart-ass word in their sentence.

I wouldn't be seeing any of them tonight, at any rate. No, I was due to pick up my mother in...

Shit! Was that the time?

I was late.

Again.

I holstered my Glock, nearly tripping over Muffy on my way to grab my coat and purse.

He followed.

'Sorry, pal, but I already said you've got to stay here.' I shrugged into my coat. 'I'm going to a *saranta*.'

Merely saying the word made me shudder.

'Trust me, you don't want to go. Absolutely no fun at all. And the food sucks.'

That seemed to be the clincher. He gave a heavy sigh and then jumped up on to his BarcaLounger, did his round and round bit, then finally lay down and stared at me through reproachful eyes.

I stuck my tongue out at him, grabbed my keys and headed through the door, somewhat surprised Thalia hadn't called at least five times already. I checked my cell as I locked up. Ooops, turned out she had. I'd put the ringer on silent while I was at the office earlier, office assistant Rosie Rodriguez's foul mood not one you wanted to mess with.

Forget tempting the Fates; it was Rosie Rodriguez you needed to watch out for. The Puerto Rican dynamo was a force to be reckoned with when she was either a) on her period, or b) pining away over a guy who had broken her heart three months ago.

The door across the hall from mine opened.

Speaking of the guy who had dumped Rosie on her heart, his nice, Jewish grandmother, Mrs Nebitz, was about to make me a few minutes later than I already was.

15

'Evening, Sofie. You're looking pretty tonight.'

'Hi, Mrs Nebitz. How are you?'

'Fine. Outside my arthritis and trick knee, I'm just fine, Sofie. Thanks for asking.'

Mrs Nebitz looked like everyone's idea of a grandmother. So much so, I was convinced it was her picture on a brand of chocolate-chip cookies claiming to be homemade. But you didn't want to mistake her for a soft touch; she could be as rigid as a tire iron when the occasion called for it. Like when rent for the other two 'legal' apartments in the building came due. I'd proven myself a completely incompetent owner when it came to collecting, caving under any excuse short of 'the money fell into the toilet and I'm air drying it now...' from the three Drake Business School students in Two-B, and Etta Munson and her Evil Child from Hell, Lola, in Two-A.

Mrs Nebitz had no problem whatsoever. I was convinced she enjoyed it, even. Claimed it gave her a little something to do.

If I noticed the way she gripped her favorite cane a little tighter when she said that, I wasn't saying.

It helped that her efforts more than made up for the fact that she was paying pretty much the same rent she had fifty years ago when she and her late, God-rest-his-soul husband first started renting the place due to New York City's strict rent-control laws.

'I was wondering if I could ask a favor of

16

you,' Mrs Nebitz said now. 'Nothing big, mind you. Shouldn't cause you too much trouble.'

'Sure,' I said. 'What do you need?'

'I have a bit of a leak in the kitchen sink, you see. Nothing major. Just a slow drip-drip, is all.'

'I'll call the plumber first thing in the morning.'

'Oh, no need to go to all that trouble. I'm sure it's something simple. Thinking my grandson Seth can take care of it.'

Ah, Heartbreak Seth. The hottie who had given Rosie's heart a good stomp.

I said, 'OK then. If he can't fix it, let me know and I'll give that plumber a ring.'

'Sure. Good then.'

I started to move toward the stairs, but something told me that wasn't the real reason Mrs Nebitz had stopped me when she heard my door open. 'Is there anything else?'

'What? Oh, no no. Of course not. You go on now. You obviously have plans. I wouldn't want to keep you.'

Yeah, I had plans: plans I wished I didn't have.

I leaned against the wall. 'I have all the time in the world, Mrs Nebitz. Please, share...'

'You're late.'

Two innocuous words, really ... had they been uttered by anyone other than my mother, Thalia Metropolis. As it was, I was pretty sure my face bore her handprint without her having touched me.

She closed the passenger door of my 1965 Mustang Lucille, but not tightly. I directed her to

17

try again.

'I don't know why you don't get a better car. Something newer. Your dad would probably give you the Caprice and get a new one if you said you wanted it.'

'Yeah, well, I don't want it.'

If I thought Lucille was a gas hog, the Caprice? The idea of keeping it filled considering the amount of running around I did was enough to make me itch.

I pulled away from the curb, the old car rocking over the deep ruts made in the tightly packed snow that was more ice now. It was after dark already and Christmas lights bled with street- and headlights, making it look like day. Almost.

My mother. As far as parents went, I supposed I could have done worse. Much worse. While she made a habit out of calling me every hour on the hour, and her top goal appeared to be marrying me off to the closest available Greek no matter how hideous, she'd done well by me and my younger brother, Kosmos, and baby sister, Efi. And, when it wasn't advent, she usually kept me very well supplied with yummy Greek food, despite my having lived on my own for nine months now.

Saying that, I could do without her treating my career choice as nothing more than a passing phase unless it personally served her, and would prefer she not guilt me into attending events like the one tonight.

And could have totally done without her asking me to investigate my father's possible

18

infidelity months back.

Thankfully, he had been arranging a surprise anniversary party with my mother's best friend and hadn't been boinking her, as even I had feared he was.

'So, what kept you?' Thalia wanted to know.

'Mrs Nebitz has a leak.'

'Uh oh. You call the plumber?'

'No. She's going to have her grandson look into it.'

'I'd call the plumber.'

'Yeah, I'm thinking the same thing. I'm going to call him in the morning.'

She moved in a way that communicated her disapproval.

'I didn't want to be any later than I already was.'

Liar.

Of course, I wasn't about to tell her I'd purposely made time for Mrs Nebitz because I wasn't looking forward to going to this ... thing.

You see, a *saranta* was the marking of the fortieth day of someone's passing. The Greek word, itself, literally translated into forty. Problem was, the person being remembered tonight hadn't been family or even a friend. He'd been the only son of one of my mother's acquaintances.

And just as she'd made me attend the funeral, she was now forcing me to go to the *saranta*, where I'd have to eat more bland food and make more casual small talk.

That is, if anyone else showed up.

19

Thalia gave a long sigh.

I slid a glance her way. 'What?'

She looked at me. 'Do you remember what we were doing a year ago this exact same time?'

'I don't know? Starving?'

She gave me a virtual swat. 'We were in the final stages of planning your wedding.'

The car tires slid on a patch of black ice. At least I decided that was going to be my story if I got into an accident as a result of Thalia's casual words.

My wedding...

Seemed strange somehow that weeks had passed since I last thought about that time, seeing as it had occupied so much of my existence after my wedding day disaster ... and since I still had the wedding gifts stacked, unwrapped, against my bedroom wall.

Hard to believe that if things had gone as planned, I'd be Mrs Thomas-the-Toad Chalikis right now. Without, of course, 'the Toad' part. I might even be pregnant, with nothing more pressing on my hands than cooking dinner for my husband and knitting baby booties.

I think I threw up a little in my mouth.

Oh, not because of the idea itself. But because of the reason I wasn't married and pregnant. Namely because on the day of my wedding, I found myself staring at the bare white bottom of my groom-to-be where he was wedged between my maid of honor's open thighs.

I'd lost what had been two very important people in my life that day. But since then I'd gained a very interesting career, a mutt-from-hell sidekick and adopted an extended family that might not want any booties I'd care to knit, but I wouldn't care if I found any of them playing the tube-snake boogie with anyone either.

My mother, however, didn't feel the same way. She'd made it very clear that Thomas' activities rated little more than a passing glance and that his punishment should have been my making the rest of his life miserable.

What she left out of that equation in her bid for little Greek grandchildren to drape in gold and feed *koulourakia* to is my own happiness.

I scratched my head, searching for something, anything that might derail my mother's speeding train of thought before someone got hurt.

'Do you remember?'

'Oh, look! *Pappou* hung the *karavi*...'

We were passing my grandfather's café, which just happened to be catty corner to my father's steakhouse, the Greek stand-off continuing away from the dining-room table. *Karavi* was Greek for boat, and most Greek men decorated boats with lights, instead of Christmas trees ... while the women starved their offspring.

'We went to your first dress fitting...'

Damn it all to hell.

My mother gasped.

Which meant I'd said the words aloud. A week before Christmas. During advent. On my way to a *saranta*.

I bit down hard on my bottom lip and mumbled something I hoped sounded like an apology.

21

Then I said, 'If it's all the same to you, I'd prefer we didn't refer to that time. Ever.'

I felt Thalia's hand on my arm. 'I understand, *koukla mou*. You're not ready yet.'

Yet?

Oh, no. No way was I going to ask. Lord only knew what she'd come back with.

'Then there's poor Dino...' she said on a long-suffering sigh.

OK, maybe we should have stuck with my ex, Thomas-the-Toad...

As far as men went, Dino Antonopoulos had probably come the closest to making me forget about my ex. Well, him and Jake Porter.

But we weren't talking about sexy Australians, we were talking hunky Greeks.

It just then occurred to me that both men currently in my life were foreigners.

Of course, Dino wasn't currently in my life, so to speak. To do that, he'd actually have to be in the country. And he wasn't. For reasons I was still trying to ferret out, he'd been deported back to Greece. Poof! Just like that. One minute he was sitting across a dinner table from me at Stamatis on Broadway making me itch by asking how many children I wanted; the next his bakery was abandoned and his next-door neighbor told me he'd been deported.

It hadn't taken long for the news to blow up my mother's calling tree. And the best I could figure it, this was the first time any of us heard of a Greek being so summarily deported. Usually there was paperwork, hearings and stays until

22

the matter could be worked out. A process that took months, if not years.

Yet three weeks ago Dino had disappeared without so much as a warning.

'Any progress finding out what happened?' Thalia asked.

'I visited the INS agent this afternoon. They're swamped, but promised to get back to me soon.'

Actually, they were no longer called the INS. Rather, a few years back the Immigration and Naturalization Service changed their name to USCIS, or United States Citizenship and Immigration Service. But the last time I'd said CIS, my mother had thought I was referring to a television show.

The 'overburdened/get back to you soon' response was essentially the same one I'd been getting since I contacted him the day Dino went missing.

Maybe I should go above him, ask for his supervisor's name.

Surely there were other resources I could tap into.

A mirror-shattering shriek nearly popped my eardrums. I realized it was my mom's. And I was unfamiliar with it solely because I rarely – if ever – heard it.

I slammed on the brakes, believing whatever she was reacting to had to do with my not paying attention to the road and my imminent slamming into something I shouldn't.

But when the car lurched to a stop, I discovered I was nowhere near hitting anything.

'What? What?' I asked, my palms slick on the wheel.

She pointed to the old Cadillac in front of us. 'Bodies. Quick! Call the police!'

I squinted through the dirty, half snow-covered windshield at the bodies in question. Sure enough, that's exactly what they were. But they weren't human. They appeared to be some sort of life-sized stuffed dolls that had been slammed in the trunk ... accidentally or on purpose. Judging by the smart-ass bumper stickers – the most obnoxious being 'Honk if You're Feeling Horny' – the neat way both the bodies were arranged, and my mother's response, I was guessing the latter.

'Are you sure?'

'I'm sure.'

I began to honk the horn to tell the double-parker to get out of the middle of the road, no matter the bumper sticker, when my door was wretched open and I was unceremoniously yanked out.

Two

OK, so this was new.

In my career as PI over the past seven months, my own client had tried to kill me, I'd been fitted with a pair of cement overshoes and nearly shoved off Hellgate Bridge, become acquainted with a mammoth wood chipper with my name apparently written all over it, and had risked being turned into a creature of the night.

But never had I been pulled out of my car in the middle of driving it.

Not while stopped either, for that matter.

Since I'd been in neutral with the brakes on, Lucille merely coughed and died when I was removed. I watched as the car that had caused me to stop pulled away, the fake bodies bouncing against the bumper as the driver negotiated the snow ruts.

'Hey, hey, hey!' I shouted, trying but failing to reach my Glock.

The guy who had both my arms held behind my back was big and reeked of garlic. At least that ruled him out as a vampire. I ousted the ridiculous thought and tried to concentrate on the situation instead.

'OK, buster, I don't know what's going on, but

if you want a girl's attention, a simple rap on the window might be a good idea?'

'Let her go!' My mother had gotten out of the car.

'Get back in and lock the doors!' I told her.

'Sofie, what's happening? Who are these people?'

'Mom, I want you to drive home.'

'I can't drive a stick!'

Shit.

Only I could be having an argument with my mother in the middle of the street while being taken captive by some beastly stranger.

'Go!' I told her. 'Now!'

My assailant released his grip enough for me to reach my Glock and elbow my way out of his hold. I turned and held the gun on him. He must have been at least six foot six and weighed three of me. And he wasn't amused.

Uh oh.

'Mr Abramopoulos would like to see you,' he said simply.

I blinked at him. 'What? Abramopoulos? As in George Abramopoulos?'

His casual mention of a name that practically every New Yorker knew was just enough to give him an edge so when he twisted my gun out of my hands, I was a second behind in stopping him.

A car pulled up in the opposite direction and I was rudely shoved into the back of it.

Great.

Well, at least I was familiar with Mr Abramo-

26

poulos. Being Greek – much less a New Yorker
– it would have been some crime, I'm sure, had
I not been. He was the Greek Donald Trump
without the hype. A regular Aristotle Onassis
without the ships. Just yesterday my mother and
I were ogling a picture of him in one of the
supermarket rags with whatever arm candy he'd
been spotted with at the time.

'Why can't you find a man like him?' my
mother had wanted to know.

'What? As old as my father with a nose you
can see coming a block before him?'

As the car door was slammed shut, all I could
hope as I checked for a way out was that the
Greek Tycoon was a lot nicer than his employees.

He *was* nicer.

Well, that kind of shiny, 'don't mess with me,
I won't mess with you' kind of nice, anyway.

At least he wasn't trying to push or pull me
somewhere I didn't want to go and wasn't trying
to take my gun.

Speaking of which, I felt naked without mine,
since the gorilla who'd taken it from me still had
it.

I didn't know much about George Abramopoulos outside what appeared on page six ...
which I'd thought was a lot until I stood shaking
his hand with nothing to say. I eyed the very
Greek, fifty-something man who knew his way
around a good tailor and hair stylist. I knew the
real-estate bust had forced him into some level
of bankruptcy last year. And that he and his

much younger ex-wife had been embroiled in a nasty divorce and custody battle. Both pieces of information rated as gossip and as such were unrepeatable in the presence of the man himself. Especially since I hadn't really followed the stories beyond the headlines.

What should I say? Perhaps: 'Congratulations on emerging from Chapter Thirteen.' Or: 'How is your little girl? Is she looking forward to Christmas break?' Or: 'Pretty picture of you and your eye candy *du jour* in the paper the other day.' But I didn't know if Thirteen was the bankruptcy for which he'd filed, and could not remember for sure if the child involved in the custody fight had been a girl, much less whether he'd ultimately retained custody of her ... and I didn't think it was a good idea for me to mention anything about the eye candy.

Damn. They should have taken Thalia hostage with me. She'd know every detail of all three stories and would have also known exactly the thing to say.

Whether it would have been the right thing was another matter entirely, since my mother was known to speak her mind without thought to the consequences.

'Glad you could make it, Miss Metropolis. Pleasure to meet you.'

I noticed his manicure was better than mine as we shook hands. I resisted the urge to chew on a hangnail when we finished. 'A phone call would have been preferable over a snatch and grab.'

His laugh was friendly enough, but his dark

28

eyes sharpened. 'I'm not familiar with the details surrounding our meeting, but my apologies if my men were a little ... forward. This matter is pressing, as you'll see.'

I noticed he distanced himself from the incident even as he stressed the importance of my being there.

'You're creating quite a name for yourself, Miss Metropolis. I've been reading of your successes these past few months.'

My successes?

'Your involvement in that bloodletting serial killer case was of particular interest.'

'Ah.'

I squinted at him, wondering if he'd tried the highly questionable and illegal blood-replacement therapy that promised to keep you young forever; a highly experimental treatment that had ultimately led to the death of those who could supply the ever-growing demand.

I was guessing yes.

'I'm hoping you'll consider using your skills now to help me out,' he said.

I couldn't imagine how I might be of assistance to him, but admit I was intrigued. No matter the motivation, it wasn't every day that a Greek of his caliber noticed a Greek of mine.

He said, 'You don't mind if I pass you on to my head of security to fill you in on what I'm interested in hiring you for?'

I didn't mind that; what I minded was that because of his thugs I'd likely have to pay a hundred and fifty to get Lucille out of the tow yard.

Without my realizing it, he'd led me to a connecting door and was ushering me through it into a reception area. Smooth. He said something about letting him know if I had any problems, then closed the door – which I heard lock – telling me he was the last person who wanted to hear from me if I encountered problems.

I looked down at my jeans, simple black cotton blouse, brown suede boots and matching jacket and frowned. Not exactly Prada. I glanced around the room. It was the first time I'd been in it. I'd been nearly carried in via a back entrance and private elevator that directly accessed Abramopoulos' gargantuan office. I did know I was on the fortieth floor of a midtown Manhattan building. One of at least a dozen of Abramopoulos' buildings.

I also knew I wasn't the only one not wearing Prada.

In the reception area I counted at least a dozen others, most of whom were eyeing me with the same intensity with which I stared at them. Had they all been grabbed the same way I had? I recognized a couple of them as fellow PIs.

One in particular stood out. He was one of those guys you couldn't quite pin an age on, somewhere between thirty-five and fifty-five who always looked sweaty. He was short, pudgy, with a bad comb-over and an out-of-date, smudged pair of glasses that made his small eyes look even smaller. He wore a forest-green blazer over a wrinkled striped shirt, but I was betting his favorite was a ratty plaid one.

I wasn't sure why he popped out from the others. Had I seen him somewhere before? Maybe with my uncle, Spyros, the real private detective in the family and my mentor? Or could it be the way he was staring at me, as if he wished he could vaporize me on the spot?

'Miss Metropolis? Hi, I'm Elizabeth Winston, Mr Abramopoulos' private executive assistant. If you'll follow me? Bruno will see you now.'

I stared at the pretty assistant wearing an expensive purple suit, her short, shiny black hair cut in one of the latest styles I'd never be able to maintain, then looked back at the locked door to Abramopoulos' office behind me and the cameras perched near the ceiling. I hadn't even sat down. A couple of snorts and sighs from the others told me they'd been sitting for a while.

What did she mean private? Was there yet another reception area off the main office? A public one with a different assistant and different people waiting to see the big man?

Then I reminded myself of the time. The bright interior lights and business-as-usual atmosphere made it easy to forget that it was well after closing time and dark outside. If the circumstances surrounding the meeting hadn't already rated a bullet on my bizarre list, the added detail would have landed it there. As it was, it was bumped up.

I absent-mindedly scratched my collarbone just under my jacket as I followed her through another door, distantly wondering if I'd entered

31

some sort of modern day version of *Alice in Wonderland* and if she was the white rabbit.

Inside I went and a man who very much resembled the one who had snatched me from my car got up from behind a desk and crossed to shake my hand. I had to blink a few times to make sure it wasn't him. First, he was dressed nicer. Second, he wasn't trying to manhandle me. And he just looked neater somehow. More civilized.

'Thank you for coming.'

'Not like I had a choice. You look an awful lot like—'

'Yeah, I get that a lot.'

'Hope your manners are better.'

His laugh appeared to catch him off guard. 'My older brother Boris, I'm afraid. And, yes, my manners are better. Please sit.'

His close scrutiny told me that while his manners might be better and his accent not as pronounced, he wasn't that far removed from his brother when it came to doing what needed done.

I sat and then listened for the next ten minutes as he quickly explained the case to me. And I sat for two minutes after that digesting what he'd said while he sat with his sledgehammer hands folded on top of his desk.

Abramopoulos' seven-year-old daughter had been kidnapped. Snatched outside her school yesterday afternoon. There hadn't been a ransom yet, but they expected one soon. Top of the suspect list was George's ex-wife.

'No police, no FBI. Is that clear?' He pushed a file from a pile toward me.

Odd. I raised my brows, taking in everything he'd just told me as I reached for the file. 'Um, yeah.'

'You even hear a word I said?'

I squared my shoulders. 'Of course, I did.'

'Any questions?'

Questions? Yeah. The first was what in the hell I was doing there.

Don't get me wrong, I'd come a very long way when it came to private detecting. But this was my biggest case to date, no matter how hush-hush. Well, at least going in. I could only hope it wouldn't be bigger going out, as some of my other cases had proven to be. Abramopoulos was a high-profile client. Do right by him and the agency stood to gain a huge up-sweep in the quality of clientele.

I gave a mental eye roll. With my luck, that would mean snapping cheating spouses outside the Waldorf instead of the Quality Inn Motel.

Speaking of which...

'What's the pay?'

He told me.

I raised my brows. 'Nothing unless I get something?'

'Zero. Zip.'

Hunh.

'You didn't think you were going to get a retainer, did you?'

'Hey, you guys snatched me.'

He smiled and a gold incisor flashed at me.

Ew.

I jabbed a thumb over my shoulder. 'And the clowns in the waiting room?'

'Same deal.'

'All PIs.'

'Most.'

'How many?'

'Every one in Manhattan and at least two boroughs.'

'Why me?'

His smile widened. 'Why not you?'

Why not, indeed...

'Any questions regarding the case?'

'Not yet. But when I have them, should I call you?'

He slid a business card across the desk. 'Day or night.'

'And I'll get you?'

'You'll get my voicemail, which is checked every five minutes. So be specific.'

'And if what I have is important?'

He looked at me for a long moment without saying anything. Then he took the card back, scribbled a number on the back and slid it back.

'Better make sure it is important.'

'Or else?' I took the card.

He smiled again.

Considering how I'd been 'invited' for this meeting, I could only imagine the punishment.

Eeek...

'Urgent only. Got ya.' I said under my breath.

Three

Rule #5,612: Don't ever take a case where the risks outweigh the potential rewards.

I was exaggerating on the number, but I'm sure I remember my Uncle Spyros reciting this rule to me, one of many I let float straight through my head and drop on to the ground at my feet before walking over it, only to later make my way back to tediously pick up what remained. Why? Because over the past few months, I'd learned that maybe it might be a good idea to heed some of his advice.

This rule in particular.

I was thinking any job that began with a snatch and grab, well, it couldn't be good.

Uncle Spyros, aka Spyros Metropolis. It was his name that graced the windows and door of the office front on Steinway Boulevard I even now drove to. He was my father's ne'er-do-well brother. A private investigator by trade who had one silent partner, Lenny Nash, who took his role literally and rarely said a word, startling both Rosie and me when we realized he was actually in his office half the time.

Silent also nailed our response to Lenny and his mysterious activities, which included large, unexplained checks he regularly deposited in the company account.

As for my uncle Spyros ... well, shortly after I hired on at the agency – choosing him over apron duty at either my father's restaurant or my grandfather's café, where I'd spent most of my working life up until that point – he had taken off for an island in Greece. That was eight months ago, and I was beginning to suspect he might never return.

And if I was also beginning to suspect he wasn't in Greece ... well, that was between Lucille and me.

It wasn't often I wished he were here so I might ask for advice. But I wished he were here now. Unfortunately, for reasons I had yet to ascertain, the only times I could talk to him were when he called the office weekly, having left no number where I could contact him.

'Go to Lenny if there's an emergency,' he said.

Rosie and I had stared at each other as if we'd rather have our salon privileges revoked for a year before going to Lenny for anything.

As I negotiated my way to the office the morning after my late-day meeting with Mr Abramopoulos' head of security, Bruno, Muffy slobbering all over the passenger window where it instantly froze there, making it impossible to see out of, I went over what I'd done so far on the case I'd been arm-twisted into taking.

Thankfully Lucille hadn't been towed, but had been parked on the side of the street a block up from where I'd been grabbed, the keys in the

36

glove box. Any other day, I might have been concerned, but it was so blasted cold outside, I doubted anyone doing any car browsing would have looked twice at my 1965 Bondo Special Mustang, much less have checked the glove box.

I also counted myself lucky I'd been given back my Glock as I left the Abramopoulos building, the ugly mug who had taken it from me grinning widely as I checked to find it unloaded.

'What, afraid I might wanna shoot you?'

His grin merely widened.

Last night I reached my limit on guys who smiled their responses.

My first destination had been the address listed for the ex-wife, even though there had been a notation she no longer lived there. The small, squat house in Kew Gardens had been barely a shack in an otherwise good neighborhood and the sidewalks and driveway had been left snow covered, giving the place more than a deserted feeling – a desolate one, particularly in the dark.

My initial reaction was shock; you couldn't have driven any farther from George Abramopoulos' penthouse offices to this small, sorry-looking house his ex-wife had inhabited. Pre-nup? Or had the ex-Mrs Abramopoulos needed a better attorney?

Any way you spun it, her standard of living had taken a marked nosedive after the divorce.

And, considering her ex owned a good percentage of prime real estate inside Manhattan, I could only imagine how she felt coming home to this every night.

But did it give Sara Canton motive to kidnap her own daughter?

The second thing I noticed was the line of cars both in front of and behind me, all of them slowing as they came to the house. I realized that every PI in a three-borough area had probably had the same idea. I'd checked my gas gauge to make sure I had enough to last through the crawl then readjusted the rear-view mirror to wait my turn. I spotted the driver of the Crown Vic behind me. Sweaty, comb-over guy from Abramopoulos' reception area, the one I thought I'd seen somewhere before. He seemed to be looking back at me. I adjusted the mirror again so I couldn't see him.

I'd supposed I probably should get out of the car, go up to the door to make sure no one was actually in the house. But since there was no sign of footprints in snow that had fallen the morning before, meaning no one had come or gone since the girl had been snatched, and the fact none of the other PIs appeared interested in sinking into the snow up to their knees, I passed.

So I'd made my obligatory stop in front of the house, stared at it waiting for inspiration, taking in the half-open mailbox that appeared overstuffed and the plastic-wrapped newspaper peeking out of the snow near the stairs, before driving along.

What I hadn't anticipated was nearly running over a kid who was pulling his younger sister on one of those oversized Frisbee sleds across the street.

'Christ, lady, we're walking here!'

'Language,' I'd said, rolling down the window to apologize and instead sounding disturbingly like my mother. 'You shouldn't be out walking like this after dark anyway. Had it been anyone else you stepped out in front of, you might have ended up roadkill. Frozen roadkill considering these temperatures. They probably wouldn't have found you until spring thaw.'

He'd stared at me as if trying to decide whether to ignore me and continue on or flip me the bird. His sister was younger, her chubby cheeks round and red, her eyes huge and overly bright in her tiny face.

'Hey, want to make a quick fiver?' I'd asked.

Had he given me the finger, I probably would not have extended the offer, but he hadn't and I had. And within ten minutes he'd met me on the next block with the mail that had been over-flowing from Canton's box.

'I think this should be worth at least ten,' he said to me.

'Five and no more.'

He sighed and handed the mail over. I'd given him seven.

'Gee, thanks, lady. You're a regular George Abramopoulos.' Then he'd gone back the way he'd come, pulling his sister behind him.

I'd sat for a minute watching him and wondering at his choice of comebacks and the coincidence of it. Then I'd sifted through the mail, thinking maybe some of it had born the name of the former Mrs Abramaopoulos. None of it had. I'd begun to go through it more thoroughly when I realized a car had pulled up, parking right behind me and shutting off the lights. I alternated going through the mail with watching for the driver to get out when I noticed the engine was still running, exhaust snaking up over the car in the cold wind and snaking around mine.

The Crown Vic.

Great. I'd been made.

I put the mail down and continued on, glad when he didn't immediately follow.

Now, I glanced at the mail still sitting on the passenger's seat that was now covered with dirty Muffy prints and then pulled on to Steinway Boulevard, finding a spot across the street and up the block from the agency.

That's when I noticed a stalker of a different color.

Jake Porter.

My heart did a funny little side to side as I visually tagged the black truck with tinted glass, cigarette smoke curling out the crack in the driver's side window like the fingernail of a carnival performer, indicating he was inside, probably watching me.

I took a deep breath, ordering my traitorous body to behave.

The hot Australian bounty hunter and I had a past, you could say.

I made a face. OK, maybe not that long of a

past, but he and I? Well, we had a good beginning of one. He'd saved my bacon bits on a couple of occasions, including the time he'd swooped in from out of the sky to prevent me from being chucked off Hellgate Bridge in my new pair of unwanted cement overshoes.

Thing of it was? I didn't want his help. OK, maybe that one time it had come in handy. But having gunmen shoot up his waterbed just moments after the first time he and I had sex? Then having his truck blow up when we made a run for it? And a growing litany of questions left without answers? Well, stuff like that I could do without, thank you very much.

Besides, I was completely capable of getting into at least that much trouble all on my own.

Of course, it didn't help that the questions at the top of that list had to do with him and his feelings for me.

Why was he trying to protect me? And what from?

What was he, officially, since I was now pretty much convinced he wasn't the bounty hunter I'd believed him to be?

And what was his interest in me beyond sex?

I'd asked those very questions one too many times without receiving an answer and told him in no uncertain terms, in his own language, to bugger off.

What he was doing parked at my curb again was anybody's guess.

And I'd long since passed the point of being tired of guessing.

41

I switched off the engine and opened the door, holding Muffy until a car passed before letting him out. He ran straight for the office front with a short detour at a fire hydrant to leave his mark. I slammed my car door, snuggled down deeper into my sheepskin jacket, and negotiated the icy ruts between me and the opposite curb without nearly as much grace. I did take some comfort in knowing I didn't have to visit the hydrant.

Another car door clapped shut. Against my better judgment, I looked to find Jake had climbed from his truck and stood leaning against it. Forget the little side to side heart movement; my entire body just burst into flame.

I squinted at him through the dim, cloud-covered morning light. He looked different. Not the scruffed-up bad boy I was used to seeing. His blondish hair was neatly cut above the collar. His jeans were newer. And he wore a crisp, button-up shirt under his leather jacket.

Funeral?

I shuddered at the thought, remembering the dozen voicemail messages from my mother the night before and the half-hour lecture I'd received for not immediately calling her back and having missed the *saranta*. Forget I'd been hauled out of my car by a gargantuan stranger and what might have happened to me; I'd ruined her night.

And somehow was made to feel guilty about that.

I realized I was staring at Jake ... and he at me. Until Muffy's manic barking reminded me I was probably failing at my dog-owner duties.

I turned to watch a woman looking a lot like ... was that Mrs Claus? Yes, as in Santa Claus' wife. Anyway, she was stepping through the front door of the agency, her dress looking not so much a costume but the real thing, complete with ruffled apron and reading glasses.

Muffy stopped barking, I thought to get a pat from the woman.

Instead, he started lifting his leg.

'Muffy, no!'

Too late.

He was already drenching her stockings.

I grimaced.

Guess that meant no presents under the tree for him this year.

Probably not for me either.

Four

'I need you to find Rudolph.'

I'd hurried to the sidewalk as fast as my size-eight-and-a-half boots could carry me over the rutted, icy terrain, nearly falling on my ass twice, my face once, my mouth opened on an apology when Mrs Claus' words caught me up short.

She wanted me to what?

Probably I was hearing things. Probably Muffy's urine had short-circuited the woman's mental wiring.

I looked down at the mutt in question, who had finished his business and stood staring at me as if he, too, were questioning the woman's marble count.

'I'm sorry,' she said. 'You must think me insane.'

She had me there.

'My name's Noel Nicholas. Every year I turn my yard into a Christmas wonderland for the kids. Free of charge, don't you know. And, well, my star reindeer has come up missing.'

I resumed squinting and noticed Muffy focusing his attention on a woman with red shopping bags walking in our direction.

'No,' I said, in both response to him and ... was her name really Noel Nicolas?

I snatched the dog up with minimal fussing – probably his feet were numb – and stepped toward the office door.

Unfortunately, I didn't close it fast enough; Mrs Claus caught it and followed me inside.

I didn't miss Rosie's expression where she stood on top of a chair and a box stringing cheesy 'Happy Holidays' garlands to hang from the ceiling. The gum-popping Puerto Rican gave me one of her trademark eye rolls even as I wondered how she could balance on her six-inch stiletto heels; boots that still only made her height somewhere around my nose.

Balance? Hell, I wanted to know how she could walk in the ice outside in them.

'Told you,' Rosie said. ''Tis the season.'

'For kooks, freaks and all things messed up,' I silently finished the sentence she'd uttered the day before after a man came in for a follow-up on a job he'd hired us for to follow his cheating wife, only to be told the photos we had of her being jolly with three other females were allowed. And that, in fact, he was in those shots in a red wig and a push-up bra.

The interaction firmly placed him in all three of the 'Happy Holidays' categories. And made me wish we had never taken him on as a client.

Although as far as cheating-spouse cases went, his was by far not the most bizarre I'd encountered.

Christmas carols played on the iPod dock Rosie had set up on the filing cabinets lining the far wall, her desk holding small piles of other decorations I assumed she planned to put up. 'Grandma Got Run Over by a Reindeer' was playing.

Considering my present company, I found the song amusing not at all.

I pulled a list of names out of my pocket and put it on her desk. 'As soon as humanly possible,' I said.

'Please,' Mrs Claus said, following me to my uncle's office, which essentially had become my office, Muffy running and barking around her legs. 'I know your assistant—'

'Executive Office Manager,' Rosie loudly corrected.

'Office Manager says you no longer handle missing-pet cases, but...'

As far as I was concerned, there were no buts. With my current caseload, I couldn't afford to go out tracking an animal that probably should not be in the city limits outside of a zoo.

Probably there was a law against it.

Not that that had stopped me in the past.

Still...

I shrugged out of my coat and hung it on the back of the door then rounded the desk.

'I'm sorry...' What had she said her name was?

'Noel Nicholas.'

'Mrs Nicholas. I'd really like to help you...' Liar. 'But the agency really can't spare the manpower at the moment.'

Was it me, or did she smell like freshly baked sugar cookies?

I glanced down at her urine-stained stocking,

thinking maybe I needed to have my nose examined.

'I understand.'

OK, that was the fastest anyone had backed down. I'd been prepared for a fight. Dreading it.

Now I felt guilty.

I fought it by taking my cell phone out and scrolling through the numbers for the one to the plumber.

'Excuse me,' I said to Mrs Nicholas and turned away.

I made an appointment for the plumber to come by Mrs Nebitz's place later that afternoon. When I hung up, I hoped to find Mrs Claus gone.

Instead, she stood in the exact place I'd left her.

'Sorry,' she said quietly. 'I know you meant for me to leave, but ... Well, I'd ask if you could recommend anyone else, but I'm thinking I'm going to get the same response from them.'

'Yeah, thinking you're right.'

'It's just that I've had Rudy for five years. He spends the majority of the time on my cousin's farm out on Long Island, but I bring him in especially for the holidays. The thought of him wandering the busy streets, no food to be had, no one to look after him...'

I didn't even want to think of what could have possibly happened on those busy streets, but the word 'roadkill' came to mind for the second time in as many days.

I shuddered.

Rosie had somehow climbed down from the chair and the box in those heels without serious injury and leaned back to stare into my office.

'Tell you what,' I said. 'Why don't you leave whatever information you have, like a photo, and I'll see if there's something I can do.'

Her face lit up like the Christmas lights Rosie was even now inspecting at her desk.

'I can't promise anything. Chances are I won't be able to do anything.'

But I just couldn't let her walk out of the office looking like someone had just crumbled her sugar cookies.

Or, rather, pissed on her stockings.

I couldn't help looking again. Only I couldn't make out the yellow stain.

Muffy got closer and sniffed then looked up at Mrs Claus as if he, too, were puzzled.

He began lifting his leg again.

'Muffy, don't!'

I shooed him away with a Manila folder I took from the corner of the desk even as Mrs Claus rattled off details, apparently completely oblivious to the Jack Russell terrier's designs on her leg.

I gave a mental shrug. Could be worse. He could have been trying to hump it.

She pulled out a photo from the pocket of the white apron edged in red. 'Here he is.'

I took the shot and began to put it down without looking at it but found myself looking closer instead.

Was that a red nose?

I shook my head and tossed the photo to the desktop. Since the shot had apparently been taken in the dark, probably it was red eye that had transferred to the nose.

'I'll call if I see anything.'

'Is there a number I can reach you on?'

Rosie did her leaning-back bit again and shook her head in stern warning.

'I think it would be better if I called you if I come up with anything, OK?'

There was that scent again. Only this time, it smelled like ... peppermint?

I led her from the office and out on to the sidewalk.

'Thank you so very much, Miss Metropolis. I can't tell you how much this means to me and the kids.'

I nodded and mumbled something I hoped was appropriate, my attention already diverted to the hot Australian still leaning against his truck across the street.

Damn.

Jake gave me a brief nod, pitched his cigarette to the street, then climbed into his truck and pulled from the curb.

Hunh.

'I can't believe you let that poor old woman believe you're going to help her,' Rosie said, hanging the lights in the front window.

'Shoot me, but I think kicking her to the curb is just a wee bit crueler.'

She tsked. 'No it ain't. Letting her believe you are going to find her stupid reindeer is crueler.'

'Whatever.'

'When do you think you'll get to that info I asked for?'

She walked to the printer, pulled paper from it and held it out, her ever-present gum popping.

There was no way she'd done all that ... when? She'd been in my line of sight since I put the list on her desk. It was impossible. There was no way...

'I think we should talk about Christmas bonuses,' she said.

'I think you should stop making this place look like a Christmas shop and get back to work.'

She raised a brow.

'Sorry.'

And I was.

Kind of.

'You're not the only one allowed to have a bad day,' I told her.

Bad day? Hell, the rate I was going, I was having the mother of all years.

'I don't never have no bad days.'

I gave her a long look.

'I don't.' She went back to hanging her lights. 'I get ... moody.'

'Oh. Is that what they're calling it now?'

'Whatever.'

I didn't have to see her eye roll in order to know she was giving me one.

I scanned down the information she'd compiled, noticing a couple of names I didn't give her.

'Why'd you run these?'

'New program. Gives you associates, et cetera. Thought you might need it.' She popped her gum. 'What's going on with Abramopoulos? You working for him?'

Probably I should tell her. Probably she could help.

Probably I was a little miffed at her and didn't feel like it at the moment.

'You gonna leave that damn dog in here all day like you did last time?'

I looked to see Muffy had grabbed a hold of a piece of garland and was running it around and around my ankles.

Great.

All things being equal? I'd prefer to eat Christmas turkey, not be trussed up like one.

'Maybe,' I answered non-committally as I clumsily extricated myself from the garland and went back into the office.

'Oh, call your mom,' Rosie said. 'She left at least five messages.'

'I will.'

'Now.'

'Soon.'

'Call her or I tell her all about that hot Australian guy always hanging out here looking for you.'

I stared at her over the paper. 'You wouldn't dare.'

She flashed a dimpled grin. 'Try me.'

I closed the door, leaving both her and Muffy to do to the outside office what they would.

Then I went to my desk and called my mother.

51

Five

'Hey, watch it! You're going to scratch baby Jesus!'

I grimaced. Lord forbid I should do irreparable harm to baby Jesus.

A half hour after I ushered Mrs Claus out of the office I reviewed the list Rosie had printed up, my mother's voice still echoing in my head (how did mothers do that?), my morning agenda roughly sketched out, and I made myself my second frappé of the morning. In order to do so, I had to move a couple of Rosie's manger animals from the top of the filing cabinets to make room.

'Is there an inch in this place that isn't taken up by Christmas decorations?' I muttered under my breath, deciding to wait for my frappé until after the client Rosie was talking to left.

'I don't understand how no one's been able to find anything,' a woman I guessed to be somewhere around thirty-five to forty said, seated in the chair next to Rosie's desk. She wore nice tan slacks and a beige sweater, her blonde hair revealing a recent visit to the salon. I resisted the urge to touch my own neglected brown hair and listened as she said, 'Five PIs and a shitload of money. And now you guys. It's been two months. Surely you should have found something by now.'

I was familiar with the case. I also knew that up until this point, all of our efforts had been for naught. Mrs Kent would call, we'd follow her husband, and get no more than her husband sitting in a bar having a drink or five.

I briefly caught Rosie's gaze as I headed back to the office as she said, 'You know, there is a chance he's not cheating on you, Mrs Kent. Have you considered that? I mean, I know, right? We women are pretty good with this stuff. We can smell another woman before he's even touched her...'

I went into my office.

'I know he's cheating. I just know it.'

The agency had a high success rate when it came to both serving court papers and cheating-spouse cases. Rare was the occasion when we didn't deliver the goods.

The front door opened and I watched the star server enter.

Pamela Coe gave me a wave and I waved back. She was tall and blonde and attractive and had a track record no one could match. Well, up until recently, that is. She'd worked for the agency long before I signed on, and while I sometimes wondered why she didn't appear interested in expanding her duties at the agency, I respected that she'd chosen her job and did it well. And, the truth was, even though I met up with her at the firing range from time to time for

53

target practice, I had no idea what she did outside serving, but I was guessing she was doing something ... and was no doubt very good at that as well.

'What if you were to tempt him into doing something?' the wife was saying.

I looked at her, Rosie looked at me, and Pamela seemed oblivious where she thumbed through the documents waiting to be served on the filing cabinets near Rosie's desk that didn't bear any delicate Christmas decorations that could be damaged.

'Like set him up, you mean? With a prostitute or something?' Rosie asked, glancing at me again.

Truth was, we'd half-heartedly talked about doing just that with some of the more challenging cases. Would land the client what they wanted with minimal fuss and time investment. Hey, if the guy was going to cheat, he was going to cheat. Right?

I looked at Pamela Coe, wheels turning.

'I don't know,' Rosie said. 'That seems a little like cheating.'

I snorted at her choice of words and all three women looked at me.

'Sorry,' I said, clearing my throat. 'I'm just going to close this...'

I slowly began shutting the office door.

'Trust me,' Rosie was saying. 'If he's cheating, we'll catch him.'

'Oh, he's cheating all right.'

'Then we'll catch him.'

54

Fifteen minutes later, the client was gone and so was Pamela and I could finally make that second frappé I was craving.

Thankfully, Rosie was busy at her laptop and didn't engage me when I opened my door and made a beeline for the filing cabinets, careful not to do any harm to her baby Jesus.

Listening to 'I Want a Hippopotamus for Christmas', which was playing on her iPod, I shook a generous tablespoon of instant coffee along with a couple of spoonfuls of sugar and a little water in my travel cup, then replaced the jars of both in the top filing cabinet where I'd extracted them with my other hand. I eyeballed the other decorations and considered tipping a lamb or a goat or two inside with them but decided against it when I caught Rosie staring at me as if she expected me to.

'I don't know how you can drink that iced coffee stuff in this cold weather,' she commented, leaning in to stare at something on her laptop screen between clacks. A state of the art piece of technology I'd gotten her when things at the agency had been going very well.

Not that they weren't going well now. It's just that, well...

No. I was stopping there. The last time I tempted the Fates by wishing for a more interesting case, I'd nearly been turned into a creature of the night.

Besides, the supposed kidnapping of Abramopoulos' kid was interesting. It might be more so if every other PI in New York wasn't also working the case.

I added more cold water and a little milk to my frappé and closed the small refrigerator door.

'If you score on any additional whereabouts of Abramopoulos' ex-wife, call me,' I told Rosie.

'Did you call your mom?'

'You know I did.'

She smiled at me.

I growled.

Funny, my mother. Last night I got an earful not about putting my life at risk by being a PI, but rather about how I'd missed the *saranta*.

I'd expected the same today. At the very least, to be bugged about picking up my *saranta* bag, an eerie reminder put together for those unable to make the event.

Instead, she'd told me Grandpa Kosmos was looking for me.

I'd scratched my head and checked my cell. It wasn't like I was hard to find.

Rather than call him, as I promised my mother I would, I decided I'd wait until he contacted me.

I'd begun to tell her I wouldn't be able to stop by today to get the bag or whatever bland, fast-inspired meal she planned to prepare when she told me she wouldn't be home.

'Anything from the CIS?' I asked Rosie after shrugging into my coat.

She momentarily looked as if she'd been hit in the face with my icy frappé – as she did whenever I mentioned the CIS, I thought maybe because she had a few relatives who were illegal.

Then she got it together.

'Nope. You expecting something on that Dino case?'

'Yeah. If the agent calls, forward it to my cell.'

Probably he would try my cell first, but I wanted to make sure I talked to him if he called. I was still working out what my next step should be since I obviously wasn't getting anywhere here, no matter how nice Agent David Hunter appeared to be.

I understood my mother had spoken to Dino a few times. He hadn't called me. Not that I expected him to after that disaster of a date. But still...

'You're not leaving him here again, are you?'

I eyed where Muffy had curled up on my old office chair at the desk next to Rosie's and he eyed me back.

'Yeah. Just let him outside to terrorize the neighbors every hour or so and piss on the hydrant and he should be fine.'

She tsked loudly, causing us both to stare at her.

'What? I'd like to know when I added "pet sitter" to my job description.'

'Look at it this way: he's protecting you.'

'From what? Women dressed like Santa Claus' wife?'

Something like that.

'You know he don't like Waters.'

Eugene Waters. One of my latest hires, the circumstances surrounding his employment a story that always inspired a smile if not an outright laugh.

OK, so the vertically challenged African-American pimp wannabe's promotion from someone on whom I'd tried to serve eviction papers to one of our process servers maybe rated a spot on the strange scale. But, in some twisted way, it made sense. Who better to get to serve than someone who knew all the ways to avoid being served? And, truth was, he was proving even more effective than Pamela Coe on some occasions, whose success rate had gone untouched by anyone before now.

Pamela had a problem? She handed the case off to him and he delivered.

'Yeah, well,' I responded to Rosie. 'That's because Waters don't like Muffy. I suspect Waters doesn't like many dogs.'

At the mention of the name, Muffy raised his head and growled.

I could relate, but for different reasons.

'Call if you need anything,' I said.

'Whatever.'

For a split second, as I stood there with my hand on the door ready to open it, I considered telling her what my next-door neighbor, Mrs Nebitz, grandmother to Seth, Rosie's heartbreaking ex, had shared with me. Something that went beyond leaky kitchen faucets and expensive plumbers and made my being late to pick up my mother worth it beyond the fact I'd wanted to be late picking up my mother.

Then my gaze settled on the cheerful Happy Holidays sign on the glass.

58

Shoot me, but no matter how foul her mood, I just didn't have it in me to tell Rosie that Seth was getting married.

Brrrr...

However hard I tried to prepare myself, that first step out into the cold always shocked me. As I walked to my car, hunkered forward against the skin-chapping wind, I put my gloves on one by one, trading off on holding my cup of iced coffee.

'Metro.'

Of course, it would stand to reason this was the one time I should have been paying attention to my surroundings. Or, more specifically, others who might inhabit my surroundings.

I looked up to find Pimply Pino Karras getting out of his NYPD police cruiser where he was parked behind Lucille.

Now what?

'Pino.'

He appeared about to hike his pants up, but caught himself. I gave a little smile. It was nice to imagine I didn't know what color his socks were. Of course, I did know; they were navy blue to match his pants since he was a stickler for rules and codes. Still, I held out hope that one day they might be purple ... with sequins.

There was a time not too long ago when Pino seemed hell bent on taking me into the precinct on something, anything, he didn't care what. Littering would have done the trick. Murder? Jackpot! Think it went back to when we were in grade school at St Demetrios, when he was pimply and I never let him forget it. Not for a minute.

But recently things between us had improved substantially.

Hungry wood chippers and neighborhood serial killers had a way of bonding people together.

'So, what's up?' he said, as if this were a summer day and we were just coming across each other, indulging in a bit of catch up.

I raised a brow. 'Other than every hair on my body 'cause it's freakin' freezing out here?'

I knew this was the way Pino operated. Why come straight to the point when you could work your away around to it? I imagined he thought he was some uniformed version of Columbo trying to get a suspect to incriminate themselves because they judged him somewhere below incompetent.

Unfortunately I was guessing most of the people Pino questioned had nothing incriminating to say.

I unlocked the driver's door of my Mustang and put my purse and travel cup inside.

'You planning on sharing what's on your mind? Or are you going to make me leave you standing here?' I asked.

'Your car.'

'My car.' I gestured for him to continue.

'You left it in the middle of the street last night.'

'Ah.' So he must have been the one to park it. Shit.

'I was in a hurry.' I got into the car. 'Like I am now.'

He caught the door when I tried to close it. 'Right.'

I grimaced at him. I supposed I should at least thank him for saving me the towing money and hassle. So I did.

'Cough it up, Sof.'

'What? Am I cat? No fur balls to be had.'

I couldn't very well tell him I was working a custodial kidnapping case and that I'd been instructed not to go to the police.

He positioned himself so I couldn't close the door without hitting him and crossed his arms.

'There was an awesome sale and I got caught behind some asshole that was double parked?' I tried.

'And left your keys in the car?'

'Yeah.' I smiled brightly. 'The sale was good, it was the last day and the shop was about to close.'

'What did you get?'

'A pair of crotchless underwear,' I said. 'Look, Pino, I'd really like to give you a full rundown, but I'm late for a doctor's appointment.'

'Nice try.'

'Yeah, my annual pap smear. You know, female stuff where that crotchless underwear really comes in handy. You want to tag along?'

That caught him off guard. As I knew it would.

Somehow his face got redder than the cold had already made it.

'Can I go now? Or would you like further

details?'

I couldn't help giving myself an inward smile. It wasn't that long ago I wouldn't have dared say what I just had to him. To anybody, for that matter. Now the words and the lies they represented slid right off my tongue smooth as could be.

And garnered me exactly the results I wanted.

He stepped back. 'I still want that explanation.'

'And maybe later I'll give it to you.'

I closed the door, started Lucille with a great deal of sputtering and ass shaking, and then pulled from the curb, the move from ice rut to ice rut jarring my bones.

My cell rang as soon as I put Pino in my rear-view mirror.

Damn.

I fumbled to get it out of my purse and nearly hit a parked car when a woman swung open her door without looking.

'Moron!' I shouted.

She flipped me the bird.

'Is that anyway to talk to your mother?' the voice on the phone wanted to know.

Great.

Hadn't I just talked to her?

No matter, I got the distinct impression the guilt trip she was about to send me on was going to be a good one.

Six

A half hour later I sat parked at the curb on a residential street in Corona where the tenements hugged the sidewalks and there barely seemed room enough to breathe, much less live. I was lucky to have gotten a parking spot at all, and might have dinged the old Pontiac behind me as I tried my skill at parallel parking while sliding on six inches of solid ice.

I sipped my frappé. 'You sure this is the place?' I asked Rosie on my cell phone.

I imagined her rolling her eyes. 'When have I ever been wrong about anything? Now is that all? 'Cause I got stuff to do and you're keeping me from it.'

'By all means,' I said. 'Oh, and thanks.'

'Yeah. Whatever.'

She hung up.

As I pressed disconnect and tossed my cell back into my purse, I came to the conclusion that the word currently inhabiting my most hated list was 'whatever'.

Of course, she was rarely off on any of the info she gave me, so I cut her some slack ... a little, anyway. While I was familiar with many of her sources, she had a few mystery contacts she liked to call 'job security'. And seeing as she'd been working for my uncle long before I ever signed on, I could only imagine what those might be.

I took another pull from my frappé, put it down between the seats and then climbed out of the car, trying to ignore the cold and failing.

Moments later I was knocking on the door to Apartment Three-B in a three-floor apartment building that had seen better days, hoping one certain ex-Mrs Abramopoulos was going to answer the door.

Nothing.

I looked up and down the dingy hall. I'd been in plenty of similar places before. Knew chances were good someone was always going to be boiling cabbage no matter the time of year. And that you didn't want to pull up the carpet for fear of what creepy-crawlies resided under them.

And I'd thought the Kew Gardens house she had resided in before was bad. This place rated somewhere between there and hell, leaning more heavily toward the latter than the former.

I knocked again, leaning in closer to try to detect movement inside over the din of cartoons from a nearby apartment, and a loud, profanity-laden argument coming from another.

I sighed. While Rosie might be right and one ex-Mrs Abramopoulos might be inside this particular apartment, she wasn't intent on answering the door. Not that I blamed her. If my daughter were missing, the last thing I'd want was company. Especially if I was suspected of taking her.

I twisted my lips and knocked again. 'Ms Abramopoulos? My name's Sofie Metropolis. I'm a PI. I'm here to talk to you about your daughter if you've got a minute.'

There've been times when I've employed more creative tactics in enticing someone to open the door, but I was guessing this particular apartment-hider would appreciate a more direct approach.

After long moments passed with no response, I supposed I could be wrong.

I was about to turn away when I heard the chain on the door.

'What is it? What's the matter with my daughter?' a small, female voice asked.

I squinted through the slight crack, unable to make anything out in the dim light.

'Hi, Ms Abramopoulos—'

'Please, call me Sara.'

'OK.' I slid one of my cards toward her. 'I was wondering if I might come in to talk to you for a couple of minutes.'

While it was entirely possible she didn't have any idea what had happened to her daughter, I wasn't going to pass up a primo opportunity to have a look around.

Only I hadn't expected it to be so easy.

The door closed, the chain disappeared and then I was motioned inside.

I went.

Either the pretty yet too-thin woman with the dark circles under her eyes was a good actress and trusted her skill, or she really was concerned about her daughter.

I decided since the straightforward route had gotten me this far, I might as well take it farther.

So I told her what I knew. Well, at least a little.

Her eyes grew even larger as she listened. 'Kidnapped? By who?'

The apartment was sparsely furnished and looked more like a man's than a woman's place. Dark furniture made the faded wallpaper and stained carpeting look even drabber. Might help if the heavy curtains were open, but they weren't. Empty beer bottles and fast food wrappers covered nearly available surface along with overflowing ashtrays.

And unfortunately for me it smelled like it looked.

I answered her question, 'By you is how I'm hearing it.'

Sara Canton's large blue eyes looked about to roll out of her head.

'Shut the fuck up out there! I need to get some fucking sleep!' a man's voice came from what I guessed was the bedroom.

Damn. We weren't alone.

Not only were we not alone, it appeared the other person in the apartment was in a foul mood and far less friendly than Sara.

She looked at me apologetically.

Boy, she really had fallen a long ways since Abramopoulos, hadn't she?

I felt a stab of sympathy for her.

But a bigger one for her little girl.

'I don't even have visitation rights,' Sara said so quietly I nearly didn't hear her.

More profanity from the other room, then the sound of something hitting the wall and breaking.

Was Sara right? Could she have not only lost custody of her only child, but any right to her at all? I knew money was capable of doing a lot of things. But I'd lived under the assumption that parental rights were parental rights and nothing short of murder could sever them.

My gaze slid toward the bedroom door that had just opened, my hand budging closer to my gun.

Then again, I supposed it depended on who the parent was.

'Didn't you hear me, you stupid bitch?'

Sara didn't flinch. Rather she looked exasperated, as if used to the treatment.

'My brother, Bubba.'

Her brother. OK. Better than her boyfriend, I guessed.

Although I couldn't tell you how that side note impacted me at all. Particularly in that moment.

'Don't go telling strangers who in the hell I am,' Bubba said. His arm disappeared inside the bedroom doorway then came back with a shotgun.

Shit.

One handed, he cocked it, then held it against his hip, the barrel pointing in my general direction.

Christ.

I held up my hands instead of drawing my gun. 'Hey, I'm no one to worry about. Just stopped by to see how Sara's doing.'

'Someone took Jolie,' Sara said. 'My little girl. Kidnapped.'

Bubba didn't say anything for a long moment, rheumy eyes slowly moving between his sister and me.

I tried to detect if the news was news to him. I was pretty sure it was to Sara.

Bubba, however ... Bubba looked like he'd cut and sell the liver out of his own dog for a drink.

'Yeah?'

'Yeah.'

I moved to get one of my business cards and the barrel of the shotgun moved, too.

'Whoa. Just giving your sister my number, is all.'

He tilted his head, apparently catching sight of my shoulder holster. 'What you got there?'

I took out one of my business cards and a pen, writing my cell number on the back of it. 'Glock.'

His smile was smug. 'Yeah, got me a couple of those. Got a few others in addition to this one, too.' He nodded the shotgun. 'Wanna see?'

'Pass.'

I held out the card to Sara.

'Call me. Anytime.'

She said something that sounded like, 'Thanks,' but I couldn't be sure.

'Always nice to meet a fellow gun lover, Bubba,' I said to her brother, hoping to disarm him. Well, figuratively speaking, since I was pretty sure he had a gun attached to him at all times. My goal was to pacify him just enough to get me through the door and down those steps before he decided he wanted a closer look at my Glock ... and I was forced to put a bullet between his bloodshot eyes.

I didn't realize I was holding my breath until I emerged out on to the sidewalk, not so bothered about the cold because I was suddenly thankful for the lungful of air, frigid or otherwise.

Damn.

For all I knew, Bubba had the kid stashed in the bedroom. Either that, or he had her stashed somewhere else.

But I was pretty sure Sara had no idea where her daughter was.

Of course, 'pretty sure' held about as much weight as a plastic colander.

A car crept by. A familiar one.

I watched it closely, trying but failing to see inside the Crown Vic.

I was kind of surprised none of the other PIs had made it this far. I made a mental note to myself to up Rosie's Christmas bonus at least by half.

Not that the information or my conversation with Sara had done me any good, but at least I had accomplished a hell of a lot more than anyone else.

I walked to my car and climbed in, reaching for my frappé.

Frozen.

Shit.

It was the second time this week that had happened. And an undrinkable frappé did not a happy camper make.

How was a girl supposed to function properly without a good, regular dose of caffeine?

My cell phone rang. I reached for my purse even as I leaned forward to look up at the window of Apartment Three-B. Sure enough, I saw the curtains move. And was pretty certain a momentary sunbeam piercing the gray sky had reflected off a gun barrel.

Yikes.

I started Lucille and bounced up and down as if the move would help her warm up as much as me.

Then I spotted the Crown Vic again, parking a half a block up.

Coincidence?

Problem was, I was coming to believe there was no such thing.

A glance at my cell phone told me my grandfather had finally decided to forgo Ma Thalia and contact me directly. I decided he could wait.

I put the car in gear and sped up to park next to the old, boxy car. Sure enough, Mr Comb-Over stared back at me through his thick glasses.

Great. Wasn't I supposed to be the one doing the following? What was he doing following me?

Then again, I'd been in the apartment for the past fifteen minutes. Surely if he had been following me, then he'd have already been parked.

No, he'd gotten there after me.

Which meant he probably had a Rosie of his own stashed away somewhere.

I thought about getting out and introducing myself, then decided against it.

Probably it was coincidence.

And probably he would get shot by Sara's brother.

I smiled and gave him a friendly wave as I put the car back in gear and sped down the street, well away from the scene of the impending crime.

Seven

Rather than call my grandfather back, I decided to drive over to his café, figuring I could kill two birds with one stone: not only would I find out what he wanted, I could get a good frappé.

I liked my coffee iced, but not solid ice.

Anyway, I needed to regroup. Rethink this case. And give a bit of attention to other agency business. It wasn't like I was sitting on my hands when that Russian heavy had dragged me from my car. I had four compensation cases to investigate, three business-viability reports to complete, two background checks to follow up on, and a partridge in a pear tree ... or, rather, a cheating-spouse case in which the spouse refused to cheat.

Right now, though, I was thankful for Grandpa Kosmos' perfectionist tendencies as I crossed his clean sidewalk. A glance kitty-corner showed the area around my father's restaurant had yet to be cleared, and it was almost eleven, nearly time for the lunchtime rush.

I opened the café door and gave a shivery sigh as heat hit me. Lucille seemed to have a hard time warming up in this frigid cold. Probably I should take her in to have her gauges checked.

Or whatever it was they did to make sure cars ran properly.

Jake Porter instantly sprang to mind.

Was it really only a few months ago that he'd been tinkering with my Sheila? That I'd come out of my apartment to find his fine ass sticking out from under the hood of my car?

That I'd taken him for a long ride when he'd told me she'd needed to be run but good...?

That I had run him but good...?

'What are you doing here?'

I blinked at my grandfather. Not only because I hadn't seen him come up, but because that's what I thought he wanted: me being there.

'Mom told me you needed to see me.'

'No,' he said, 'If you had listened to my message to you, left on that stupid mail voice or whatever it is, you would know I wanted you to call me.'

I blinked ... slowly.

'I don't get it.'

The ever-present coffee klatch in the back shouted hellos and I greeted them back, all of them like uncles to me since I'd known them as long as my real ones, and most of them better since I'd spent half of my teen years as a waitress there, and the other half as a waitress at my father's.

Grandpa Kosmos moved closer and lowered his voice although no one was near enough to hear. 'The matter I have to discuss with you is better done ... in private.'

Oh.

I wasn't sure if I'd said the word aloud or not.

'OK. So I'll call you,' I told him.

'Good. Good.'

He walked away.

Hunh.

OK, as far as crazy family members went, Grandpa Kosmos rated among the sanest. In fact, I counted on him to be less zany than the rest of them. But this...

I shook my head and moved to the end of the counter, taking a stool and placing an order for a frappé. When it came, I sucked half of it down in one slurp.

Ah, yes. Much better.

Even Grandpa Kosmos' odd request no longer seemed so odd. So he didn't want anyone in here to know whatever business he had to discuss with me; nothing wrong with that.

I glanced at where he had rejoined his friends in the back, laughing as if nothing had just happened.

And nothing had.

Had it?

I dialed Rosie.

'So was she there?' she asked without saying hello.

'Yeah.'

No response.

'Pete come in this morning?' Pete was my cousin, Uncle Spyros' biological son from a previous marriage. Things hadn't always been good between the two of us and there was a time not long ago that, when I saw Pete, it usually meant something was going to come up missing around the agency. Most often cash. And once out of my own purse. Which is when I finally put my foot down, no matter what absentee-father guilt Uncle Spyros felt.

My cousin could steal from my uncle all he wanted; take from me, and we had a problem.

That's when I gave him a job.

I know, it's probably never a good idea to hire someone who already had a reputation for stealing – especially from you – but I figured it might be a good way to nudge him in a direction other than the one he seemed intent on taking. So I put him to work painting and fixing up the offices. He'd grumbled and moaned. But he'd done a good job. And I paid him.

Then he went to work at the agency.

Speaking of the agency, still no response from Rosie on the other end of the line.

'You still there?' I asked.

'Yeah. I'm waiting for a thank you.'

'For a what?' I sucked on the straw, draining the rest of the frappé. 'Oh. Yeah. Thanks.'

She tsked. 'You gotta work on those people skills.'

What people skills? I'd labored for years as a waitress. The extent of my people skills were 'Ready to order?', 'Want fries with that?', 'Anything else?', 'Thank you', and 'Come again.'

Oh, and on occasion, 'I'll tell management', when a customer complained, and, 'I'm sorry', when I spilled something, usually on the customer and usually very hot or very cold. Thankfully neither was a regular occurrence and mostly happened on purpose in the case of the latter.

When it came to revenge against a particularly annoying customer, some servers spit in their food. I chose to spill it on them.

'Whatever.' I used her favorite response in response to her. 'Did Pete come in or not?'

'Yeah. Put him back on the Kent case. He's not happy.'

'Tough. What else is going on?'

'That INS agent called.'

'CIS,' I corrected. 'Thanks. I'll call you back in a few.'

I hung up on her irate response and immediately dialed the CIS agent, hoping he was still available.

Boggled the mind to think it had been three weeks since Dino was deported back to Greece without explanation ... and that I still hadn't been able to discover why. I was a PI, for God's sake. Surely I could at least accomplish that, if not clear a path for him to return.

Putting aside my personal connection to him, he was an honest, hard-working citizen. He loved this country – sometimes I feared more than I did – and owned a bakery that was fast becoming Astoria's most popular, which was saying a lot because the borough boasted some awesome bakeries.

And he was hot.

And brought me chocolate tortes.

And ate them off of me.

I bit on my straw, reminding myself I'd determined to put the personal connection aside.

Problem was, that connection was oh so good. Despite his recent favorite topic of conversation: all things commitment.

It wasn't all that long ago that I'd nearly stood in front of an altar with somebody else. The future? Held no altars at all. Hell, the word altar was no longer a part of my vocabulary.

No matter how hot the sex.

The CIS agent picked up on the third ring. 'Hunter.'

I snapped upright and tried to focus. 'Hi, Agent Hunter. Sofie Metropolis here.'

'Ah, yes. Hello, Sofie. Please, call me David.'

I sat for a moment squinting at the air in front of me.

Not for the first time, I wondered if I knew him from somewhere. He was maybe five years older than me and I was sure we hadn't, but the almost ... too friendly way he spoke to me left me thinking some kind of groundwork must have been laid. Because I certainly hadn't been friendly. If anything, I'd been rude, looking for answers that seemed to be very hard in coming.

Don't get me wrong. David Hunter was good looking. No, he was hot. At around six foot three, with dark red hair and the bluest of blue eyes, he looked more Wall Street than CIS material. And he had a grin that...

I blinked. Was I really inviting romantic thoughts of another man when I already had my hands full of a mess caused by two others? Never mind that just a moment ago I was revisiting the chocolate torte experience.

'Thanks for getting back to me so fast,' he said. 'I got some information on Dino Antonopoulos' case.'

'Good,' I said, proud I didn't say what I wanted to, which was, 'It's about time.'

'I was hoping we could meet for lunch to discuss it.'

I squinted harder.

Lunch?

Since when did CIS agents invite anyone out to lunch to discuss a case?

'Sure,' I found myself saying, and then also found myself squinting at myself.

OK, this was getting weird.

'Great. How about Stamatis at noon?'

'Twelve thirty. And which one?'

'The original one. Date.'

He hung up after saying he'd see me then. I wasn't sure I responded. Probably because my eyes had closed altogether at his choice of words.

Had I really just scheduled a date in the middle of everything going on?

No. I was meeting with the CIS agent who would finally tell me why Dino had been deported.

Nothing more.

Nothing less.

I ordered another frappé, took my notes out and then stared through the front windows at Broadway beyond.

Weird. Just plain weird.

I paid for the second frappé and slowly sipped, thinking about Sara Canton in that dingy apartment, her gun-happy brother casually pointing his shotgun in my direction. I checked my notes. A late-model BMW was spotted picking up little Jolie from school ... a car so similar to the one driven by the nanny it hadn't been given a second glance. Until the nanny arrived late at the school after encountering not one but two flat tires to find the girl had already been taken.

I absent-mindedly scratched the back of my neck, thinking again of that apartment and of the rental house I visited the night before. Yes, while I'm certain you can rent such high-end vehicles, I could only imagine what the cost was. And the flat tires indicated there were at least two involved. Or one very fast worker.

Sara and her brother were two. But did they have the resources to rent a BMW?

And if they did, where had the girl been while they were at the apartment?

I was pretty sure she hadn't been in there with them. Sara would never have let me in if she had been. And her brother would never have let me out.

I considered the street outside again, watching as a dark Crown Vic cruised slowly by outside the cafe.

It caught me up short.

Nah ... It couldn't possibly be...

I shook my head and then looked down at my notes, figuring I had a good two hours before my, um, date.

'So sad about little Miss Jolie,' the Hispanic nanny said to me a while later at Abramopoulos' apartment in the Upper East Side of Manhattan, where the towering residential buildings had a hard time keeping up with the modern-day titans who'd built and lived in them.

I'd already inspected the underground garage and possible access points to get an idea how two of Abramopoulos' nanny's tires had been tampered with. The place was more secure than Kennedy airport. OK, maybe I was exaggerating a little, but not much. You needed key-card access at two points, both with three security cameras pointed at the driver and any passengers' direction following any and all movement, along with two two-man security details, one between gates, the other inside the garage itself.

Yes, while one flat tire could have been a coincidence – a huge one considering what happened that day – two of them? Definite wrongdoing.

I wasn't entirely sure what I hoped to find out about the nanny and what she might or might not know. What I was really after was a good look inside Abramopoulos' private quarters. I was more than a little surprised when I was given instant access. I figured Abramopoulos' guys had already questioned everyone immediately involved and would have blocked my and the others' access to them.

Of course, I hadn't exactly contacted anyone and asked for permission. I'd called the house directly, asked for the nanny and gotten her.

The sixtyish Latina looked nothing like how I imagined she might. Weren't nannies typically college-aged English exchange students with cool accents, large breasts and double-zero-sized wardrobes? The Argentinean-born Mrs Garcia looked more like a housekeeper with questionable resident status than a nanny. Then again, she could be pulling double duty. If that was the case, I hoped she was getting paid double for it. Although I doubted it.

The apartment itself was as amazing as I expected, the penthouse spanning at least two very large floors in a building named after the owner and built to order. While there wasn't anything ostentatious like gold leaf covering the ceiling as The Donald had (Eugene Waters talked about it often ... along with his latest plan to get inside so he could chisel it off and sell it), everything was very expensive and very uncomfortable looking. And there wasn't a TV on display anywhere, although I knew there was probably a button somewhere that would open a full wall to reveal ten of them.

Give me an overstuffed couch, the remote to one workable television, takeout from my favorite *souvlaki* stand and a *Seinfeld* DVD and I was a happy camper.

Of course, outside professionally shot and framed photos on a large fireplace mantle decorated for the holidays, there was no evidence a seven-year-old girl lived there.

Probably she had her own private wing.

The difference between this place and the

apartment I found Sara in earlier contrasted so profoundly my brain was almost incapable of the comparison.

Had she lived here? Had she been the woman of the house being waited on hand and foot? Morning brunches with the girls and afternoon spa appointments, with nights out at Lincoln Center and the opera?

I couldn't even imagine the woman I'd seen earlier gaining access to this apartment, much less living there.

Then again, I'd gotten in.

While I hated to admit it, just being there cast Sara in a darker light. How did you go from this ... to that? And what would you do to recapture even a bit of it?

Then again, Abramopoulos himself wasn't looking too good either. What kind of man did something like that to the mother of his child? I'm thinking it would have been less cruel to throw her from the thirty-story window.

The nanny surprised me by leaning in closer where we were sitting together on a red-velvet sofa in the main salon and whispered, 'I read about you in the paper a couple weeks ago. That story about those women ... all that blood.' She gave a visible shiver. 'So glad you caught the monster who did all that bad stuff.'

Hmm. So it stood to reason that's why I had been let inside.

'Have you spoken to anyone else, Mrs Garcia?'

She shook her head. 'Oh, no. Mr Abramopoulos, he tell me not to. I mean, I talk to his people...'

'Then why did you let me in?'

'Because I had to talk to somebody about it. Little Miss Jolie ... I love her like she's my own little *m'ija*. If anything bad happened to her...'

Her big dark eyes boiled over with tears. Genuine? Yeah. I found myself digging in my purse for a Kleenex. She took it and mopped at her cheeks.

'I need you to tell me what happened that day. Everything, no matter how insignificant you think it is. If there was a run in your stocking, I want to hear it.' Mrs Garcia nodded, listening intensely. 'And I want you to tell me everyone Jolie comes into contact with on a day-to-day basis. And who she might have seen over the past month. Doctors, teachers, the neighbor with the Great Dane, security personnel ... doesn't matter. I want to hear about them. And I want to hear what you think about them.'

She continued nodding for a full minute. Then her face contorted, a mixture of hope and worry. 'You find her, yes?'

'I hope to find her, yes.'

And I did. If only because this one woman seemed to love her more than anyone else I'd encountered so far.

And everyone should be where they were loved.

The thought inspired an inward squint of a whole different color...

Eight

'Sorry I'm late.'

I breezed into The Original Stamatis ten minutes after the time I had rescheduled; Mrs Garcia had taken me at my word and told me about everybody, but everybody, with whom Jolie had ever crossed paths. I'd been afraid it might take the entire afternoon, but thankfully she hadn't so much slowed down as she had come to a complete stop.

Just like that. No, 'Oh, one more.' She had outlined each individual with perceptive detail during a consistent, fast-talking roll, then closed her mouth and smiled. That was it.

I'd managed to hold up my hand and halt her for half a minute while I called David Hunter and asked to push back our lunch an hour. Then she continued on as if she'd never been interrupted.

All I could say was I was glad I'd set up my cell voice recorder. I can't imagine trying to take more than the occasional note while she was talking. Probably I'd have cramped up. Probably I'd need carpel tunnel surgery.

Now I smiled at David Hunter.

I'd half expected him to be upset. Most men

would be. And he was a CIS agent, after all. Didn't that require that he have a sour disposition to begin with in order to heartlessly deport innocent people?

'That's OK. I just got here myself,' he said.

I noticed the newspaper open in front of him and the half-drained glass of water and raised a brow.

Although I did get the impression he hadn't ordered yet, you know, just in case I didn't show. Which had loomed a very real possibility. I still wasn't sure I liked the idea of this being misinterpreted as a date. Especially by me.

As it was, I had to stop myself from kissing his cheek when he got up to greet me and invited me to sit.

It was a Greek thing.

But he wasn't Greek and I didn't know him much less date him, so it wasn't appropriate.

Of course, I would have preferred he not seem to register the fact that I had almost kissed him and respond to it with a sexy smile.

'Have you ordered?' I asked, scooting my chair up to the table.

'No. I thought I'd wait for you.'

'Better than ordering for me.'

'I'd never do that.'

'Good. I find it irritating as hell.'

'Me, too.'

I smiled at him. He smiled back.

How come I'd never noticed how hot he was before? OK, maybe I had. But it struck me all over again as I sat across from him. It was hard not to notice he was handsome in an All-American kind of way. Bet he played varsity football in high school. Probably the team captain. Dated the head cheerleader. Had sex with her on a blanket at the fifty-yard line at midnight under a full moon. Maybe even dated her for years after...

I cleared my throat and reached for a menu.

'Have you been here before?' he asked.

'Yeah. It's required to come here at least once a week when you're Greek. You?'

'First time. You recommend anything?'

I put the menu back; I already knew everything on it anyway. 'Depends on what you want. Herbivore or carnivore?'

'Oh, very definitely a carnivore.'

I nearly choked on the water the waitress had brought me and suddenly felt hot all over at the way he looked at me as if to demonstrate dead animal flesh wasn't the only thing he wanted to tear into.

'Lamb?'

'Love it.'

'They, um, do great chops.'

'Sold.'

I had the sneaking suspicion that I could have told him they served dog and he would have been all over it.

Which flattered me more than any direct compliment would have.

We ordered and I decided it would probably be a good idea if I got a takeout carton after the food arrived. It was one thing for me to entertain the idea that this was a date. Another for it to actually appear to evolve into one.

I only wished I had instructed Rosie to call at a certain time so my departure would be easier and less obvious.

Why? Well, number one because I wasn't there to play 'getting to know you' with a CIS agent. Two? I was attracted to him – mightily so – and I didn't want to be ... also mightily so.

'So you're a PI,' he said, turning his cup over so the waitress could pour him coffee. I ordered a frappé.

'So I'm a PI.' I smiled. 'Did I tell you that? I can't remember.'

'No, you didn't.'

'Weren't looking into my residency status, were you?'

'No. Just looking into you.'

I was glad for his honesty. 'Yes, well, considering the resources available to the agency where I work, I can only imagine what you can get at the stroke of key.'

He chuckled. 'A lot.'

'I bet. And not sure I want to know what you dug up on me.' I crossed my legs under the table and found myself rubbing them together.

I immediately stopped.

OK, so I liked his laugh. And his smile. And the way he leaned forward as if wanting to get closer to me, hear every word I said.

Then I realized why this meeting seemed so odd, out of the ordinary. It had been a good, long time since I'd been out on a date. Well, a *date*

date, anyway. With someone I didn't previously know. Yes, in that way.

With Jake ... well, our paths just seemed to keep crossing (it wasn't until later I discovered it was by design), and one thing led to another (read: I determined to back him into my bedroom as soon as humanly possible), and we'd skipped straight to the sexy stuff without all the other boring date stuff.

Then there was Dino...

I stopped for a moment, slowly sipping my frappé.

When I'd first encountered the yummy Greek baker on my parents' sofa, I'd been told he was there to meet my younger sister, Efi, a victim of one of my mother's many doomed-to-fail matchmaking attempts. Turned out he'd been there for me. Something else I hadn't figured out until much later.

What he and I had went well beyond his loving to bake and my loving the things he baked ... and never mind the way he ate them off of me.

I quietly cleared my throat, wondering if my cheeks burned as red as they felt.

Of course, there hadn't been any baking or eating recently since Dino was now back in Greece; abrupt travel plans made possible by the agency the guy across from me worked for.

I looked across at Agent David Hunter, hoping I had managed to turn down the flame of attraction at least a hair.

'And you're a CIS agent,' I said.

He was watching me curiously. I couldn't help wondering what he'd seen on my face during my mental journey to lovers past.

He said, 'Yep. Didn't have to do any digging for that.'

'How long?'

'Five months.'

I smiled. 'I knew it.'

'Knew what?'

'That this job wasn't your first choice.'

'Oh? If you thought that, then you must have tagged me for something else. What might that be?'

I ran my fingertip along the rim of my frappé then dipped it inside, scooping out a bit of the froth, and sucking on it. It didn't occur to me how sensual the move might be interpreted until I watched David's eyes darken as they focused on my mouth.

I picked up a napkin, wiped my lips and my finger, nearly apologizing.

So much for cooling things down.

'Um ... I don't know,' I said. 'Thought maybe something on Wall Street.'

'Close. Fleet Street.'

'As in London?'

He grinned. 'As in London.'

Impressive.

'What brought you back here?'

'Family.'

I gave a silent shrug. OK, this was the part where he was going to tell me he married the head cheerleader and they had three kids all under the age of five.

'My mother had a stroke.'

'Oh, I'm sorry!'

The information was so different from what I expected, I was knocked off guard. I couldn't imagine what I'd do if something like that had happened to my mother.

I looked to find my hand was covering his on the table.

He easily slid his to rest on top of mine instead. So big. So warm.

I withdrew my hand.

'Thankfully it was a mild one. But it was enough to remind me what's important.' He picked up his coffee cup. 'Besides, by that point even Fleet Street had landed in the crapper.'

I laughed. A genuine, open one I didn't recognize. Mostly because I couldn't recall the last time I used it.

Wait. Yes, I did. Back the last time I dated. Back when I'd met my no-good almost-groom, Thomas Chalikis.

The idea was enough to send me into dating shock just as our food arrived.

I'd ordered a heaping piece of moussaka and now stared at it feeling like I couldn't take a single bite of the eggplant and ground beef casserole. And it was one of my favorites.

'These do look great,' David said.

I blinked to find his chops did, indeed, look good.

And so did he.

'So,' I began, forcing myself to pick up my

fork. 'What did you find out on Dino's case?'

Peripherally I noticed his movements slow momentarily, as if he, too, had forgotten the reason we were there.

'I'm not entirely clear on why, but it seems Mr Antonopoulos landed high on the suspected terrorist list.'

If it weren't bad enough I couldn't taste the moussaka, now I couldn't swallow it either.

I coughed and spat the mouthful into my napkin as delicately as possible. Which was probably indelicately.

'What?'

He nodded. 'Yeah. That's what I said.' He took a bite of chop, and his expression reflected he found it good, but I was glad he didn't say anything. 'I don't have access to a lot of the information since most of it came from Homeland Security and is deemed top secret, but there's no doubting that's why he was sent back.'

'Dino's not a terrorist. He's not even Arab.'

I realized how dumb the comment was the instant the words were out of my mouth.

'God, I'm sorry. That was so stupid.'

He smiled. 'No worries. I probably might have made the same statement myself if our roles were reversed.'

I sipped water. 'No, you wouldn't.'

'You're right. I wouldn't.'

I toyed with my food, then gave up and put my fork down. 'So what do I have to do to get him off the list and back here?'

He went momentarily silent as if processing

my question and perhaps even my motivation for asking it.

Then finally he said, 'I'm unclear on that. I explained I was new, right? But I have feelers out. I'm waiting for Homeland Security to get back to me this afternoon for more information.'

I nodded throughout, as if I understood what he was saying, when in reality my brain was stuck on those three words: suspected terrorist list.

What? Did they think Dino was going to try to blow up the UN with an explosive torte? While I agreed they were good – I highly recommend the triple chocolate – they weren't *that* good.

I rested my face in my hands, giving a good rub.

'I'm sorry...' I said. 'This is all a little much to take on all at once...'

He put his fork down, too. 'I understand.'

We sat in silence for long moments, the mundane sounds of the few remaining diners around us seeming suddenly loud ... suspect.

'This Constantine...' David said quietly. 'I know I asked before, but ... what is he to you?'

I slowly blinked. 'Dino?'

He nodded. 'I mean, I know you're a PI. And you're both of Greek extraction. Him a little more directly than you. But...'

But...

That about covered it.

'He's a family friend,' I finally said.

I inwardly winced. Yes, while Dino was that, he was also much more to me. Much, much more. Although even I wasn't sure what all that encompassed.

And now that he wasn't even around.

David's smile was immediate, but didn't completely reach his eyes. 'Good.'

'Good?'

He nodded. 'Yeah. Because I'd really like to see you again.'

My stomach pitched to somewhere in the vicinity of my feet and then bounced back up again.

'Outside working hours...'

Nine

Back at the office an hour later I still couldn't quite grasp the implications of what had happened during lunch. I'd gotten the moussaka to go, albeit for different reasons than I planned, and then passed it on to Rosie. I now sat in my office, absently watching her try to feed pieces of eggplant to Muffy – slimy! Disgusting! Was Muffy's take – while she dug into the rest, Adam Sandler's Hanukkah Song playing on her iPod dock. One of her many gossip mags was open at her elbow and she was talking to who I was guessing was her sister Lupe via her cell phone on speaker.

Suspected terrorist list...

The mere possibility of someone mistaking Dino for a terrorist was enough to freeze my brain for ... well, for a good hour. And that was so far.

The first thing I did upon my return was look up Homeland Security's website on my uncle's desktop computer. Now the home screen glowed at me. Probably my merely accessing the site had landed me on some kind of list.

Was I, too, at risk of being deported?

It made no sense. Absolutely none at all.

Neither did my agreeing to see David again.

My cell phone beeped. I picked it up and saw I had a text from an unknown number. I accessed it:

SECURITY BULLETIN #1: No progress. The first with a line on Sara Canton earns a bonus. Status reports should be sent via text to this number.

Hunh.

I scratched my head and read it again. Well, I suppose I should count myself lucky he hadn't signed it *Love, Bruno.*

My guess was the number couldn't be traced back to him, anyway.

Another beep. Another text. This one from a Charles Chaney.

I have the address of the ex-wife.

Idiot. Sent it to everyone rather than just Bruno.

And very obviously after that bonus offer.

I, on the other hand, thought maybe I should be concerned I wasn't interested in the bonus offer at all.

My guess was Mr Sweaty Comb-Over Guy was the Lucky Winner of Security Bulletin Bonus #1.

I picked up the agency phone and dialed the number that had come with the address Rosie had given me earlier.

'What the fuck do you want?'

I wasn't surprised I'd gotten Sara's gun-happy brother on the second ring.

'Your fucking sister. Put her on the fucking

phone.'

I wasn't sure my ruse would work – truthfully, I'd never spoken like that to anyone in my life – but it was my knee jerk reaction. Just as reaching for my Glock had been my reaction to his shotgun earlier.

Not that I'd drawn it. I could just imagine what might have happened had I acted on that instinct.

'Sara! Get the fucking phone!'

Go figure. It had worked.

I stared back at where Rosie had leaned back in her chair to stare at me.

'Hello?'

'Sara. Sofie Metropolis. You've been made. I'd advise you get out of that apartment as soon as possible.'

'Now?'

'Now.'

'Thank you.'

'Sure. Stay safe. And call to let me know where you land.'

'I will.'

I hung up and sat back in my uncle's leather office chair, wondering why I had done what I had. And what it might yield down the line.

Of course, it all depended on her getting out of there within the next two minutes. Because I was pretty sure that was all the time she had before her ex-husband's heavies showed up at her door.

Maybe five minutes. Depended on how long it took Mr Sweaty Comb-Over Guy to barter his

96

bonus amount.

At any rate, I'd done what I could. If she got nabbed, it was no skin off my nose.

My cell chirped again, this time a phone call. I picked it up on the first ring.

'Hi, Pappou,' I greeted my grandfather.

'You didn't call me.'

Yeah, he had me there. 'I didn't call you.'

'I wanted you to call me.'

'We're talking now.'

In a series of odd events, this one more barely rated a blip on the radar. Although it did rate one. I'd noticed earlier Grandpa Kosmos seemed a little off his game, somehow. He might be known for occasional outrageous behavior (socking my ex-groom in the nose and breaking it, being one example), but out of nearly everyone in my family and my life, he'd always been the one who made the most sense.

I sincerely hoped that wasn't about to change.

'Are you OK, Pappou?'

'Come to the café. Ten tonight.'

I hesitated at the strange request. 'OK...'

Hadn't I just been at the café earlier? And hadn't he insisted I leave and call him instead.

OK, I was really beginning to worry.

'Don't be late,' he told me.

I opened my mouth to respond, only to find he'd already hung up.

Double hunh.

Was it just me, or had he whispered his end of the conversation?

I think he whispered it.

I decided I needed to get out of the office before something else strange happened.

Not that my leaving would prevent that, but being out and about always made me feel better. Despite how cold it was.

'Where you going now?' Rosie wanted to know, forking the last of the moussaka into her mouth.

Suddenly I felt hungry.

Of course.

'Out. Why? Having trouble holding down the fort?'

She stared at me.

I placed a short list of names on her desk that included Bruno and his brother and asked her to run a background check, just out of curiosity, then glanced down at the gossip rag she had opened, my attention drawn to a shot of Abramopoulos and his latest gal pal. She'd been among the earlier batch of background checks I'd had Rosie make. I leaned in closer, noticing another familiar female. Abramopoulos' personal executive assistant – I think that's what she'd called herself – Elizabeth Winston, was a step behind the couple carrying a briefcase.

To a charity ball?

'I'm on break,' Rosie said, closing the mag.

'Did I say anything?'

'You don't have to.'

She returned to chatting with her sister about horror gifts of Christmases past and I let her.

It was only natural that while department stores enjoyed a spike in business around the holidays, others suffered. Private investigating was one. Oh, we weren't suffering. But cold, off-the-street inquiries took a bit of a nosedive, Mrs Claus' request notwithstanding. For a couple of weeks, priorities shifted, whatever detecting plans put off until next year, which now wasn't as far off as it sounded ... yet somehow felt forever away in light of all I had on my plate.

'I know you're not leaving without him,' Rosie said.

I looked at her, and then at Muffy, who appeared perfectly content sitting where he was begging for yummy scraps.

'Come on, boy,' I said half-heartedly. 'Let's go.'

He wagged his tail at me, but didn't move, looking back at Rosie and licking his chops instead.

'See, he doesn't want to come.'

Rosie held out the empty container to him. He gave it a lick and then whined. She threw the box away.

Muffy got up and walked over to me, his entire rear end now wagging in what I imagined was the 'Where we going? Where we going?' song of his own making.

'Have fun,' Rosie said, waggling her red fingernails at me.

'See if I bring you moussaka again.'

'See if I care. Oh, and that Chaney guy you have listed here? Stay away from him.' She slid a photo at me, then opened her magazine again.

'What?' I hadn't even seen her look at my list, which included his name. There was something very familiar about the guy...

'Bad blood between him and Spyros. Goes back a ways.'

'PI?'

'Yeah. At least in his version of his so-called life. Just saying.'

'I'm not following you.'

She held up her hand to indicate the conversation was over.

'Whatever,' I muttered under my breath, deciding to wait for the report or when she was in a better mood, whichever came first.

I slid into my coat, pulled on my gloves and opened the door, Muffy preceding me outside. I looked for the telltale dark truck, but didn't see it. If I experienced a stab of disappointment that Jake Porter wasn't out there, I wasn't saying.

OK, maybe I was.

Odd...

Very definitely odd.

I led the way to where I was parked at the curb and unlocked the passenger's door, letting Muffy in first. He jumped inside ... and then ran over to the driver's side to bark at a passing car.

I gave an eye roll. I'd let him in so he wouldn't get wet footprints on my seat.

I should have known better.

I rounded the car and got in, not caring if I had dirty paw transfer prints on my backside. I was too cold to complain about anything but the frigid temperatures. I started Lucille, then watched as that all-too-familiar navy-blue Crown Vic rolled slowly by in the opposite direction.

I couldn't be one hundred percent certain, but I was pretty sure it was Mr Sweaty Comb-Over Guy.

And that Mr Sweaty Comb-Over Guy was, indeed, my uncle Spyros' friend, Charles Chaney.

Muffy ran over my lap and barked at the car.

Yeah, think he was sure, too.

'Come on,' I said, putting the car in gear. 'Let's go get some souvlaki.'

Muffy barked in approval and licked my chin.

'Ewww. Keep that up and you don't get any.'

He moved to his seat and plopped his furry butt down as if to say, 'OK, I'll behave.'

I wiped my chin and pulled away from the curb, not daring to wonder if my day could get any stranger. I learned that whenever I did that, The Fates had a way of answering in a peculiarly affirmative way.

Ten

'What happened to you?'

While I was out and about, Eugene Waters called my cell and I met up with the five-foot-nothing African-American who probably weighed as much as Muffy on a good day outside a motel on Queens Boulevard, his newly adopted hairstyle of retro-Afro making him look like a burnt matchstick, his single gold tooth flashing in the light of the neon 'Vacancy' sign. It felt late, but I knew it was only around five thirty. Early by anyone's standards. Except when it came to my stomach, which was reminding me I hadn't eaten anything but a couple of gritty bites of the moussaka I had during my non-date with David Hunter.

'Aw, this?' He motioned absently to his face, which even the dim light revealed his right eye was nearly swollen shut. 'One of my ho's decided to get uppity with a niggah. Ain't that some shit?'

I had a hard time hiding my answering laugh, amused that his 'fro wasn't the only retro item he'd recently adopted; his language also emerged like something out of a seventies movie.

'One of your ho's, huh?'

'Uh huh. Bitch had the gull to ask me for money. Too new to understand she's the one who's supposed to be supplying me with some green, you know what I mean?'

'Mmm ... indeed. More like your old lady got upset and hit you upside the head for being late for supper.'

He gave a quiet, 'Heh heh,' and shuffled his eight-inch platform shoes on top of the cleaned and salted sidewalk, his Caddy puffing exhaust fumes our way where he'd left it running at the curb. 'You comin' to know me too well. And it wasn't for being late, it was for forgetting her mama's birthday.'

The exchange reminded me of the first time I'd crossed paths with the wiry man. I'd been serving eviction notice papers; he'd been wearing a too-short pink women's robe edged with feathers and matching mules ... while a woman at least three times his height and five times his weight yelled profanity at him from a back room, and whose shout had blown my hair back when I'd come face to face with her.

Who'd have thought after that fateful first meeting we'd now be working together?

He jumped up and down. 'Damn, it's colder than a witch's tit out here.'

'I'll take your word for it. So what do we got here?'

While I'd hired him on for process serving, he'd been so effective he'd quickly worked his way to cheating-spouse cases, which is what I was guessing this was about.

103

'I followed the Menendez wife here. I hate this motel 'cause it got both a front and a back entrance and you can't see the room doors from here.'

I merely stared at him.

'OK, night manager don't like me,' he said.

'What did you do?'

I'd found out quickly that low-paid motel and hotel clerks were a valuable resource and prided myself in cultivating relationships with them.

Eugene had been particularly good at it, too. Or at least I'd thought so.

He said something so low I could barely make it out.

'What was that?'

'How was I supposed to know the maid was his girlfriend?'

How, indeed.

Yeah, that would pretty much burn any resource.

If I found it ironic Eugene had cheated while working a cheating-spouse case ... well, I wasn't telling him that.

'OK, let me go get you in,' I said.

'Just get me a back door key. I'll take care of the rest.'

I nodded.

Within minutes I'd gone in and come back out with the card key, having slid the manager the usual twenty for the trouble.

'Thanks.'

I crossed my arms. 'You could have taken care of that. May have taken you another couple of bills, but that's the price you pay, I guess. So what did you really want to see me about?'

He pointed a finger at me and smiled, sliding the card key into his front shirt pocket. 'You good, you know that, Metro? I don't care what they say about you. You know what you're doing.'

Who was saying what about me?

'I need some money.'

'Oh?'

'Yeah. I mean, I don't like to say nothing negative about a girl, 'cause you know I'm all about the ladies, especially pretty ones, but that Rosie ... she been something else lately.'

I agreed.

'With it being Christmas and all, I could really use some cold hard cash, you know? My lady ... well, she got her eye on this fur coat.' He chuckled. 'And you seen my woman. For one her size, I gotta fork over some major shekels.'

'Rosie not giving you enough work?'

'Aw, nah, she giving me enough. I was just hoping you'd throw a little something extra a brother's way, you know? Something maybe that pay a little better than serving and photographing people doing what nature intended.'

Nature intended?

I wasn't going to argue the point. After catching my ex-groom with his pants around his ankles on the day of our wedding, I'd argued it enough with myself to last a lifetime.

But considering his little problem with the night manager, I was hoping maybe he might have learned a personal lesson.

Apparently, he hadn't.

Another point I wasn't up to arguing just then.

While I'd used Waters a couple of times out-side normal parameters, I'd stopped about a month ago. Back when he'd called me from a dark alley downtown one night, swearing bats were chasing him, then essentially abandoned me when I went to rescue him – ending up with a huge block of time for which I couldn't account, resulting from a sort of trance mumbo-jumbo the neighborhood vampire's creepy nephew had put me under – I really hadn't used him since.

Hey, you couldn't blame me, could you?

I looked toward Lucille parked at the curb to find Muffy practically licking the inside of the driver's window in a bid for freedom. At this point, I wouldn't be surprised if his saliva could freeze the glass and a simple tap from his paw could shatter it. It was that cold.

And the day was working out that odd.

Before I'd taken Eugene's call, I'd stopped by my parents' house, figuring I'd better pick up that *saranta* token and whatever bland, un-desirable food my mother had prepared that day that I'd pretend to eat.

But she hadn't been home.

And my sister Efi said she'd pretty much been AWOL all day.

Hunh.

Where could my mother have been all day without pelting me with messages designed to make me feel guilty?

'Actually,' I said to Eugene now. 'I'm working a big case now. Let me see what I can throw your way, OK?'

'Cool. Cool. I'll take anything. No matter how dirty.'

'Now would I give you something dirty?'

'You haven't yet. But I keep hoping.'

A car rolled by on the street next to us, slow enough to catch my attention.

The Crown Vic.

OK, now this was getting downright creepy.

'All right. I'll be in touch. Once you get the pics, go home and make good with your wife.'

'Nah. Think I'm gonna let her stew a little.' He sniffed and straightened the lapels of his tan leather jacket that was probably as effective in battling the cold as my own brown one. 'Let her miss me.'

'OK. I can only hope I don't see you with a matching black eye tomorrow.'

I watched him strut back to his Caddy, presumably to get his camera equipment, and then headed back toward mine. Peripherally, movement caught my attention. I turned my head and gaped at an unfamiliar sight on Queens Boulevard. Hell, in all of New York City, period.

A deer.

More specifically, a reindeer.

Rudy!

What were the chances?

I hadn't even thought about Mrs Claus and her missing reindeer since she'd given me a photo I really hadn't needed the day before. Yet here he was, large as life and twice as impressive, standing across the street looking back at me.

What a majestic creature. For just a moment it was easy to imagine he was standing in the snow of some rugged mountainside, the cars a fast-running stream, the buildings behind him rocky outcrops.

How did one go about catching a reindeer?

I didn't know, but I figured now would be a good time to figure it out.

I quickly opened the car door, prepared to give chase ... and Muffy zoomed out, heading straight for the Santa standing outside a half a block up ringing a bell outside a drugstore, his collection pot left untouched for as long as I'd been there.

'Muffy!'

Too late. I watched in abstract horror as he lifted his leg and released a stream worthy of Guinness attention on the unsuspecting Santa.

When I looked back across the street, Rudy was gone.

A while later I trudged up the stairs of my apartment building, an unrepentant Muffy in tow.

My apartment building. Amazed me to think how easy it was now to view the three-story structure in those terms. It had been given to me as a wedding gift by my parents, and while by rights I should have given it back, I hadn't. Like the unopened gifts still piled against my bedroom wall, time had entered into a warp of sorts when it came to that part of my life.

` Besides, since everyone – including my mother, probably – had known about Thomas' extra-curricular activities, I figured it was only right I take a while to figure things out.

So I'd moved into the apartment upstairs, taken the job at my uncle's, and moved through the hours, days, weeks and months until I stood where I was now.

Which was where, exactly?

Muffy barked, his little body a coil of tension where I held him tightly in my arms lest the need to raise his leg on someone or something else he shouldn't take hold. Although I was pretty sure there was nothing left in his bladder, given the puddle he'd left dripping from the drugstore Santa's pants leg.

There went another twenty spot I'd never see again. And the unhappy Santa still hadn't looked any happier.

'Do you have any idea how much it costs to have this sucker cleaned?' he'd asked.

I'd plucked up my crazy dog and left, thinking maybe the Santa trick had been taught to him by his previous owner and my mother's late best friend Mrs Kapoor, who had never believed in men wearing red suits.

Of course, a lot of people didn't. But they didn't train their furry friends to piss all over them.

'Bad dog,' I said to him again, in case I hadn't gotten my point across the other half dozen times I'd said it.

He barked again and licked my chin.

I put him down.

'Sofie. You didn't have to come.'

I reached the second floor to find Mrs Nebitz waiting in her doorway for me. I opened my apartment door, waited for Muffy to go inside after he did his sniffing, circling bit around the elderly neighbor's legs – that he thankfully left urine-free – then closed the door after him, ignoring his whine of protest.

Turd.

I turned back to Mrs Nebitz. 'I figured it's the least I could do. Is he here?'

I'd called the plumber again to confirm the time of his visit earlier and was glad it happened to coincide with my ability to be there to oversee things.

'Yes, yes. But it was unnecessary, really. You see, my grandson Seth is here, as well. I'm sure he'll be able to fix it. It is only a leaky faucet, after all.'

'Better to make sure. Are they in your kitchen?'

'Yes, yes. Come in.'

If Mrs Nebitz appeared a little animated, I put it down to the unaccustomed activity she was being treated to, which I suspected wasn't altogether unpleasant.

I smiled. The way I saw it, she deserved to have an unleaky faucet.

Along with the attention of two young, attractive males.

'Hey, Joe,' I said to the young plumber I'd inherited with the building. So far I had no complaints and I could only hope that would hold.

'Hey, Sof,' he said back from where he was under the sink.

'You remember my grandson, don't you, Sofie?' Mrs Nebitz said.

Of course I remembered her grandson. Even if he hadn't looked like the statue of David come to life with all that blonde hair, blue eyes and chiseled physique, there was that whole Rosie heart-stomping thing.

A little hard to forget.

Especially since mine had been the shoulder she'd soaked in tears.

Several times.

Not to mention her insufferable moods as of late.

'Sofie,' he said, sounding awkward.

'Seth,' I said back, avoiding meeting his gaze where he messed around with the faucet head.

'Seth was just telling the nice Mr Wurzel-bacher he thinks it's the soap.'

'The washer,' he corrected.

Joe's voice was slightly muted from under the sink. 'Never hurts to check a little further.'

'I agree.'

The room fell strangely silent considering there were four of us in there. Nothing but the sound of metal tools scratching against metal objects.

'Sofie, would you like some knish?' Mrs Nebitz asked. 'Seth brought some fresh.'

'I'd love some.' I jumped at both the chance to leave the room and to enjoy some knish, which was, no doubt, from Knish Nosh, the best in town.

We sat together in her living room that reminded me of my mother's, handmade doilies covering nearly every available surface along with photographs, mostly old black-and-white and sepia prints, but some new. The small television was tuned in to *Wheel of Fortune* but the volume was low, so I watched a voiceless Vanna White pretend to turn letters.

Wait a minute, Vanna was always voiceless.

OK, maybe it was the fact that she was sans bells and whistles and dings that made it seem strange somehow.

'So,' Mrs Nebitz said after cutting me a square of knish and handing me a plate. 'How're things?'

'Things are good. How about with you? You looking forward to Hanukkah in a couple of days?'

'Yes, yes. Things couldn't be better.'

I found it curious she didn't launch into a blow by blow of her coming schedule as she normally did.

Probably she was distracted by the two men in her kitchen.

Probably she wanted to stay alert in case they said something.

'So ... how is your friend Rosie?'

I nearly choked on my knish. Probably I was wrong.

The last thing I expected was for her to enquire after the feisty Puerto Rican who had nearly upset all of her plans by falling in love with her beloved grandson.

Hey, I'll be the first to admit even I was surprised by the odd pairing. The two couldn't have been more different had you plucked them from rival gardens.

But when they'd met at my apartment some months ago ... well, even I, the skeptic, recognized the signs of love at first sight.

Oh, Rosie had thought she'd hidden the fact they were secretly dating from me – OK, she'd succeeded to some extent – saying she didn't want to jinx the relationship by sharing too soon, but I'd known that, whoever it was, it was nowhere near a passing fling.

Of course, I don't think even Rosie suspected Seth's reason for keeping their relationship a secret had been a little more substantial.

Namely, the staunchly traditional woman opposite me.

'Rosie?' I asked now, wiping whatever crumbs there may have been from my mouth with the back of my wrist.

Mrs Nebitz handed me a napkin.

'Thank you.' I swallowed the bite lodged in my throat. 'Rosie ... she's fine.'

She nodded. 'Good. Good.'

Was it me, or did my chewing suddenly sound unusually loud?

I committed the mother of all sins by eating the rest of the knish in one bite, then said to fill the silence, 'She has that new nephew of hers. She and her sister plan on spoiling him to death over the holidays.'

Mrs Nebitz nodded again. 'Good. Good.'

I pretended an interest in cleaning my hands.

While I wasn't entirely sure what had gone down a couple of months ago that had resulted in Seth's tossing Rosie's heart to the floor and doing the *hora* on it, I did know that Mrs Nebitz' role had been a large one. She only had the one good, Jewish grandson. And she wanted him to marry a good, Jewish girl. And go on to produce plenty of good, Jewish great-grand-children.

And Rosie was as far away as you could get from Jewish.

And probably as far away from good as well.

I understood the mentality. My own family demonstrated enough of it for me to be very familiar with it. I comprehended that it wasn't so much about racism as it was traditionalism.

Still, I couldn't help thinking Rosie's ongoing pain transcended all that.

What about love?

When both men appeared in the kitchen doorway at the same time, Mrs Nebitz and I couldn't have moved any quicker to stand.

Which meant I leapt up, and she got up in stages.

'I replaced the washer,' Seth said.

'And I tightened the pipes and checked the pressure,' Joe said.

'And the leak?' I asked.

They both smiled.

'Taken care of,' Seth said.

114

'Gone,' Joe said.

'Good, good,' Mrs Nebitz was clearly pleased. 'Now, why don't you two nice, young men come have some of this knish. It's the best in town, you know...'

A couple of hours later, I was back at my apartment, unrolling twinkling lights, an old episode of Seinfeld in the DVD player, *souvlaki* wrappers crumpled up on the coffee table. A sated Muffy was curled in his chair, idly watching me.

So maybe I'd caught the Christmas bug.

OK, at least the sniffles.

I was thinking spotting Mrs Claus' reindeer might have something to do with it. Even though a street-by-street search following the sighting had turned up nothing.

Of course, I purposely banned any thoughts related to his being anywhere near Queens Boulevard, which was also unaffectionately called The Boulevard of Death. I argued that anyone else would be sure they were seeing things and would give him a wide berth.

A human being, on the other hand, they would hit.

I'd happily called Mrs Claus and reported the news. Why, I don't know. To let her know I'd spotted him, apparently alive and well? She'd been so overjoyed even I smiled.

Of course, that didn't mean that tomorrow he wouldn't end up sausage or reindeer jerky if the wrong person crossed paths with him.

Damn. Now why did I have to go and think

that? Yuk.

I thought that perhaps there was something I should be working on related to the kidnapping case, perhaps beating the bushes or pounding the pavement, but since so many others were also on the case, I didn't like the thought of fighting with anyone the way I had to at department store sales.

As far as I was concerned, they could have the last pair of red, suede boots at a killer price.

As for me ... well, I planned to wait until the holiday crowds dispersed and a regular clearance sale would get me the same pair without the fight.

Guess the same could be said of my method of detecting. While chasing down leads yielded important clues, they also led down many a wrong road. I was satisfied for now that I had enough information to work with until I figured out my next step. Since no ransom demand had been made yet, there wasn't all that much to go on.

The idea that the little girl might have been taken by a child predator...

No. Chances of that were so slim, they weren't worthy of consideration.

And considering the money at stake, my thinking was she would be well looked after.

Hopefully.

Anyway, I certainly wasn't going to solve the case tonight. So I had my notes and background checks and photographs spread out on the back of the sofa, passing them often and pausing here and there to leaf through a page or two while I decorated.

I didn't have plans to buy a tree – artificial or otherwise – but while I was out picking up a couple of smaller gifts for my family, I put a few holiday decorations in my basket. Nothing major. Just some colored strings of lights, a couple of cookie trays with Santas on them (which I hoped Muffy would refrain from watering), and two fragrant table arrangements of live pine branches that filled the space with at least the scent of Christmas; one for me, one I planned to take to my mother.

Seeing as this was my first Christmas on my own, I wasn't sure how big or how small I wanted to keep it. But while I'd grumbled at Rosie's overboard efforts, truth was for the most part I liked the little touches around the office. Made it feel more festive somehow.

Festive. Now there was a word I hadn't been compelled to add to my vocabulary lately.

Truthfully, I don't think I'd used it before.

'...then there's Miss Platterpot, she live downstairs. She no like kids. Always tell Jolie "keep quiet"...'

I'd set up my cell phone to play my earlier interview with Jolie Abramopoulos' Argentinian nanny. I was a half an hour into the nearly uninterrupted monologue of names and details and had essentially tuned out about ten minutes ago, much as I had during the conversation itself.

As with then, nothing glaring stuck out at me. But I still had an hour to go on the recording.

And if there was something there, bookended with inconsequential details about the night security man's bathroom habits (seemed he liked to relieve himself on tenants' car tires), and the nice new mailman who always gave Jolie a head pat, I was determined to find it.

A knock at the door.

Lights still in hand, I looked in that direction, then at where Muffy didn't even raise his head from his paws.

A friendly.

Then again, with the security door downstairs, what was I expecting? A hostile?

I put the lights on the kitchen table, pressed pause on my cell phone and went to see who it was, although I was already pretty sure it was Mrs Nebitz, probably to thank me again.

I smiled and opened the door, only to discover I was wrong.

Oh, boy, was I ever wrong...

Eleven

OK, this was getting old.

As I was ushered into Bruno's Manhattan office, snatched and grabbed for the second time in as many days – this time from my own apartment – and transported downtown, I glowered at the men responsible, and then turned to stare at Bruno, who for all intents and purposes should be dressed like a street thug, but instead looked like he was ready for a business meeting with foreign heads of state.

'Miss Metropolis. We must stop meeting like this.'

He crossed the room and held out his hand.

I really wished my Glock wasn't hanging in its holster from the coat tree back at my apartment so I could shoot him.

Hell, I didn't even have a coat.

Not that I'd needed one. I'd only felt the cold during those brief moments when I was between warm buildings and warm car.

Still, I felt ... odd, somehow, without one.

Not to mention stupid standing there in my bare feet.

And he wanted to shake hands?

I didn't think so.

'Ah, you're upset. Understandable,' he said, crossing the room and rounding his desk. 'And it also puts you in the right mindset to see why I'm also upset.'

'You're upset? You're fully dressed...'

My sentence flapped in the proverbial wind as he held up a report of some sort. I stalked toward him and snatched it out of his hand.

Oops.

There in black and white was the record of my calling Sara Canton mere seconds after Mr Sweaty Comb-Over Guy's text saying he had found her.

'What's this?' I tried playing off. 'I recognize the agency number. Who does the other belong to?'

Bruno slid the paper from my fingers and dropped the report to the desktop. 'Let's not play games, shall we, Miss Metropolis? I can guarantee I'm much better at them.'

'You ever pick up a baseball bat?'

My reference linked back to another man who was convinced he had me beat ... until the last thing he saw before passing out was a baseball bat swinging in his direction.

I leaned my hands against his desk, feeling far braver than I probably should have. Anger and adrenalin were dangerous on their own; lethal when mixed together.

'Look, Mr ... Bruno. I have no idea what you're referring to. My agency makes at least a hundred calls a day. That number could belong to anyone.'

'So it's a coincidence then that it happened to belong to Sara Canton's brother? And that it occurred not even a minute after my text bulletin offering a bonus for her location.'

'Normally I don't believe in coincidences,' I said, crossing my arms over my chest. 'But in this particular case, it's true.'

I could have tried pointing out there were others in the office, in addition to staff that came in and out, that it could have been any one of a number of individuals, but where six months ago I might have over-explained, embellished a lie too thickly, now I was learning to keep it simple.

Besides, what did it matter? Both he and I knew I'd dialed that number.

He sat down, considering me long and hard.

I stood my ground, offering nothing more.

'I've got a proposition for you...'

I squinted at him.

He remained silent.

'I'm sorry? I'm not sure I heard you correctly.'

'I said I have a proposition for you.'

I gestured for him to go ahead, hoping he wasn't going to offer me a choice between being hung out the window by my feet, or being fitted for another pair of cement overshoes.

'A ransom note came in a half hour ago.'

'So the case is officially a kidnapping now,' I said.

'The case is officially a kidnapping.'

'How much they asking for?'

'Two million.'

I raised a brow. Hardly worth all the pain the kidnappers were going to suffer once they were found.

And I was pretty sure they would be found.

'And?' I asked.

'And Mr Abramopoulos would like you to make the drop, when one's arranged.'

More than my bare feet suddenly felt cold.

'No.'

Bruno smiled and rocked back and forth in his chair. 'It wasn't a question, Miss Metropolis.'

'What is it then? An order? Because the last time I checked, I wasn't directly employed by the Abramopoulos firm. In fact, I'm not even indirectly being paid by it, either.'

'It's atonement,' he said.

'For what?'

Oh.

For calling and warning his ex.

Shit...

What had I gotten myself into this time?

A half hour later I was being unceremoniously dumped outside my apartment building, bare feet and all, and told I would be contacted once a drop had been arranged. Something that wasn't expected for at least twenty-four hours, when the kidnapper was scheduled to call back.

By 'contacted', I assumed they meant collected in whatever state I was, at whatever time.

Probably I shouldn't be in the shower.

The late model, black, four-door sedan's tires spun on the ice before racing down the street in a cloud of exhaust.

I was strongly considering flipping it and its occupants the bird when red-and-white lights flashed behind me.

Damn.

Damn, damn, damn.

I slowly turned to watch Pino roll to a stop in the street in front of me.

Did the guy ever have down time? Was he on the job twenty-four/seven, for cripes' sake?

Leaving the lights flashing, he got out of his car and walked toward me.

'Metro.'

'Pino.'

I scanned the neighbors' windows, wondering if anyone else found the scene as ridiculous as it felt. Me, standing without a coat and barefoot on the ice in the middle of the street ... Pino walking toward me as if I were some sort of dangerous criminal, his hand on his firearm.

Dino's handsome face drifted through my mind. What must he have experienced when those Homeland Security officials – or FBI agents – or whoever had picked him up at the bakery, handcuffed him and taken him directly to the airport and put him on the first plane out. Had he been scared? Confused? Pissed?

I was guessing a combination of the three.

Pretty much what I was feeling just then.

'OK, I'm thinking you should be just about ready to tell me what's going on,' Pino said.

Over his shoulder, I caught sight of another recently familiar sight.

Parked two cars behind him to the right, sat

the Crown Vic, the exhaust smoke snaking through the cold air telling me my new friend was sitting inside, probably laughing at me.

'Just about...' I said non-committally. 'Can it hold for a minute? There's something I need to do...'

'Sofie...'

'A minute. That's all I'm asking for. Sixty seconds. Can you give them to me? How far am I going to go without a coat and shoes?'

He stared at me speechlessly.

OK, maybe I was being hard on him. He'd had the bad fortune to be the closest available object and I needed to vent.

I cleared my throat. 'Thanks. Be right back.'

I stalked around Pino and headed straight for the Vic. When I was about ten feet away, the driver figured out he might not like my intentions and the red taillights glowed against the car behind him as he put the Vic into gear.

'Oh, no you don't,' I said, picking up my pace.

He hit the car behind him. Not hard, but hard enough to set off the alarm. I recognized the ten-year-old Chevy as belonging to the jarhead who lived across the street. The car was a piece of shit, but he treated it like it was a showpiece.

He was not going to be happy.

And when he wasn't happy, nobody was.

I knocked on the driver's-side window even as Pino came rushing up behind me, thankfully distracted by an honest-to-God crime in progress.

Or an accident, anyway.

The window slid part-way down.

'Hi,' I said, thrusting my hand through the window. 'My name's Sofie Metropolis. But I'm guessing you already know that. I'm also guessing you're Charles Chaney. What I don't have a clue about is what you're doing following me...'

Pino stopped a couple of feet away and was opening his ever-present mini-notepad, writing down the Vic's plate number.

I was just glad he'd climbed off my back for a second.

'I'm not following you,' Mr Sweaty Comb-Over Guy said, looking suddenly twice as moist at the sight of a uniformed officer.

'Sir,' Pino said, having apparently finished his notation business and moving on to the next step in the police officer's procedural. 'I'm going to have to ask you to step out of the car.'

I smiled at Chaney. 'I'd say it was nice to officially meet you, but I have a feeling I'm going to be running into you again soon.' I leaned back and stared at the Chevy where John Cain, its short-fused, ex-Marine owner had somehow made it outside in record time and was surveying the damage, his profanity-laced tirade telling me Mr Chaney was, indeed, going to have his hands full for a while.

'Hey,' Pino said as I stalked toward my apartment building. 'Where are you going?'

I stared at him. Then I gestured toward my feet. 'You want I should tell your mother you contributed to giving me frostbite?'

John started yelling at Chaney and Pino.

In the resultant confusion, I pushed Mrs

Nebitz's bell. Within two seconds, she pressed the buzzer to let me in.

'Thank you again, Mrs Nebitz,' I said after explaining to her satisfaction what had happened ... or at least something that matched up with what she'd seen through her front window, probably drawn there by the police cruiser's flashing lights.

'Thank you, schmank you. You go get into a nice, warm shower – not hot. And put something warm on. You want I should bring you a cup of chicken soup? I made a fresh pot this morning. It's Seth's favorite, don't you know.'

Yes, I did know, mostly because she told me every time she made it. 'No, thank you, Mrs Nebitz. I'll fix myself a nice cup of tea.'

Her gaze was drawn to her front apartment windows where the lights still obviously flashed. I was glad she appeared to want to get back to it.

'Good night, Mrs Nebitz.'

'Huh? What? Oh, yes. Good night, Sofie.'

She closed her door, my frost-bitten feet apparently forgotten. Which was OK with me, because just then I would prefer not to be fussed over. I needed to get in, get warm, and figure out how I was going to get myself out of this mess.

The door closed behind me and I froze.

Leaning against my bedroom doorjamb was none other than Jake Porter.

And for the first time since I met him, anywhere near my bedroom was the last place I wanted him.

126

Twelve

OK, the Fates appeared to have it in for me today ... big time.

What had I done? And how in the hell did I go about undoing it? Because right then ... well, I'd far surpassed my monthly quota of odd happenings.

I stared at Porter, completely at a loss for words.

In this case, I suppose there was some comfort in knowing any minute Pino would be up here and Porter would have to leave.

What was I talking about? I was going to kick him out now.

'Well, I'd say hello, but I think that's something you do when you open the door to a visitor, not open your door to find him already in your apartment...'

My feet felt like ... well, they felt like nothing. Mostly because I had stopped feeling them about five minutes ago.

'You really should put something on those,' Jake said.

I gave a massive eye roll. 'Yeah, thanks.'

I opened the hall closet door. The only things inside were galoshes and a pair of the pinkest, most hideous slippers known to man, that also just happened to be the warmest.

I put on last year's gag Christmas gift from my sister one by one, leaning against the wall for support as I did so.

Jake raised a brow and a grin quirked his full mouth.

I gave another eye roll and headed for the kitchen. I checked the kettle for water, added a bit, then put it on to boil.

'And to what do I owe the pleasure?' I asked.

He shrugged. 'Just dropping in to say hello to a mate.'

'Yeah?' I turned and leaned against the counter. 'Decided to turn over a new leaf?'

I recalled Bruno's earlier reference to coincidences and decided this was another one that wasn't going to fly.

Problem was, I didn't currently have the figurative ammo to shoot it down with any type of guaranteed satisfaction.

But that wasn't going to stop me from trying.

'So what do you know about the Abramopoulos case?' I asked.

'Pardon me?'

I went to the dining room where the window was open (had he opened it for Muffy? Or is that how he'd gained entrance?), peeked out, then back in again. No sign of the mutt.

Damn.

I left it open.

'You're not pardoned. Give.' I took only one cup out and plopped a tea bag into the middle

128

of it.

'You still have those blasted ... things in here,' he said.

I grimaced, finding him looking into my bedroom. Things ... I guessed he meant gifts.

The first time he was inside my apartment, he'd been put off by the fact I'd kept my wedding gifts. Said something along the lines that I was stuck in the past and until I moved on...

Until I moved on, what?

We'd have a chance at a relationship?

Depended on your definition of the word.

And it was obvious mine varied greatly from his.

In his world, he could pop in and out whenever the mood moved him, never answer any questions, and remain a mystery. In mine, I revealed my second grade teacher's name, how old I was when I first kissed a boy and what my mother was fixing for dinner that Sunday ... as well as expect him to go with me to said dinner every now and again, even if goat was on the menu.

'What do you want, Jake?' I asked.

He slowly turned back to look at me, a somber expression on his handsome face. I'd noticed he looked different, but now I saw the extent of the changes. Yes, his hair was trimmed, but he was also closely shaved, lending an almost baby-like quality to his striking face and emphasizing how very blue his eyes were.

The color where the Greek sky meets the Aegean Sea, my mother would say.

I quietly cleared my throat and went back into the kitchen.

OK, so I wasn't as immune to him as I pretended. And accepted I probably never would be. From the get go, he'd touched something inside me. Some sort of animalistic, fundamental shadow that made me crave all things dark and mysterious.

Made me ceaselessly yearn for him.

'You not seeing that Greek baker bloke any more?' he asked quietly.

The kettle began to whistle. I shut off the burner, and against my better judgment took another cup out of the cupboard.

'No,' I answered just as quietly.

I poured the water over the bags to steep, then stood for a long moment, trying to interpret the myriad currents running through my veins. Part of me very much wanted to walk up to Porter, curve my fingers over his strong jaw and kiss the ever-loving stuffing out of him.

Another wanted to toss the hot tea down the front of his shirt.

I was having a hard time deciding which track I should take.

I removed the tea bags, took out sugar and milk, and put them and the cups on the kitchen table.

'Black, please.'

I added sugar and milk to mine then took him his, close enough to smell his tangy lime cologne.

Was that humming I heard? I was pretty sure

130

that was humming. And I was also pretty sure I was the source of it.

With me in my hideous slippers, he towered over me by about nine or ten inches, every bit of him hard, raw male.

Double damn.

I forced myself to sip my tea.

'Whatever Abramopoulos is asking you to do?' he said quietly. 'Don't.'

I squinted at him.

'I knew it! I knew this had something to do with Abramopoulos.'

I began to turn away, but he caught my arm, strong enough to stop me, but not too much that I spilled either of our teas.

'No, Sofie. This has to do with you...'

Was he going to kiss me? It really looked like he was going to kiss me.

Yeah, he was...

I tried to decide whether or not I'd let him when his mouth pressed against mine ... and my body decided for me by sighing against his.

God, he tasted so very good...

Every part of me melted on the spot, including my feet, which were now tingling inside my slippers for reasons not having to do with the cold.

I'd pretty much figured out that even if I lived to be a hundred and two I'd never figure out what it was that drew me to Jake Porter. No matter what stunts he pulled, or secrets he kept, there was no fighting my attraction to him. In fact, the more I battled, the greater it grew, like a snowball rolling downhill.

If only the sensation that an icy wall lay at the bottom of the hill would go away, I might have been able to stop fighting and surrender to him.

There was that humming sound again.

His tongue slid against mine and my core temperature rose even higher, igniting thoughts of finally making it to my bed in the other room, unopened wedding gifts be damned...

A loud knock at the door.

I found I'd gotten up on my toes in order to kiss him more fully. I now stood flat-footed.

He slowly pulled away.

'You've got a visitor,' Jake said, grinning.

I resisted the temptation to wipe the drool I was sure was dripping from the left side of my mouth. 'Um, yeah ... that I do.'

Another knock, then Pino said, 'I know you're in there, Metro. Don't make me force entry.'

Jake hiked a brow even as I longed for a whole different type of entry that had nothing to do with Pimply Pino Karras and everything to do with the hot Australian in front of me.

'I dare say you'd better let him in.'

I didn't want to. I wanted to kiss Jake again. And again. And again.

Unfortunately the insistent knocking proved Pino was more determined than I was.

I let out a soft breath that seemed to carry out with it some of the longing pressing against my insides.

'I'm coming, I'm coming,' I called out when I heard what sounded like scratching against my doorknob. Probably Pino had gotten out his lock-picking kit.

I reluctantly put my tea down on the kitchen table and went to open the door.

'What took you so long?' he demanded, looking more upset than I'd seen him in a while.

'Pino I'd like you to meet...'

I turned around ... only to find Jake was gone. Hunh.

No matter how many times he did that, I'd never get used to it.

Pino picked up what had been Jake's cup on the kitchen table next to mine.

'For me?' he asked.

'What?'

He raised the cup.

'Yeah.'

The ghost had left the building ... again.

Jake's words swirled around my head in an endless stream as I tried to calm an agitated Pino, promising him I'd let him in on what I was doing when the time was right, then again during the drive over to Grandpa Kosmos' café; an appointment I'd nearly forgotten about and probably would have entirely had Pino not interrupted that kiss.

I found my fingertips lingering against my lower lip.

'Oh, for Pete's sake, stop it,' I told myself, nearing my grandfather's place.

Probably I should be thinking more about his words than the sinful mouth from which they'd exited. I nearly plowed into the back of a car that had stopped suddenly in front of me. Probably I should be paying attention to where I was going.

I looked closer at the dark corner coffee shop. That was odd. Why were the lights off? I knew he was closed Tuesdays, but it wasn't Tuesday, and, even if it were, there would be some lights on.

I found a parking spot on the side street and got out of the car. I'd thought about calling to cancel our appointment, but considering how odd my grandfather had sounded, I didn't dare. Besides, it had given me the excuse I needed to get rid of Pino ... and to remove myself from an apartment with walls I would probably climb wondering where that kiss might have led had circumstances been different.

OK, it was official: I was insane. Just lock me up in a rubber room in one of those white jackets and leave me there until I started thinking with a part of my brain that worked properly.

Or worked at all when it came to Jake Porter.

What had he meant by don't do whatever Abramopoulos had asked me to? And how would he know I'd been asked to do anything?

Why was it Jake Porter knew more about what was going on in my life than my mother?

Speaking of which, where was my mother?

I stopped in the middle of the sidewalk and dialed the house.

No answer.

I knew my father wasn't home yet. Could see his steakhouse was still open for business across the street, and odds were his car was still parked out back.

And my black-clad grandmother – better known as Yiayia – never answered the phone because she didn't speak English. Or, rather, pretended she didn't.

But my mother?

Someone picked up on the tenth ring. 'Hello?'

'Mama?'

'Sofie?' She sounded decidedly groggy. 'What is the matter, *koukla mou? Ti simbeni*?'

She asked me in Greek what was wrong.

'I was hoping you could tell me that. What's going on? Are you in bed already?'

She never went to bed without my dad. Unless...

'Are you sick?'

'Sick? Knock wood. What would make you ask that?'

What, indeed.

'I just had a long day, is all. Went to bed early.'

I squinted into the dark as if it would help me make sense of everything.

'Can I call you back in the morning?' she asked.

'Sure ... OK.'

'Kalinikta.'

'Good night.'

I hung up and looked again at my grand-father's dark windows.

Had I fallen asleep and woken up in some sort of parallel universe? Because right now, nothing was as it should be.

I got out of the car and walked to the front door of the dark café. I pressed my nose against the glass, my hand shielding my eyes against the street light. The door opened slightly inward.

I started and slapped the same hand against my chest.

What was the door doing unlocked?

Oh, boy. This was not boding well...

'Hello...?' I called out, opening the door. *'Pappou*? Are you in here?'

As many times as I'd been in this place, I'd never entered in the dark and I lost all sense of perspective. I bumped into a stool, the screeching of the legs against tile sending icy tentacles up my spine.

Oh, this was ridiculous. Probably Grandpa Kosmos had forgotten about our appointment. Probably he'd gone out somewhere with a couple of his friends. Or despite the darkness of the overhead apartment, was upstairs, maybe even sleeping, like my mother.

Right...

Having one of them in bed this early was enough. Both of them? I was calling a doctor.

I reached for my cell phone, thinking I should call him, see what was going on.

A sound in the back.

I couldn't tell exactly what. Why did things sound different in the dark than they did in the light? It was similar to the stool legs against the tile ... but not.

What if he was lying on the floor in here in the dark? If he'd fallen and hit his head?

136

My heart expanded to block my air passage.
'Pappou...?'

I whispered the word so softly, I barely heard it.

Another sound ... this time a kind of wet plunk...

All things dark and sinister leapt to mind.

What if the reason why the front door was unlocked was that he'd been robbed? And the assailant was even now still in there?

I reached for my Glock and considered running for the front door, the thought of dialing 911 floating around in there somewhere...

'Please ... Come in, Sofie...'

Thirteen

'Pappou, what are you doing sitting in here with the lights off?'

The instant I recognized his voice, I sighed off my fears, re-holstered my Glock and walked to the end of the counter where the light panel was located on the far wall. I flicked the first switch I came to, which illuminated him where he sat in the back at the table his friends claimed during the day.

He lifted his hand to ward it off. 'No, please. Turn it off.'

'No.'

He stared at me.

I turned it off.

Now that I knew where he was, it was relatively easy to make my way back to where he was sitting.

'How come you didn't answer me when I called?'

He sighed heavily. 'I must have fallen asleep. Sorry.'

I held my hand out in front of me, feeling around for the chair backs. Then I pulled out the one next to him and sat down.

'Are you OK?'

'What? Yes, yes. I am fine. How are you?'

Right then? I was so not fine it wasn't funny.

Was it something in the water? The reason for the funny way everyone was acting?

If so, I determined I should stay away from it. Then again, perhaps if I downed a good gallon of it, everything would make sense.

'Fine is not sitting in your café in the dark,' I told him. 'What's wrong?'

'Nothing. Really. It's nothing.'

I tried to come up with a few reasons to explain his strange behavior. 'Is it the café? Is everything all right? Business is good?'

'Huh? Yes, yes. Business is very good.'

'Is it ... my grandmother?'

My grandmother had died some years ago, but occasionally my grandfather slipped into a funk and sometimes didn't re-emerge for days. But usually it was around the time he'd lost her, which was spring, not winter.

'Can I make you something?' I asked. 'Warm milk, maybe?'

My mother had sometimes made it for me and my siblings, including lots of sugar and some sweet bread dunked into it. Every now and again my brother and I would pretend we couldn't sleep just to get the treat. I was pretty sure Mom was wise to us, but she'd always made it.

'What? What do I look like, a kid? Or, worse, an old man?'

The one thing I hadn't asked him about was his health. Partly because I was afraid to. Mostly because I was afraid to.

'Of course not,' I reassured him.

He made some disgruntled sounds that were at least reassuring in their familiarity.

'So ... what did you want to see me about?'

Silence.

'Pappou?'

'I heard you.'

'But you didn't answer.'

He leaned forward, causing his chair to creak slightly. 'You remember last summer? I asked you to find something for me?'

Yes, I remembered. All too well. He'd requested I find an old war medal of his.

'Well?' he asked.

I realized I hadn't answered him. 'Yes, yes. I remember.'

'Good. Because I need for you to find it for me now...'

When I finally returned home, I was beat ... physically and mentally. I mean, how much was one person really supposed to take?

I looked up at the ceiling while I climbed the stairs to my second story apartment.

My feet protested my every move and I had the sinking sensation I might end up catching more than the Christmas bug before this day was over, no thanks to Bruno and his gorillas.

I half expected Mrs Nebitz to crack open her door as I unlocked mine; I was thankful when she didn't.

I let myself in and then collapsed against the closed barrier, imagining it was some protection against me and the rest of the world.

140

I'm not sure what it was about the cycles of life that always catch me unawares. You get a long, dull stretch of nothing much, then BAM! Everything is lobbed at you at once, with little hope of catching half of it.

I slowly blinked, looking for the energy to push from the door when I became aware of two things: the lights were out; and it was freezing.

I always, but always left the lamp on the side table on. There were few things worse than coming home to a dark house ... or café, as my earlier experience bore out. Or a cold one.

I watched where a frigid breeze billowed the sheers on Muffy's open window. I was surprised they hadn't frozen. Or maybe they had and I wouldn't see for sure until I went over there.

Something I couldn't seem to muster the motivation to do.

Had Porter come back? I took a deep breath, trying to detect his cologne on the cold air. I couldn't make out anything but the scent of the pine boughs.

'Muffy?' I whistled softly. 'Come here, boy.'

Nothing.

Shit.

OK, surely it was written somewhere that a body shouldn't have to enter a dark place twice in one night. Especially if said dark place was her own apartment.

I slowly slid my hand across the door and over to the light switch. Click. Nothing.

I brought my hand back and took my Glock from its holster for the second occasion that night.

OK, time to see what was going on in my own apartment. Although the option of driving up the street to stay the night at my parents' until dawn broke was mighty tempting.

That, however, wasn't going to help Muffy.

I remembered a time not so long ago when I'd returned to find the Jack Russell duct taped in the bathroom.

My heart gave a sharp squeeze.

I crept slowly forward, my eyes adjusting to the dark. I considered opening the door, allowing the hall light to illuminate my way. Problem with that is it would also outline me like a close target.

No. Better to do it this way.

Creak.

Funny how you never realized how much noise your floorboards made until you were walking across them in dark silence. I mean, I was familiar with old buildings; the house I'd grown up in was at least as old as this place and it had taken teenaged creeping to learn where to step without waking my parents or Yiayia.

One night I'd made it down the stairs and was breathing a sigh of relief when I'd run straight into my grandmother.

I'd screamed.

She'd merely stared at me, arms crossed, brows raised, her gray head shaking.

I'd slunk back upstairs without a word ... and didn't try sneaking out again for at least two weeks.

Now that I was on my own ... well, some-how it didn't hold the same innocent appeal. Although I would still prefer the floorboards didn't creak as loudly as they did.

'Here, Muffy, Muffy, Muffy...'

I wasn't clear on what bothered me most: that Muffy wasn't responding to my calls or that the lights were off. Maybe it was a toss up. Maybe one amplified the other.

Maybe I was just overtired and in dire need of a hot shower and a good night's sleep.

I cleared the coffee table and sofa and nearly tripped over something that shouldn't be there.

I held steady, taking deep breaths I hoped weren't too loud in the otherwise quiet room.

Please, please, please don't be a body...

I really didn't want to see Pino again tonight.

I nearly giggled, wondering if a ruptured gas line could be responsible for the silly ping-ponging of my thoughts.

Then it occurred to me the object could be Pino...

Holding my gun tightly in my right hand, I slowly knelt down, blindly feeling around. I didn't realize I had my eyes tightly closed until my fingers touched something cold and metal-lic.

Not a body.

I shuddered with relief as I felt out the lamp I usually left on.

Well, that explained why there was no light.

As I quietly turned it upright, I reminded my-self that what went unexplained was how it had

143

ended up on the floor.

I stood back up, reasoning out other lights should be in working order. I stepped the few feet toward the kitchen and tried the switch.

I was so relieved the apartment was no longer pitch black I nearly let my guard down with my gun.

Not so fast...

I moved around the apartment, turning on lights as I went, aware of every movement. Or rather, non-movement.

Until I reached my bedroom.

There, in the middle of the bed, lay the last thing I expected to see...

Fourteen

Hunh.

OK. I suppose in the scheme of things, this was the least odd thing to have happened today. Still, seeing Muffy curled up with the large black cat – very large! – in the middle of my bed was still unusual.

Both of them looked at me, Muffy excitedly wagging his tail, my one-time visitor Tee the Cat giving himself a lick or two between blinks. I hadn't seen Tee since October, when he and I had crossed paths seemingly at every turn, until one day he'd popped up in my apartment through Muffy's open window ... much as he'd presumably done again tonight.

Then, just as abruptly, he'd disappeared again.

'Did you two break my lamp?' I asked.

They stared at me.

'Just so you know, it's coming out of your kibble.'

They both lay their heads back down as if to say, 'Yeah, right,' and I gave an eye roll, wondering if I was always going to be a pushover.

I took in the wedding gifts still stacked against the wall on the other side of the bed. They'd been sitting there so long, a couple of the towering piles had begun tilting, the boxes starting to collapse under the weight of those on top of them. I absently scratched my head. Most times, I didn't even notice they were there. But after Jake's pointing them out – again – well, I supposed it was past time I decided what I was going to do with them.

I considered Mrs Nebitz's grandson Seth and his engagement announcement. I could give the gifts to him...

Then again, no. Seth was Jewish and these particular gift givers were Greek Orthodox, which stood to reason at least a few would hold religious icons of a Christian nature.

I don't think Mrs Nebitz would appreciate a portrait of the Virgin Mary holding baby Jesus, even if it was etched in gold.

I went into the other room and closed and locked the window, pausing for a moment to scan the street. No black trucks. No Crown Vics. No dark sedans. Everything was as it should be.

Did I dare hope that meant the day's strangeness had reached its end? I glanced at the clock to find it nearly midnight.

I dared to hope.

I headed for the bathroom and the shower beyond, propping my cell phone on the sink and setting my earlier conversation with Geraldine Garcia to play, even as I reviewed everything else that had happened that day. Up to and including Jake's warning: 'Whatever Abramopoulos is asking you to do? Don't.'

Trust me, the last thing I wanted to do was be

146

anywhere near that ransom drop. I had a very bad feeling about it.

Then again, what was there to feel good about?

Which was why I intended to figure out who had grabbed little Jolie outside her school before that drop was arranged.

Or work my ass off toward that end, anyway.

I stripped down, climbed into the shower and emptied my mind of everything but the sound of the water and Mrs Garcia's almost melodic words.

If every now and again Jake Porter and his phenomenal mouth slid through my mind, and my hands took a little longer than necessary to soap certain areas of my anatomy ... well, that was between me and my shower head.

'This is a list of everything I need you to do,' I said the following morning, dropping what was essentially a notepad full of names and information I was looking for on to Rosie's desk. 'And I need you to get Pete and Waters in here as soon as possible.' I shrugged out of my coat. 'Let me know the instant they get here.'

I was halfway to my uncle's office when I realized I hadn't heard a 'tsk' or a 'sigh' or an 'eye roll', (yes, you could hear Rosie's). I turned in the doorway and looked back at her ... and wished maybe I hadn't.

The petite Puerto Rican dynamo looked even smaller still sitting in her office chair staring off into space, snowflake-sized tears sliding down her cheeks unchecked.

Oy.

I didn't know how she'd found out, but she'd found out.

I put my coat in the office and then pulled my old desk chair closer to hers.

'Rosie...?'

She finally seemed to register my presence and looked vaguely in my direction. 'Huh?'

'You OK?'

It seemed to take her an inordinate amount of time to process my question; she appeared confused. 'What? What kind of stupid thing is that to ask?'

I smiled – inwardly, because I was sure an outward one would earn me a slap or a whack or some other physical rebuke. Her sarcastic response proved she wasn't too far gone.

'You're not OK?'

She glared at me. 'I'm sitting here with no make-up on, looking like a bargain basement reprobate, *crying* ... I'm peachy. You?'

This time I did smile.

And she smiled back, albeit only slightly.

'What happened?' I asked, hesitant.

She sucked her bottom lip between her teeth, telling me I was losing ground.

Then again, I honestly had to gain it in order to lose it.

'Seth is engaged.'

The words seemed ripped from somewhere deep inside of her and the tears virtually launched themselves from her big, dark eyes.

I rolled my chair backwards, took tissues from

one of my drawers, then rolled back, offering the box to her.

She began yanking them out one by one. 'He called me last night to tell me. Can you believe it? I saw his name in my cell display and my heart ... well, it nearly flew from my chest. He's back, I thought. He wants to see me.'

She continued yanking, short, angry jerks while her tears dropped on to the front of her top, soaking it.

'But no. Instead, he tells me he had something to say ... something he wanted to make sure I heard from him first, rather than someone else.'

I didn't know what to say, so I said nothing.

'She's Jewish, of course. Someone that old bitch of a grandmother – excuse my French – introduced him to.'

'Mrs Nebitz?'

She stared at me, her hands finally halting their frenetic movement.

Of course, Mrs Nebitz. Who else could she possibly be talking about? It had been Mrs Nebitz who'd played the starring role in her grandson's break-up with the unacceptable Puerto Rican girl. I could almost hear her voice in my ear now: 'Sofie, dear, Seth is the only grandson I have. It's so very important he choose the right girl to be his wife. Someone who shares his values. Who can make him happy. Who, while he might not love in the beginning, he will grow to love ... just like my late husband, dear one that he was, and I. Kids throw around the word "love" all the time nowadays. But that's not real love. That's not what lasts.'

I'd listened with half an ear, because I'd heard the same thing from my mother ... again and again and again.

Of course, I'd never really heeded it.

Or maybe I had.

Had my acceptance of Thomas Chalikis' marriage proposal been a way to appease my Greek parents?

Eight months ago, I would have answered no. That my falling for a Greek had been a coincidence. Nothing more. Nothing less.

Now?

'You knew!'

Rosie's loud words nearly catapulted me from the chair, much less my thoughts.

'What? Or course, I didn't know. How in world would I know? Seth doesn't have my number.'

'No ... but you live across the hall from that old battleaxe of a grandmother of his. She told you, didn't she? She told you Seth is going to marry somebody else.'

OK, the way I saw it, there were two kinds of lying: the one you did when your ass was on the line, usually to strangers; and the one you did for personal reasons, to keep from hurting someone more than they already were.

I was coming to see both were equally important.

'No, Rosie, she didn't. Don't you think I would have told you if she had?'

A heartbeat of a pause.

Then she launched herself into my arms and started sobbing in a way that made me want to cry.

An hour later I was in my office working at my combination white board/cork board, flipping from one side to the other as my theories flew fast and furious. I leaned back to look through the doorway into the outer office; Rosie was explaining our fees to a new client. I'd overheard enough to know the woman was interested in knowing if her husband of two years was cheating with an old girlfriend. And that Rosie had grabbed on to the case like a drowning man a floating piece of driftwood.

'Oh, girl, it don't look good,' Rosie was saying. 'Trust me. If he's got his dirty paws in the cookie jar, you can rest assured we'll catch him with his paw prints all over those biscuits.'

After she'd cried on my shoulder (and my sleeve and the front of my shirt) I was afraid I'd have to send her home until she felt well enough to work. The mere prospect had made me want to sob. While I knew much of what she did, I knew nowhere near enough to do what I'd asked her. Research and background checks that would take me days if not weeks.

And I didn't have either.

I had till the end of the day today, best I could figure it.

Thankfully, the phone had rung and Rosie disengaged herself from her shirt-drenching activities and answered as if she hadn't shed a single tear, calmly telling the person on the other end that, yes, we worked cheating-spouse cases, and, yes, they were open.

I was guessing the woman in the office now had been the caller.

My eye caught on a stack of the usual agency newspaper subscriptions on the corner of the desk. More specifically, my attention caught on a picture and caption in the upper right-hand corner: one of Santa's reindeer spotted in Queens, along with a shot of what I guessed was none other than Mrs Claus' Rudy.

I leafed through the paper until I came to the piece, took note of the publication and the reporter and then closed it again.

I realized I'd lost my place in listening to Mrs Garcia's recorded interview. I stepped to my desk and slid it back a hair.

There, that's it.

She was going on about the front deskman and how he always had a piece of candy for Jolie, you know, that expensive chocolate stuff. I'd asked how long he'd worked there and she'd told me seven years.

I returned to my board, continuing my flow chart of people who surrounded Jolie on a daily basis per one very observant nanny, Geraldine Garcia.

'Then there's Sara ... you know, Mrs Abramopoulos. So very sad what happened there. She was such a nice lady.'

I paused, then went back to my cell and re-played that portion again.

I wondered how nice Mrs Garcia thought she was. Nice enough that she might have taken Jolie to visit her mother every now and again, despite what the custody decree held?

'What's shakin', bacon?'

I looked up to find Eugene standing in my office doorway looking even gaudier in the light of day.

He sucked his teeth. 'Whatcha think?'

He opened his black leather coat and did a twirl of sorts, stopping every ten degrees to shift his weight from one platform-heeled foot to the other.

'I think you should have saved the money for that fur coat you're planning on buying your wife.'

He tsked. 'Oh, she gonna get that coat, all right. 'Cause I'm guessing you got something for me, don't ya? Something juicy.'

'You mean like those bats last month?'

His bug eyes bugged out farther. I capped my marker.

'Don't worry. That's history.' I leafed through the items on my desk. 'While it's not as juicy as you might like, there is a bit of meat to this one.'

A brief knock and my cousin Pete peeked his head around. 'You rang?'

I smiled. 'I definitely rang.'

With Rosie working one angle, and me and these two guys the other, I might just stand a hope of discovering something that would save my ass before Bruno and his guys took another bite out of it.

Fifteen

A phone call had netted me what I was looking for regarding Geraldine Garcia's taking Jolie to visit her mother on the sly.

'Oh, no, Miss Metropolis. I would never do that. Mr Abramopoulos, he would be very mad if I did that.'

Which meant she had.

What bearing that had beyond satisfying the small voice in the back of my head, I didn't know.

I leaned back from the board to glance at Rosie. Pete and Waters had left a while earlier, if not happy with their assignments, accepting of them. Thankfully Rosie seemed better. The Christmas carols were playing at a lower volume than usual, but at least they were playing. And she seemed busy at work with something on her laptop.

'That Kent woman called again,' she said.

I raised my brows. How'd she do that? Know I was looking at her without looking at me?

'Says she's going to fire us.'

I made a face. While I hated to admit defeat, I was beginning to think in this particular case, throwing in the towel was my only option.

The front door opened, letting in the agency's long-standing star process server. Or, rather, one-time, since Eugene seemed to be out-serving her lately.

Pamela Coe was likely there to collect her pay for the morning's work.

I eyed the pretty blonde, a revisiting idea tap dancing around the edges of my thoughts.

Rosie looked at me and the idea tapped right into the spotlight.

'Bait,' she said at the same time I thought it.

If the thought of not delivering on a case bothered me, I suspected it actually kept Rosie up nights. Well, OK, probably she wouldn't lose any sleep over it, although probably she did file her nails a little too vigorously.

'What?' Pamela asked.

Rosie swiveled on her chair and smiled at her. 'Oh, nothing. But I'm guessing Sofie might like to talk to you once we've concluded our business.'

Pamela looked at me and I smiled, as well.

She appeared dubious. Understandable. Probably I would have run for the door had I encountered what she was right now.

I happily switched off the monotonous drone of Mrs Garcia's voice and focused on something other than the kidnapping case.

'I can't believe I let you talk me into this.'

I'd instructed Pamela to go home and change into something sexy; she'd met me outside the Queens restaurant – where Mrs Kent's husband

155

regularly took his lunch – looking ready for an upscale cocktail party. The simple black dress and pearls made her more Abramopoulos-ready than cheating-husband bait.

Probably I should have called Debbie Matenopoulos, another sometimes process server. I could have told her to dress for a cocktail party and she'd have showed up looking like a two-dollar whore.

I felt slightly guilty for thinking that about a girl who'd gone to school with my younger brother Kosmos, but facts were facts and the bleached blonde that even Jake Porter used on occasion to work cases that were a mystery to me filled a certain criterion I thought would come in handy now.

Pamela, the gun-toting natural blonde, looked a little too conservative for the role of bait.

Who knew she cleaned up so well?

I reached out and tried to push up the dress a bit.

'What are you doing?' she protested, stepping away from me.

'Trying to shorten your hem. What are you, an uptight librarian?'

What went without saying is that I couldn't have done any better. In fact, once I'd outlined what I had in mind back at the agency, Pamela asked why I didn't go ahead and act as bait if I was so convinced the ruse would work. The question had stumped me for a good minute. Then I explained that I was the boss, and bosses didn't do items of that nature.

No, we just got ourselves drafted into making dangerous ransom drops.

I grimaced inwardly, wondering how in the hell I was going to get out of that one.

Besides, I'd added, I'd garnered more than my fair share of media attention as of late, and I couldn't risk Mr Kent's recognizing me.

Still my arguments hadn't held much sway; it had taken me a good ten minutes, promise of a hefty bonus, and a Rosie pep talk to convince Pamela to do this.

Now she looked a snowflake away from changing her mind.

'Alright then,' I said, throwing a wary glance at the cloudy sky. 'Here's his picture.' I held out a casual shot of a nice-looking guy in a button-down shirt throwing a football. 'He usually sits at the end of the main bar, which should make your job easier.'

'And my job is, exactly?'

'To get him to come on to you like gang-busters.'

She looked back at the street where she'd parked her car then back at me. 'And that'll prove what, again?'

'That he's a rat, cheating bastard.'

'Because he comes on to me?'

I nodded.

At this point, I'd settle for a good come on.

Have I mentioned I didn't like not delivering on cases?

I wasn't sure if it was the cold and the fact that she wore very little or if I'd finally convinced her to do the job, but finally Pamela walked toward the door of the simple, American-style restaurant a half a block up. I waited until she disappeared inside, then reached inside Lucille to collect my purse and other gear. Then I followed her.

I entered the establishment some five minutes after Pamela. I spotted Clark immediately, seated on a stool at the end of the bar just as he had been the other dozen times I'd had Pete or Waters follow him. Pamela had taken the seat a couple up from him. Why hadn't she sat right next to him?

Damn. This wasn't going to work. I could tell already.

I chose a stool a couple up from her, close enough to hear any conversation, but far enough away not to be too obvious.

I hoped.

I placed an order for a chocolate shake after verifying they didn't serve frappés and asked for a menu.

'I'm sorry...' Pamela said.

I watched in the mirror behind the bar as she reached for something she had apparently dropped between her and Clark.

'I've got it,' he said.

He bent at the same time and they bumped heads.

Quiet laughter and apologies then Clark was handing her what looked like a small, black appointment book.

'Thank you. If I'd lost this...' Pamela shook

her head.

'No problem.'

They both looked straight ahead again.

Damn.

Probably that was as good as it was going to get. Probably I should have snapped a picture of the head bump. Probably Pamela didn't know how to get a guy to come on to her like gangbusters and this was going to be a complete bust, period.

As long as I was at it, probably I'd have been better off staying at the agency trying to figure a way out of the mess I was in.

I ordered a burger and fries I didn't plan to eat but thought Rosie might appreciate.

My cell vibrated in my jacket pocket. I took it out, half expecting my mother. Instead, it was a text from Waters telling me I was crazy. I was about to call him to ask what he was talking about now, since no bats were involved in the assignment I'd given him, when I noticed Pamela and Clark were not just talking, but she had moved to take the stool next to him, to his smiling consent.

Wow.

OK, maybe I'd underestimated Pamela's abilities.

I took out a small camera that looked like a pen from my purse along with a notepad, silently thanking Waters for his 'five-finger discount' supply access.

I snapped off a few shots, trying not to be too obvious as I squinted into the small display on the back of the silver pen.

'I'm here for a business meeting but she must be running late,' I heard Pamela say.

The legs of the stool to my left screeched against the floor and a heavyset Latino man sat down, talking loudly in Spanish on his cell phone.

Great.

I only caught snippets of Pamela's conversation with Clark after that, nothing I could follow with any certainty.

'Excuse me, may I borrow that for minute?'

I blinked to find my new neighbor motioning toward the camera pen.

'Sorry,' I said, continuing to pretend I was writing on my notepad while I snapped another shot.

'I'll just be a moment.'

Damn.

I discreetly switched off the camera and handed him the pen.

'And a piece of paper?'

I wanted to ask if he wanted me to write it for him, too, as I tore off a piece of notepad and held it out.

He spoke into the phone in Spanish again, holding the pen at the ready.

Problem was, he didn't appear in any hurry to use it for what he intended.

'Excuse me?' I said.

He held up the fingers of the hand holding the pen to wave me off.

Then he started messing with the sensitive

buttons on the end, as if looking to click the pen open.

I snatched it from his hand, hoping he hadn't inadvertently deleted anything. 'Just tell me what you need written down,' I said.

He stared at me.

I raised my brows.

He said something into the phone, waited, then looked at me, speaking in Spanish.

'English, please?'

I noticed Pamela was getting up from her stool.

I hurriedly wrote down a number, shoved the paper toward my neighbor, then messed with the pen until I hoped I got the camera working again.

'Thank you for keeping me company,' Pamela was saying.

'It's I who should be thanking you,' Clark was saying.

Pamela turned toward me, her gaze briefly meeting mine before she dropped the coat she was putting on.

'Seriously, I don't know what's gotten into me today,' she said as she reached to pick it up.

'Please, allow me.'

The money shot.

I clicked away as Clark picked up Pamela's coat then reached up to drape it over her shoulders. She leaned back, turning her head slightly to say something to him I couldn't make out.

And then my unwelcome neighbor filled my vision, along with the pen's.

'I need your help again.'

I said something I'm sure wasn't very polite as I pushed from the stool, grabbed my own coat and made for the door, snapping photos as I went.

A few minutes later, Pamela joined me up the block next to where our cars were parked.

'Did you get what you needed?' she asked.

I mumbled something under my breath and then said, 'I hope so.'

'Good. Because I never want to do that again.' She gave a shudder I was sure had nothing to do with the cold.

'It couldn't have been that bad.'

'No? Then why do I feel like I need a shower?' She turned toward her car. 'That man rates up there as one of the nicest I've come across in a good, long while.'

'You mean he didn't come on to you?'

'Come on to me? He couldn't have been more of a gentleman if he tried.'

'Maybe that was his come on.'

She stared at me. 'No, Sof, what he did was second nature. He couldn't have been less interested in me as a woman. I didn't pick up a single untoward vibe from him.'

'Maybe he's gay.' I searched my mind for a suitable piece of gay bait.

She gave a rare eye roll. 'I'm going home. Don't call if you need anything.'

She got into her car and began driving away.

I realized I'd forgotten to thank her.

I was too busy trying to double check the pen

cam, silently cursing myself for not having requested a takeout carton for the burger and fries for Rosie, and noticing my least favorite Crown Vic was once again on my tail.

A short time later I drove Lucille down Steinway, on my way to Ditmars to pick up something for Rosie for lunch, trying not to think of the perfectly good burger and fries I'd forgotten to take from the restaurant and the Crown Vic on my tail.

The sky seemed to be hugging the tops of the low apartment buildings, and big, flat flakes started to fall. Great, more snow. The city hadn't completely dug out from the last storm. I reached out and turned down the police ban radio I'd taken to listening to lately and instead switched on the radio. Of course, there were no weather reports anywhere to be had in the canned broadcasts. Probably I should have read those newspapers this morning outside that reindeer story. Which probably wasn't a bad idea beyond even the weather reports. For all I knew, there was something related to the Abramopoulos case in there. I was thinking not, though. If there were something in there, I'm sure I would have been the victim of a snatch and grab for the third time.

Speaking of which...

I took my cell phone out of my purse and checked my messages. No daily bulletin. Which meant they weren't daily, but rather whenever the mood moved Bruno.

Of course, he'd instituted them before I'd

warned off Sara Canton and been drafted to make the ransom drop.

I dialed information, giving them the name of the newspaper that had run the reindeer story. Within a minute, I had the reporter who had written the piece on the line.

'Wendy Wyckoff.'

I began by telling her I knew whom the reindeer belonged to, then told her about Dino's story.

I didn't know what I was hoping to accomplish. Maybe that a little negative coverage might light a fire under the CIS and David Hunter? Get Dino off that list and back home?

'Tell me more about the reindeer,' Wendy said.

Someone honked at me from behind. I stared in the rear-view mirror to find I was holding up traffic. I spotted a free spot at the curb and pulled into it to talk. The driver behind me flipped me the bird as he passed.

'Yeah, and Happy Holidays to you, too,' I mumbled to him, then returned my attention to Wendy. 'What I'm thinking is a kind of "Bring Him Home for the Holidays" human interest piece.'

'Sorry, but do you have any idea how many stories I get basically the same as yours? My editor wouldn't run it if it were my own father, and he was born here.'

'But...'

'Seriously. Two weeks ago I wrote up this real tear-jerker of a story. Woman was born here, but, because her parents were foreign, she spoke with an accent. They deported her to Mexico. She had three young kids they put in foster care. Harry – that's my editor – wouldn't even look at it. Dime a dozen, he said.'

'A lot of stories like that coming from Mexico, I bet.'

'This woman's parents were from Portugal.'

I winced.

That was the second time I'd mistaken a person's country of origin.

Was I a racist?

'Look, unless you want to tell me about this reindeer, I'm going to have to ring off.'

I thought for a moment, weighing my options. Depending on how well I worked this, I might very well be able to kill two birds with one stone yet.

And that's exactly what I set out to do, telling her just enough about the missing Rudy, without many supporting details, to keep her interest ... then telling her if she wanted the rest, she'd have to agree to run something on Dino.

'I'll see what I can do,' she said grudgingly.

'Not good enough.'

'Look, it's not in my hands. But if I can slant this Rudy story the way I'm thinking I can...? Well, your friend Dino gets a run.'

I smiled.

'Well, then, let me tell you the rest of the story.'

Five minutes later I had a happy reporter, had contacted Mrs Claus to let her know she would be getting a call from Wendy and likely a visit from her and a paper photographer, and was sitting back in my car sipping a frappé I'd picked up when I realized where I was: up the block from Dino's bakery.

Were those lights?

I squinted through the snow that was falling more heavily now, then rolled down my window a hair, catching a familiar scent of...

Was that *Christopsomo*? Greek Christmas bread?

It couldn't be.

I shut off the engine and got out of the car. Dino hadn't made it home somehow without my knowing ... had he?

I took in the 'Open' sign on the door, the bustle of activity inside and especially the full window display of baked goodies.

My mouth watered.

My heart beat harder.

My stomach was too small for the bird that fluttered around inside it.

I pulled open the door and walked inside, looking for signs of Dino.

'Excuse me,' I said to a girl in a white apron and hair net stocking the breadbaskets behind the counter. 'Who's in charge?'

A head popped up next to her.

And I found myself staring at none other than my mother, Thalia Metropolis.

I sat at the round table set up for customers across from my mother, trying to digest what she was saying while wishing instead I were digesting one of the many delicious concoctions in the display just to my left.

Fast-forbidden delicacies Thalia wouldn't let me have.

I suppose I was lucky I'd been given a frappé. Surely even that was forbidden?

'I didn't even know you could make all this stuff,' I said absently, thinking of all the goody-gobbling sessions I'd missed out on growing up.

'Of course, I know how to make them. But with so many great bakeries nearby, I didn't have to.' She sat back and wiped the table with the corner of her apron. 'Anyway, don't be over-dramatic; I make some of this stuff from time to time at home.'

I looked over at the fresh tortes. 'Not those.'

'No, maybe not those.' She smiled. 'They look good, don't they? Took me a while to get back into the swing of things, but I'm back in good form.'

'Define "a while"?'

'Three crooked and inedible tortes.'

'Three?' I could probably make a hundred and not one of them would come out the way they were meant to.

I took a hefty sip of my frappé, giving serious consideration to tackling my mother and making a run on the chocolate torte decorated with strawberries, whipped cream and cherries in the top-right corner of the case.

'So let me get this straight: one morning you just decided to open the doors and take over management of the bakery?'

She nodded, her expression wary. 'I hadn't

told you, I talk to Dino every day. He was saying if he wasn't allowed to come back soon, his business would be sunk; he'd lose everything.' She squared her shoulders. 'Of course, I couldn't allow that to happen.'

'Of course,' I mumbled.

I wasn't sure which bothered me more: that she was talking to Dino and I wasn't, or that it hadn't even occurred to me he might suffer financially without someone to look after his interests.

I decided it was a toss up.

'Why didn't you tell me?' I asked.

'When?' she asked pointedly. 'You're always running here, running there, working, doing God only knows what all. You haven't had time for me lately.'

Because I didn't want any of the bland food she was forcing me to eat.

Because I was busy.

OK, mostly because of the bland food.

How shallow was that?

I didn't particularly like myself at the moment.

One of the girls motioned to my mother. She waved back and told her she'd be there in a minute.

'And the staff?' I asked.

'All Dino's. They were happy to have the work.' She smiled. 'It is Christmas, after all.'

That, it was.

Not that you could tell by my actions.

Of course, not everyone was working a kidnapping case either.

'Bakeries are always busiest during the holidays,' she said. 'And you should see the orders. I'm certainly going to have my hands full over the next week or so.'

'If Dino doesn't come back.'

She nodded. 'Yes. How's that coming, by the way?'

I said something under my breath.

'What?'

'It's coming. I'll share something when I have it.' I didn't have the heart to tell her he'd somehow earned a key position on Homeland Security's suspected-terrorist list.

'Yes, well, word on the street has it he was set up.'

I squinted at her. Not only was my mother using contemporary lingo, she was picking up gossip I wasn't privy to? 'Oh?'

Why was I getting the feeling she already knew about the list?

'Yes. And...' her words drifted off and she looked away from me.

Oh, please don't stop now. I waited. 'I'm sorry? Didn't I say anything? Thought I said something.' I gestured with my hand, wondering why she was hesitating. 'And...'

She looked at me. 'It's one of the orders...'

What did any of this have to do with tortes? 'Yes?'

I got my cell out to check for messages.

'It's for Thomas.'

I froze.

Thomas? As in my Thomas?

I cringed at my description of my ex-fiancé. Thankfully Thomas wasn't mine and never would be.

Still, the fact the tortes were meant for him could mean one thing and one thing only.

Thalia's speech quickened as if now that the words were out, she was required to follow them with more. 'The order's for the day after Christmas. You know ... It's for his wedding.'

My cell slipped from my fingers and clattered to the floor. I stared at it as if unable to work out that it was actually mine and I had dropped it.

She picked it up and handed it to me. I took an inordinate amount of time dusting it off, checking to make sure it still worked, which of course it did.

'Kati?' I said. Or thought I did.

She nodded. 'Yes.'

'Is she pregnant?'

'Not so far as I can tell.'

My ex-groom Thomas was marrying my ex-best friend Kati almost nine months to the day when I caught them messing around on the day of my wedding? And she wasn't pregnant?

My mind filled with the image of Rosie nearly blowing her nose into my sweater that morning.

Only I didn't want to cry.

Did I?

'Small church wedding, I guess. They only ordered ten tortes.'

I nodded at my mother's words, but truth be told I barely heard her.

'Anyway, I'd better get back to work. Just

170

thought you should know, is all. Hear it from me before someone else.'

My mother got up and I followed suit, automatically picking up my frappé glass to take to the counter and wiping up any residual condensation with the napkin that had been under it. Thalia went behind the counter and I gestured toward one of the girls.

'I'll take that torte over here,' I said, pointing to the one in question.

'No, she won't.'

I stared at my mother. 'It's a gift.'

'For whom?'

'For my co-worker, Rosie. She needs some cheering up.'

'Uh huh. Go cheat on the fast somewhere else. Your business isn't welcome here until Christmas Eve.'

'You're helping others break fast.'

'Others are not my daughter.'

I made a face at her. 'Fine.'

'Good.'

'I'm leaving.'

'*Sto Kalo.*'

'I'll talk to you later.'

'Have a nice day.'

My scowl deepened as I stalked outside and into the cold. The snow had picked up further, blanketing the street and sidewalk in more white stuff. I looked over my shoulder at the bustling bakery. The restaurant on Ditmars was only a couple blocks down from another popular Greek bakery. I was thinking I should stop and do

171

exactly as my mother suggested and pick up a torte from there.

A knock on the window. I looked to find my mother shaking her head and wagging her index finger.

I stuck out my tongue at her and stalked to Lucille.

What she didn't know wouldn't hurt her.

Problem was, I'd know.

And considering my recent self-awareness of my own shortcomings as a friend and a daughter ... well, I didn't want to hurt her.

Sixteen

'Where have you been?' Rosie asked with an exasperated eye roll when I finally returned to the office. 'And where's my lunch?'

I blinked at her as if she'd sprouted a third eyeball in the middle of her forehead. Eye rolls from two were enough; the idea of an additional one was nightmare material.

'I forgot.'

She tsked. 'Thought as much. Got Phoebe to deliver me a soup and a sandwich. On the agency. On account of I worked through my lunch hour to get you all the stuff you needed.'

'You got it?'

She appeared insulted.

Of course she had.

At least she wasn't crying.

I accepted the stack of paper she'd compiled, wondering what I'd gotten myself into. It would take forever to get through all of this. Much longer than the few hours I had.

'Where'd you go?' she asked.

To hell and back ... can't you tell by the burn? I wanted to say. Instead, I offered, 'On that bait thing.'

'You finished that an hour ago.'

How did she know that?

Oh.

Probably she had talked to Pamela.

She held out her hand. I fished the camera pen out and laid it in her palm.

I could only hope the photos came out and that my rude bar neighbor hadn't accidentally deleted the best shots.

'Where'd you go after that?'

I left out the bakery part in case she'd nail me for not bringing her something and said, 'Manhattan.'

'You didn't drive, did you? 'Cause it ain't looking too good out there.'

'No, I didn't drive.'

I stared through the front window at where the snow came down in thick waves and was accumulating quickly, even though I'd just come in from it, and shook the large flakes that hadn't melted from my jacket and hair.

Still, it was one thing to plow through it, another to look at it from the inside. She was right; it wasn't looking good out there.

In more ways than one.

'Here,' I said, handing her a fresh list of names. 'When you get a chance.'

I went inside my uncle's office and closed the door, shrugging out of my coat around the documents I held as I went.

Dare I hope the ransom drop would be cancelled due to bad weather?

Ha!

I cleared my throat, put the pile in my hands

down on the desk then stood staring at everything ... nothing.

What would my uncle do?

Probably he would quote me some sort of silly rule ... that would turn out to be not so silly after all.

'Hey.'

Pete popped up from behind the desk and my head nearly hit the ceiling I jumped so high.

'What are you doing?' I demanded.

He chuckled, sitting upright in the chair. 'I was picking up a pen I dropped. You?'

'Checking to make sure my heart is still in my chest, thank you. What are you doing here?'

'You asked me to check in. Remember?'

Now if that wasn't a turnaround, I don't know what is. A few months ago Pete's being in my uncle's office meant he was looking for money or probably something to steal in order to get money. Now there could be a twenty on the desk and he wouldn't touch it.

Well, OK, maybe I wouldn't go that far. At any rate, I didn't intend to put the theory to the test so the point was moot.

'A phone call would have done the trick,' I told him.

'Yeah, well, I lost my subject.'

Great.

'Here,' I said, handing him a file. 'Now I need you to follow her. She knocks off at around five, I'm guessing.'

He accepted the file that held little more than a brief info sheet and a driver's license photo.

'You plan on telling me what this is about?'

'Maybe. Don't let her – or others – spot you.'

'Others?'

'Yeah.' He came out from behind the desk and I moved behind it. 'Trust me, you'll know them when you see them. And you'll want to make doubly sure they don't spot you.'

'Reassuring.'

I smiled at him half-heartedly.

'Later.'

'Yeah, later.'

He opened the door and walked through it.

'Close it, please.'

His eyes narrowed as he looked at me, but then he did as I requested, the catch giving a satisfying click.

I just needed a few moments to myself.

After my bakery visit, I'd taken the subway downtown, the trip serving two purposes: meet with Abramopoulos' personal executive assistant; and catch up with the Greek waitress rumored to be his current girlfriend.

The girlfriend had taken me all of ten seconds, but had required twenty minutes of my presence and an expensive meal breathed on but otherwise untouched. Melina Christides was about as Greek as my big toe, stamped with the label due to her dark beauty and the fact that her father – whom she'd never really seen – bestowed her with his Greek name by nature of sperm default. She was an aspiring model/actress/singer (of course) and had been dating Abramopoulos on and off for the past three months. As near as I could figure it, eye candy for whenever he went to public events ... and perhaps a cooperative bed bunny for private ones when the public ones went well.

I normally didn't write people off so quickly, but I did her. Honestly, I couldn't imagine her working anything more complicated than a MetroCard ticket machine, and more times than not, I'd bet she boarded the wrong train.

Now Abramopoulos' executive personal assistant Elizabeth Winston had been another matter entirely...

As I suspected during my first involuntary visit, there was a separate, public entrance to Abramopoulos' domain, with a separate 'professional' executive assistant who took care of it. Fortunately for me, the woman hadn't known me, and I'd altered my image just enough by way of twisting my hair up into a Mets ball cap and sunglasses I hoped anyone else watching on the umpteen security cameras wouldn't recognize me either (namely, Bruno, who I hoped would be busy with other matters. The FBI agents sprinkled about the place didn't concern me much, since I'd suspected they'd been contacted, probably at the outset. And they didn't seem overly concerned with me, another plus).

I'd asked for Miss Winston ... and gotten her.

She, of course, had known me, not surprising considering I was the only female PI in the room that night. But my unexpected visit had given me the edge I needed to glide right into her office and begin speaking with her before setting off any loud warning bells.

Most professional females I encountered enjoyed talking about their résumés. To a certain extent I respected and appreciated it. And in Elizabeth's case, she had an impressive one: Harvard Business grad, *summa cum laude*. Five years with the Trump organization in acquisitions. Abramopoulos' junior then executive personal assistant for the past three.

I'd enquired about what happened to the previous personal executive assistant and been given my first freeze out. One of many while I spent the next half hour carefully probing her.

When it came to creepy smiles – which people like Bruno, and even Abramopoulos himself, mastered – hers ranked right up there.

And likely revealed more about her than anything she did or didn't tell me.

'Great city, isn't it, New York?' I'd asked after one of her frostier freeze outs.

I'd walked to her expansive windows and looked out over the city, straight down the street over the domino of buildings stretched seemingly as far as the eye could see. Nope, this Broadway was nothing like mine in Astoria. And I could relate to the sway it held over some people, say like those from Peoria, Illinois, whose persuasive dream while growing up in a small town was seeking out the big city.

'I bet your place is nice,' I said quietly.

I'd watched her reflection in the glass. Was it me, or did her back stiffen just a tad?

OK, maybe her place wasn't so nice.

Comparing her response to the pride she'd taken in sharing her resume, I'd say Miss Winston wasn't being paid nearly the salary she thought she should be.

And, unlike the model/actress/singer wannabe arm candy ... well, she had the wits to pull off something, oh, say like a kidnapping?

The two million dollar ransom, however? Hardly worth the trouble to someone of her caliber and ambition.

'Does Bruno know you're here?' she finally asked, indicating our impromptu meeting was drawing to a close.

I turned from the windows. 'No. And if it's all the same to you, I'd prefer he not know.' She'd looked a little self-satisfied, revealing the first thing she was going to do when I left her office was tell him. So I'd shrugged. 'But if you feel compelled to tell him, by all means, go ahead.'

Now, an hour later, I sat back in my uncle's Astoria office, a place not so far removed from Miss Winston's ivory tower physically, but planets apart otherwise.

All things being equal, I'd take this over that never-enough fantasy land any day.

Of course, when I'd indirectly inquired about Elizabeth Winston's living quarters, I'd already known the answer: she had a small, one-bedroom walk-up in TriBeca that she'd paid half a million for a year ago.

Not exactly a place where you'd entertain New York movers and shakers.

And, judging from the information Rosie dug

up, she'd also shared the place for a few months with a live-in boyfriend, one Daniel/Danny Butler, who appeared to have changed residences a month back, whereabouts unknown, and had been a guest at an upstate correctional institution for a two-year stint up until a year ago. I'd noted the detail, but not what crime he'd been incarcerated for.

I hadn't asked about him. Had I, I'm sure she immediately would have put an emergency call in to Bruno, who likely would have pulled an on-premises snatch and grab and kept me until the ransom drop.

Speaking of which...

I stared at the clock on my cell phone. The twenty-four-hour grace period was coming up fast.

Damn.

I got up and approached the board ... then my mind went blank.

OK, maybe it hadn't gone blank. Rather, it filled with items I'd been fighting not to think about.

Say, like my mother's not only working Dino's sweets shop, but doing a bang-up job of it as well, and leaving me foodless, even if it was bland food.

The fact there was a message on my desk from David Hunter saying he wanted to meet to discuss further information he'd discovered: dinner tonight at seven?

My grandfather's medal case, which I knew was very important to him, and as such important to me, but not more so than figuring out how to save my own hide.

My new and old housemates who had taken over my bed so that I woke to each of them on either side of my head, jockeying for position in the renewed game of 'Claim That Human'.

And last, but certainly not least, the fact that my ex-groom would be marrying my ex-best friend in less than a week.

Double damn.

I flipped the board over to the cork side and the various notes I had fastened there, then back to the dry-erase side, reading but not registering what I'd written.

Then I went to the door and opened it.

Instantly the sounds from the outer office invaded mine: Rosie's familiar voice talking on the phone (to a client from whom she was attempting to collect a debt, apparently, the occasional 'tsk' punctuating her speech), the canned ting of Christmas carols coming from her iPod dock, the long, angry honk of a horn outside on Steinway, the jingle of the door bells as a delivery man came inside.

I closed my eyes for the briefest of moments and smiled.

Ah, yes: peace on Earth.

Maybe now I could concentrate...

Seventeen

'Does your friend Konstantine have any enemies?'

I'd talked CIS agent David Hunter into coffee rather than dinner and now sat across the table from him at one of my favorite Greek cafes on Broadway enjoying a tall, frothy frappé and a plate of *diples*, which is a cross between a doughnut and a funnel cake, drenched in honey syrup and sprinkled with walnuts.

'Want one?' I asked, hoping he'd say no.

He said no.

'I don't think "enemy" is a word in Dino's vocabulary,' I said in answer to his question, sucking the honey syrup from my thumb. 'Everyone loves him.'

David was watching my movements, especially my mouth ... a little too closely.

Ooops.

Note to self: do not lick honey-covered digits in the company of males ... unless you're interesting in licking them, of course.

I'd never thought of myself as the sensual type. But I suppose that was one of those traits determined by someone other than you. Take the finger-sucking bit: I'd always done it. Not sure why. And Lord knows my mother had tried breaking me of the habit. Yet, here I was, still doing it.

'Why do you ask?' I tried to redirect his attention to someplace other than my mouth. Partly because I was beginning to feel awkward. Mostly because it made me notice his mouth, which looked like it might be very nice to lick, indeed.

It would be good to keep in mind licking had landed me more than my fair share of trouble. And this meeting and the motivation behind it stood as a stark reminder of that.

'What? Oh.' David shifted in his chair and sipped his coffee – regular with just a dab of cream. 'Just that my investigation shows he was turned in by a reliable source.'

'Turned in?'

'Yes. For suspicious activity.'

'Such as?'

He shrugged. 'I wasn't able to obtain that information. But I'm guessing enough to not only put him on the list, but to have him placed on the first flight out.'

'Who was it?'

'Additional information I wasn't able to obtain.'

I was beginning to think I might have better luck going straight to Homeland Security, no matter my fear of finding myself sitting in a Greek airport eight hours later looking for a way to call Dino to come pick me up.

This is what was so important for me to meet him about? I had things to do. People to see.

Ransom drops to wriggle out of...

'I don't have time to date,' I said.

David nearly choked on his coffee. Which made him all the more attractive in an odd kind of way.

And, sitting across from him again, it was hard to ignore how very attractive he was.

And difficult to remember why I shouldn't welcome his interest beyond the obvious reasons.

'This isn't a date,' he finally said.

OK, I wasn't up to arguing the point. Probably it wasn't a good idea, either. While I was reasonably sure he didn't have the authority to deport me anywhere farther than Canada, I didn't want to try him.

Then again, being in Canada just then might not be a bad idea...

'You know, my mom says she's hearing rumors Dino was set up,' I said.

'Your mom would be the one running the bakery?'

'You've met her?'

'I was going to suggest we go there.'

This time I was the one who nearly choked on her coffee.

Me? David? Seen out together? By my mother?

'Yes, that would be her.' Imagine how I might have responded had I not happened by the bakery and discovered for myself what everyone else seemed to already know. 'At any rate, I'm thinking maybe we should stick to meeting at your office from here on out.'

'I see.' His gaze drowned in his coffee cup. 'I'm sorry if I offended you. It's just, since I moved here six months ago I haven't really been out much. Oh, sure, I've been downtown. But not here. After you came into my office, I thought you might be the perfect person to show me around, since you know Astoria so well.'

OK.

Now I felt bad.

Which seemed to be happening a lot lately.

'I'm not offended,' I said. 'I'm flattered. But...'

He looked at me hopefully.

'Well ... but.'

I smiled.

My cell phone chirped and I glanced to find a text from Waters.

'I should really get going,' I said.

'Oh. Sure. Let me walk out with you.'

I smiled and let him help with my jacket then I led the way out, allowing him to open doors as we went.

'I'm hoping to hear on my reconsider request by tomorrow,' he said when we both stood on the cold sidewalk. 'I'll leave a message at your office on the decision.'

It had briefly stopped snowing and the evening was one of those where your breath turned into an ice sculpture before it could evaporate.

'Thank you,' I said.

He really did have nice eyes. The kind that seemed open to laughing. And I was flattered he was interested in me. For reasons I wasn't entirely clear on, I found myself leaning slightly in toward him. To kiss his cheek, I told myself. Something quick and not too friendly.

Problem was? I missed his cheek and hit his mouth.

And there was nothing quick or unfriendly about it.

Mmm...

Yes...

There was something gratifying in knowing I was right: David was a good kisser. A considerate one. He allowed me to decide how far I wanted to go.

Well, until he leaned into me and deepened the kiss but good, making off with my breath entirely.

Whoa...

Suddenly I was no longer aware of the cold. To the contrary, I felt very warm.

We both stopped at the same time, pausing for a moment, noses nearly touching.

I felt him smile rather than saw him. 'Glad you had time for ... that,' he said.

I smiled back. 'Me, too.'

There was something hotly intimate about our standing in the middle of the sidewalk enjoying our first kiss.

I waited for fear or exasperation or another objectionable emotion to hit, to remind me why I really wasn't interested in dating anyone.

There was nothing.

Hunh.

My cell chirped again.

David chuckled as he drew away. 'You'd better see to that bird in your pocket.'

'Yeah. Ravenous beast.'

'I'll call you,' he said. 'I mean, tomorrow. When I hear on that reconsideration.'

I nodded. 'OK.'

'Good night.'

'Good night.'

I did experience something I wasn't prepared for: shyness.

And it didn't dissipate until after he turned the corner and moved out of sight ... and only then minimally.

I sighed and turned to walk in the opposite direction.

That's when I spotted the dark truck cruising by...

Jake.

My heart dunked into my stomach.

Then it rebounded.

How long since the last time I'd found myself in nearly this exact same position?

Right before Dino was deported.

My brain seized.

No...

There wasn't a chance that...

Never in a million years would Jake...

Would he?

My cell chirped again.

I fished it out, saw Waters' name in the display and answered.

'I quit!' he said, then hung up.

'I swear, woman, I ain't seen anybody get them-damn-selves in as much trouble as you do,' Eugene said after I finally managed to get him to take my call. It had taken no fewer than ten tries and five voicemail messages promising a bonus in addition to hazard pay.

'What's going on?'

I'd arranged to meet him outside a bar in Jamaica, Queens. Was it just me or did his dark skin look a little lighter? Then again, it could be the cold.

'Ain't you gonna offer to buy a brother a beer?'

I looked at the low, squat building pulsing with hip-hop music and then looked back at him. 'Here? No.'

'Fine, then.'

He reached inside his new leather coat and took out what, to all intents and purposes, look-ed like a cigarette. But when he lit it up, it smelled like anything but.

I noticed his hand trembled as he filled his lungs, held it, then exhaled. His shoulders drop-ped at least three inches before my eyes.

'You want some?' He held out the joint.

'Nah. Pass.'

Mostly I limited myself to contact highs. And just being near Eugene right now, his blowing the smoke in my direction, guaranteed I'd get a good one.

Oh, screw it.

'Yeah, hand it to me,' I said.

He did.

I took a tentative puff, tried to hold the acrid smoke in my lungs, then coughed it out.

I handed it back.

He chuckled softly. 'Good you don't smoke. Can't imagine what kind of trouble you get into if you did. Probably get a nigga killed.'

'So are you going to tell me what happened or not?'

'I'm thinking we should talk about that bonus you mentioned first.'

My turn to laugh.

I'd had him tail Sara Canton. Yes, I knew where she was. She'd called early this morning to tell me and ask if her daughter had been found yet. I withheld mention of the bonus attached to her, and my second snatch and grab after warning her away, and shared as much as I could.

Then I put Eugene on her.

I was guessing his skin-whitening experience? Had to do with her gun-loving brother Bubba.

'Sum-a-bitch tried to fit his shotgun up my mutha-fucking ass,' Eugene confirmed.

I giggled at the image.

He did, too, shaking his head. 'I ain't even joking. I fell asleep in my car. Hell, been watching the boring-as-hell woman, keeping all discreet and shit ... the next thing I know, I'm being hauled out by the ugliest white ass gorilla you ever saw.'

Yep, definitely Bubba.

'It ain't even funny!' he said, although he was laughing. 'Swear to all that's holy, that guy bent

189

me over the front of my own car and looked like he was gonna fuck a nigga right there in front of God and everyone.'

I laughed harder, more at him than the situation. I wouldn't put it past a sicko like Bubba to do exactly that.

'If I'm lying I'm dying.' Eugene held his hand up as if taking an oath. A gesture that may have held much more weight if a joint wasn't squeezed between his index and middle fingers. 'Shit. Tell you, I ain't ever been so glad to see the NYPD roll up in my life.'

'The police showed up?'

'Showed up? That cop friend of yours? He was all over it.'

'Pino?'

'Yeah, that be him.'

I imagined Pino going toe to toe with the likes of Bubba. Almost worth the price of admission to watch the dick-measuring contest up close and personal.

'What happened next?'

'What do you mean what happened next? Shoot, ain't that enough?'

I waited.

'Nothing happened. That Bubba guy couldn't have run faster back into that rat hole they staying at. Didn't say two words. All I knew is that damn gun of his was missing from between my goddam legs and he was gone.' He pointed at me. 'And that Pino guy wasn't too happy that I didn't want to talk about it.'

'I bet.'

The squeal of tires.

We both turned toward the street, laughter gone as the tire of a black SUV. bounced against the curb and three guys got out, grabbing me and stuffing me into the back seat.

Not again...

The last thing I heard was Eugene's scream. At least I think it was his scream. Sounded so feminine, I had to wonder about it.

Talk about a buzz kill.

I could only hope that my buzz was the sole thing on the chopping block.

Eighteen

Ransom time already?

That was the first thought that popped to mind when I came to Lord only knows how much later to find myself propped in a chair, hands bound behind my back, ankles tied to the chair legs.

OK, this was new.

I looked around the plain, windowless room that held nothing but the chair I was sitting in, a small table and then another chair across the way, currently empty.

The silence was absolutely deafening.

Aw, hell. David Hunter had been offended by my rejection and now Homeland Security was going to deport me. I could only hope to go someplace warm and friendly.

I rolled my too big tongue around my teeth, hating the pillowy feeling. Chloroform was my bet. But who knew nowadays.

At any rate, I was mildly glad Bruno wasn't behind this latest kidnapping.

The door opened and I found myself hoping I was still glad when he was done with me.

I silently watched him. At six foot something, with a slender build, I guessed he'd look like a runner if he were wearing something other than a plain, navy blue suit.

Crud.

FBI.

He put a pitcher of water on the table along with a glass. No file. No notes.

I had a run-in with the Feds a few months back. They hadn't caught up with me, but I suspected it was because they really hadn't wanted to.

Of course, this could also be Homeland Security.

Nah. This guy had Federal Bureau of Investigations stenciled all over his too calm, too collected butt.

He finally sat down, back rigid, attention finally focused on me.

'Water?' he asked.

He picked up the pitcher and slowly filled the glass.

It made me want to pee.

Which, I suppose, might be desired response Number Two.

Pun intended.

I felt the ridiculous urge to giggle. Which told me my buzz hadn't been entirely killed. In fact, I was beginning to wonder if maybe the chloroform had enhanced it.

'What's next? Waterboarding?'

'Wrong agency.'

'Right. Because that would make you with...'

He didn't answer and his face didn't shift. But I caught the slightest trace of amusement in his dark eyes.

'If you're going to deport me, you might as well just put me on a plane now and get it over with. Just make my destination someplace nice.'

He blinked.

The door opened and a woman looking exactly the same as the agent across from me, except for the bun at the nape of her neck, entered, putting a file down on the table and then leaving again without saying a word.

The agent didn't move.

'Mine?' I asked.

My arms and legs were beginning to go numb, but I determined to ignore them. Asking to be freed wouldn't get me anywhere anyway. The way these guys worked was you show me yours and I'll grant you one wish.

And I wasn't showing anyone anything.

'Yours,' he said.

I stared at the file. It must have been at least an inch thick.

Wow.

Of course, I knew that elementary and high school transcripts, printed email correspondences, utility bills and medical records could easily account for most of what was in there.

I also knew it wouldn't account for all of it.

I moved my hand to scratch my head but got a chair squeak instead.

'How thick is yours?' I asked.

A whisper of a smile.

He got up, took a pocketknife out of his jacket, and cut my restraints without my asking.

194

Cool beans.

I told myself not to do anything as unoriginal as rub my wrists, but I couldn't help myself.

He sat back down and slid the glass of water my way.

'Pass. Thanks.' I nodded toward the file. 'But I wouldn't mind a look at that.'

'Not on offer. But something else is.'

I took some comfort in knowing that why I was pulled in had nothing to do with anything I had done wrong. Well, nothing they knew about, anyway.

Although I was pretty sure they could have pressed the issue of tampering with a federal case. Because those had definitely been FBI agents at Abramopoulos' office.

'Oh?' I asked.

So they wanted to know what I did about the kidnapping. Good enough. Problem was, they likely knew more than I did.

I narrowed my eyes. Or did they?

'What is it? And what do I have to do in exchange?'

'Do as Abramopoulos asks. And keep your cell phone on you at all times.'

I winced.

While I'd basically resigned myself to my fate as official ransom dropper, I was coming to think maybe I should take a taxi to Homeland Security strapped with fake explosives and shout at them in Greek.

'That's it?'

'That's it.'

I had the sinking sensation I was being set up for something.

'And in return I get...?'

He smiled. 'The name of the person who set up your friend the baker.'

I went cold.

Was there anything these guys didn't know about?

The sound of my cell phone ringing in my coat pocket made me jump. I was surprised they hadn't taken it off me.

'Go ahead,' he said.

I warily slid my cell out to see PRIVATE CALLER displayed.

I answered, watching the agent's face as I did so.

Bruno. 'Date's been cancelled for tonight.'

'Why?'

'Weather.'

I recalled my earlier wish that there would be a snow delay and nearly laughed, but it would have revealed my nerves, so I didn't.

'Tomorrow night. Same time.'

He hung up.

I stared at the agent. 'Why do I have the feeling you knew exactly who was calling and what they had to say?'

He moved the file to sit in front of him, his nicely manicured hand on top of it.

Why did I suddenly have the sinking sensation that my making the drop wasn't what was truly behind my little involuntary visit?

And why was it I also feared that by the end of

all this I was going to regret trading my waitress apron for a PI apprenticeship?

I was dropped off the same place I'd been picked up, Lucille exactly where I left her, Eugene nowhere to be found.

Not that I expected to find him. I was thinking it would be a downright miracle if I ever saw him again.

Still...

'You wanted juicy,' I told him when he finally picked up his cell phone.

'Sweetness, that ain't juicy; that's flat out, motherfucking suicide.'

I laughed and asked him for a favor.

'You ain't putting me on that Canton woman again?'

'Now that you've been made? Nah.'

I did want to switch him with Pete, however.

I pondered whether or not I should tell my cousin about Waters' experience, then decided against it. I had a feeling Bubba fell a bit on the racist side and probably thought Eugene's interest had been strictly of the larceny variety, even though from what I saw, the guy didn't own anything outside his guns that held any value.

I told him what he wanted and he reluctantly agreed.

'Thanks, Eugene.'

'Thanks ain't what I want. What I want is a big fat check to make up for today's mess.'

I rang off without saying anything, although I fully agreed with him.

I stood for long minutes on that sidewalk,

ignoring the looks I got from those exiting and entering the bar behind me and the fact that it was freezing cold and snowing again. There was such a stillness about moments like these. Quiet. The snow muffling the sounds of the cars rolling by on the street in front of me. Softening the lights from the bar behind me.

All things being equal, I would have preferred the drop have been made tonight. In fact, had it gone ahead as planned, I might have been done and be home in bed right now.

OK, maybe it was too early for bed, but...

The thought of my bed – or more specifically the gifts behind my bed – brought three things to mind: first, that I needed to get rid of them; second, that my ex-groom was marrying my ex-best friend; third, that had the drop happened tonight, I'd know the name of the person who had set Dino up.

I blinked against a random snowflake that had drifted into my eye.

But I already knew the name of that individual, didn't I? It had been sitting back there, parked at the back of my brain since that morning I stopped by and saw the 'Closed' sign on Dino's bakery. I just had been ready to turn the key.

Now, I was.

I started walking toward Lucille, thoughts and ideas swirling around in my head as lazily as the snow around me. But my mind was focused on one thing and one thing only: confronting the person responsible for the closing of my favorite bakery.

Well, until my mother reopened it. Now it was the one bakery I could go to.

'You got a cigarette?'

A girl about my age asked as she passed. 'Nah, sorry. Don't smoke.'

But something did make me reach inside my coat pocket and pluck out a tenner.

'What's say you go buy a pack and enjoy it for the both of us.'

She squinted at me and then the money, as if unsure what to say.

'Merry Christmas.'

I got into Lucille.

'Same to you,' she said, standing and watching as I pulled away from the curb.

Nineteen

Forty minutes later I sat in my car near the East River, damning myself for not having thought this all the way through; I was freezing! And I couldn't turn my car on to warm up.

As far as bright ideas went, this one was turning out to lean toward the dim side.

Oh, wait. Here he comes.

My heart valve closed as I watched Jake's truck drive by. At least I think it was his truck. Sure looked like it. As dark as it was, I couldn't get a good look at the plates, but...

I rubbed my forehead. If it was Jake's truck, why wasn't he stopping?

The vehicle disappeared down the road. I slumped down in my chair remembering my phone conversation with him twenty minutes ago, right after I arrived at the park.

'Hey,' he'd said upon answering on the first ring.

'Hey, yourself. Need a favor.'

He'd fallen silent.

OK, so my calling him asking him directly for something? Part of what made this idea so dim.

Wasn't it me who was usually asking him to go away, butt out, leave me alone?

And now I was calling him?

Headlights flashed in my rear-view mirror. I looked to find the truck approaching again.

Was he checking to make sure I hadn't been followed?

Couldn't say I blamed him. I'd had so many people trailing me lately I was considering charging a fee.

Speaking of which, I found it interesting that I hadn't spotted Chaney behind in a good, long while. I wondered what was up. Had Pino finally scared him off me? Or had that jarhead given him a beating that left him in the hospital after scratching the bumper of his Chevy?

The truck drove by again.

'Come on, come on, Jake. I'm one degree away from hypothermia.'

Finally, he swung around again, parking directly behind me.

I got out of my car the same time he climbed from his truck.

Was it me, or was he wary?

Then again, I could be projecting.

'Car problems, huh?' he asked.

'Yeah.' I motioned to where Lucille'd been sitting dormant for the past twenty minutes. 'I don't know what's wrong with her. She just wouldn't start when I turned the key.'

His eyes narrowed. 'Uh huh.'

We stood face to face, no more than two feet separating us. The wind was colder here next to the East River and I swore I could feel the frigid dampness coat my skin with ice.

201

'And you were here because...?'

I had chosen there because it was remote, I couldn't hop a subway, and it wasn't within walking distance of my apartment.

'Meeting a source.'

'Uh huh.'

It's the second time he'd said that and I was growing even more irritated than I already was.

Especially since I was the one who was supposed to be doing the interrogating.

That's right. I'd called Jake here to grill him. Not on what he'd done. I was already sure on that. No, I wanted to understand his motives.

'You know,' he said simply.

He knew that I knew.

I wondered if I ever was going to get the jump on anyone or if I was doomed to go through life revealing my cards the instant I picked them up.

Still, it didn't mean I couldn't learn how to play them better once they were in my hand.

'I know,' I said.

He looked out over the river, his face drawn in hard lines.

'What I want to know is why?'

It appeared he hadn't heard me.

'Why would you go through the trouble of getting Dino deported?'

'...I did it because I love you...'

I tossed and turned and tossed again for good measure, wanting out of the dream but not sure where the exit sign was. It took a good Muffy face-licking to finally snap me out of it.

I jackknifed upright, sputtered and coughed

and pushed him away.

'Ewww. That's some morning breath you've got going on, dog. And I don't even want to know where your tongue has been.'

Tee got up and shook himself on the pillow next to mine, flicked his tail at me, then snuggled up presumably to go back to sleep. I squinted at the clock on my bed-stand. Six twenty-eight. Two minutes until the alarm was due to go off.

Damn. I felt like I hadn't slept a wink although I'd crashed somewhere around midnight. Probably it had to do with my non-stop dreaming about all that was going on in my life at the moment, one scene morphing into the next and the next so that it had been my mother who had been kidnapped, David Hunter who had been deported and Eugene Waters who had kissed me outside the restaurant last night.

Double ewww.

The words I'd woken up to circled my mind like one of those air banners pulled around by small planes you usually saw while you were at a baseball game.

'...I did it because I love you...'

I snatched the blankets back from my legs and Muffy commenced running back and forth over my bare legs, excited that it was time to get up.

Of course, Jake hadn't said those words. He'd said very little at all. Merely stood there gazing at me as if the key to the universe lay somewhere there if he only knew where to look for it.

All I wanted to do was sock him one.

The alarm buzzed, scaring the holy hell out of me.

I smacked it off, further exciting Muffy and annoying Tee. I told them that if they weren't happy with it, they were more than welcome to go find another room. And that, in fact, there was another room to be had. The second bedroom that I'd turned into Muffy's dog cave.

Not that he ever used it.

I pushed from the bed, wincing at the coldness of the floor before putting on my slippers, and then cut a path for the bathroom, Muffy zigzagging in front of my legs and leaping up to lick my chin.

Damn fool dog.

I got to the bathroom, ducked inside and closed the door enough so he couldn't get in, before saying, 'Me first. And, no, you can't watch,' before closing it all the way.

Actually, it was more like listen, because he really couldn't watch, could he?

Still, he wasn't doing that either. No matter how much he tried to. It was just ... weird.

I saw to my business, jumped in the shower, brushed my teeth, blew my hair dry and applied make-up before emerging again.

Muffy was lying on the floor directly outside, looking at me from his paws before popping back up as if spring loaded and resuming his manic actions.

'All right, all right, to the window, Batman...'

I had hoped to get dressed before giving the icy air access to my skin, but I could tell Muffy was going to make that impossible.

Besides, it probably wasn't a good idea to make him wait any longer than he had already. I'd stepped, barefoot, into a warm puddle or two and swore just thinking about it made the area between my toes feel damp and yucky.

That was the thing about pets, I was finding: no matter what nonsense was going on in your life, they had a way of reminding you that nothing was more important than bathroom breaks and kibble.

I opened the window and moved back, allowing Muffy the space he needed to leap out. I shook my head before popping it through the window to have a look at the day.

Seven o'clock and all's ... well?

OK, maybe I wouldn't go that far. But at least it had stopped snowing. And by the looks of the purple sky, it was going to be sunny.

I chose to ignore the three inches of fresh snowfall that had accumulated overnight. And the fact that, without cloud cover, it was even colder.

Then there was also the fact that the Crown Vic was back and ... was that Jake parked up the block?

Jake Porter...

Despite the cold, I remained where I was.

When it came to mysteries, was there a bigger one than the hunky Australian?

Truth was, he had been an enigma from the start. And I'd be lying if I said that that hadn't appealed to me in some fundamental, primal way that made me want to bag him and mount him on my wall.

Or just mount him, period.

I'm sure if I did some digging, I'd find out what he really did for a living, since it was obvious he wasn't the bounty hunter I once believed him to be. But there remained a part of me that didn't want to know, that wanted him to remain that mysterious, commitment-phobic bad boy who looked after me, even when I didn't want him to.

And that part was bigger than the parts that wanted to know more. At least for the time being.

Of course, none of that touched the fact that he had crossed a line by seeing that Dino was deported by coming up with some trumped-up suspicious-activity charge.

Oh, he hadn't admitted to it. Not in so many words. He never admitted to anything. But we both knew he had done it. The instant the FBI offered the identity of the one responsible, I'd known. Who else in my life had that kind of power?

'There's nothing wrong with your car, is there?' he'd asked me after a long silence while we were standing between the park and the East River last night.

I'd held up the spark plug I'd popped out.

His grin made my toes curl inside my boots.

'You know,' I'd said quietly, 'I had this plan to get you to admit to me why you'd done it, but, well, I won't get anywhere with that, will I?'

No.

He didn't have to say it, but we both heard it nonetheless.

'So I guess I'll just say this: get him back.' I'd searched his face and discovered somehow my hand had ended up pressed against the hard stone of his chest. 'Please.'

I'd kissed him then. A wet, lingering one ... before I turned and walked back toward my car.

'Sofie?'

I stopped.

'Merry Christmas.'

I'd smiled, then continued walking.

Yeah, I'll admit it. In some strange way, I found his wanting to eliminate the competition ... well, sweet.

I made a face and ducked back inside, leaving the window open just enough for Muffy before going into the kitchen to make my first frappé of the day and then back into the bedroom where I eyed the contents of my closet for what to wear.

It was going to be a busy one today. Outside the ransom drop later, I had myself a kidnapper to catch (which would hopefully negate the need for a ransom drop), a medal to unearth (Grandpa Kosmos had left three messages on my cell last night) and a reindeer named Rudolph to find (note to self: check out *The Ledger-Times* to see if Wendy ran the piece), not necessarily in that order.

I stood in front of my bedroom mirror, fixing the top of my black turtleneck, and strapping my shoulder holster on, the wedding gifts looming behind me. I really did need to do something about those.

A low hum captured my attention. What was that? The apartment building ran on steam radiators I paid good money to have a heating guy check on regularly. Was that what was making the sound? I inched closer to the bedroom unit, but couldn't make out anything.

Then I remembered Mrs Nebitz and her leak. Water?

Since when did water hum?

I gave myself an eye roll then went to make my bed up enough so my furry room-mates couldn't make too much of a mess out of my sheets. I noticed the sound got louder.

I leaned over my bed, then pulled back, my eyes widening.

It was Tee.

And he was purring so loudly I could hear it across the room.

Hunh.

I smiled and gave him an affectionate scratch behind the ears before shooing him from my pillow so I could cover it with the comforter.

I'd set up the litter box I'd bought in October for him again in Muffy's room. I reminded myself to check it out before leaving, and also to put extra food out for the two of them.

Sipping my frappé and walking back into the living room, I became acutely aware of an absence: my Glock wasn't on the kitchen table where I'd expected to find it when it wasn't in my holster.

Then I remembered: the FBI hadn't returned it to me.

Great.

I idly wondered if there was something Jake could do about that.

Twenty

'Oh, you so gotta see this,' Rosie said, launching from her chair the instant I entered the office.

She blocked my passage to my uncle's office and held up the paper. Splashed across the front page was a picture of the lost Rudolph and his forlorn owner Mrs Claus.

I mean, Mrs Nicholas.

The headline read: *Will Rudolph Be Able to Find His Way Home in Time for Christmas?*

'Isn't it the coolest?' Rosie was, well, looking back to her rosy self.

I had to admit, it was pretty cool.

I put the items in my hand down on my desk and took the paper, leafing through it for the other story. I didn't find it on the first go through and had to start again from the beginning.

'He'll be found for sure now,' Rosie said, returning to her desk. 'Mentioned us in the piece, too. Mrs Nicholas talking about how nice we were and everything.'

I paused to stare at her. 'You tried to kick her to the curb.'

She shrugged as she popped her gum and returned to whatever she was doing on her laptop. 'Must have been nice when I did it 'cause she likes me.'

I gave an eye roll as I went through the paper again.

'There's a box for you on your uncle's desk. Waters dropped it off.'

'Thanks.'

There. Tucked away in a tiny corner on page thirty-three was a small piece on Dino's deportation. One whole paragraph.

Damn.

'What? What happened?' Rosie asked.

I showed her the piddly piece.

'Bring it here. I can't see it.'

I moved closer.

'That's that baker guy, right? The one you were dating?'

'Yeah.' I closed the paper so abruptly I startled her, earning a tsk for my efforts. 'She was supposed to do something bigger.'

'She who?'

'The reporter. In exchange for the Rudolph story, she was supposed to run something to get under the skin of the CIS.'

'You made a deal on Rudolph?'

'Yeah. Got a problem with that?'

She shrugged. 'I don't. But Santa Claus might.'

I slapped the paper on her desk. 'Anyway, that piece isn't even big enough for a bird to poop on.'

'Whatever.'

Morning festivities over, I gathered my things from my desk and moved into my uncle's office, where I didn't plan to stay long. I hung up my coat, took in the board and then looked over my desk.

'Rosie? You get that info I asked for yesterday?'

'Printing it up now.'

I used a letter opener from my uncle's drawer to open the box Eugene had dropped off. Just as I asked, there were two cell phones inside, charged and ready to go.

'You know, you ain't supposed to have me doing personal stuff for you.'

'Who said it was personal?'

'Come on. I remember that medal thingy you were working on last summer for your grandfather. This is related to that.'

'Yeah, well...' I wasn't up for an argument. I was just glad she'd gotten me the info I needed. 'Anyway, it was a small part of what I asked you to do.'

'What's that?' she asked, looking inside the box.

I handed one of the phones to her. 'Personal communications device.'

'What?'

'That's the only way you'll be able to contact me.'

I opened the other, entered the number for hers and pressed call.

'That would be me.'

She stood staring at it. 'This has to do with that case you're working on, doesn't it?'

'What case?'

'What do you mean "what case"? The one you got nearly everybody working on and won't tell me about.'

I ignored her as I toyed with the cell.

'That Abramopoulos kidnapping case.'

I nearly dropped the phone.

'Don't look at me that way. You know I got my sources. I knew two minutes after you came into the office that day what case you were working on.'

'What case? For all intents and purposes, there isn't a case.' Not an official one, anyway.

She stared at me.

'Why didn't you say anything?'

'What? And ruin your fun?' She popped her gum. 'Anyway, everybody knows his ex-wife done it.'

I leaned against my desk. 'Define everybody.'

'Everybody I know. You know, my sources. My friends.' She shrugged. 'Everybody.'

'And the reasoning behind this belief is...'

'On account of what that pig did to her. I mean, all that money and she got nothing ... *and* lost custody of her kid?' She crossed her arms under her breasts. 'I don't blame her, really.'

'So if that's the case then she doesn't plan on giving the kid back.'

'Would you?'

'Two million isn't enough to hide from the likes of an Abramopoulos.'

'Two million? I heard it was twenty.'

Could it be true? Could the amount be ten times what I'd been led to believe?

213

And if it was, why hadn't I been told the correct amount? And why was I the one being asked to deliver the ransom?

'He can't have any more kids, you know that right?' Rosie asked as she turned to leave.

No, I hadn't known that.

She tsked again, louder. 'Don't you even read the stuff I give you? It's in there.' She gestured toward the nearly untouched documents on the corner of my desk.

I stared at the pile. 'Is there anything else I should know?'

Rosie grinned as she pulled up one of the visitor chairs. 'Thought you'd never ask...'

An hour later I was ready to put my hastily sketched out plan in motion. Only now, I had some excess baggage for which I hadn't planned. More specifically, Rosie's take on the situation sat on my shoulders as solidly as if she, herself, had climbed up there.

I tried to be careful with second-hand information; which was a big reason why I hadn't included her directly in the investigation in the first place. While I respected her sources for facts no end, the rest ... well, whatever additional commentary tended to be little more than gossip fit only for grocery store rags.

Thing was? Sometimes even they got it right.

Anyway, I left Lucille parked at the agency, my cell phone locked inside, and walked up the block where I caught the subway, getting off at the next stop and then hailing a taxi to my parents' house where I arranged to pick up my sister Efi's car.

The way I figured it, if I was being tracked via my cell or my car, ditching both would guarantee my freedom until I decided what to do.

One of many drawbacks was I felt naked without my Glock. I hadn't realized the FBI had kept it after our little chat until after they'd dropped me off.

How, exactly, did one go about retrieving one's firearm from the FBI?

I wasn't sure, but I needed to find out.

I'd gone inside my parents' house to get the car keys only to run head on into Yiayia, who looked none too happy with me.

My grandmother, my father's widowed mother, was, at the risk of sounding disrespectful, weird. I understood she was uncomfortable speaking English, but what about Greek? For as long as she'd lived with my parents, which was a good ten years, I'd barely heard her utter a word. Mostly she communicated with stares, the occasional mumble and wooden spoon swats to the wrist or backside, usually when I was trying to get a taste of, or steal altogether, something from the stove.

She'd indicated she'd made dinner and I was to take a plate. I told her I'd get it when I swung back that way. Which hopefully wouldn't be until tomorrow judging by the unappetizing smells coming from the pot on the burner.

I'd grabbed Efi's keys and took off in her little ten-year-old, putt-putt, subcompact car, rolling my eyes when I found the gas gauge on 'E'. I'd filled it up and then pointed the car in the direction of Brooklyn.

One thing I'd learned is that when you reached a mental roadblock, thinking about something totally unrelated often helps. So I was going to do a little legwork on my grandfather's missing medal case in the hopes of oiling the mind gears.

It took me a half hour to reach my destination in the busy, pre-holiday traffic. Last night's snow had been pretty much cleared off the main streets, but despite sunny skies, more snow was forecast for today and tonight.

Tonight. As I parked my sister's car in the spot closest to the brownstone I was visiting, I wondered what the ransom drop would have in store for me. If, that is, I couldn't get out of going.

At any rate, I ousted the thought that served more as rust than lubricant as I climbed the stairs and rang the bell for the first-floor apartment. I was immediately buzzed in, as if Mrs Liotta had been waiting there ready to press the button. I entered and the apartment door opened, revealing a woman I knew was about my grandfather's age, but looked more like my mother's.

I knew her husband of fifty years had died five months ago and that they had moved to Boston shortly after they married. And that she had relocated back here, her hometown of Brooklyn, a few months ago, making my job of finding her that much easier.

'Miss Metropolis?' she said, blue eyes bright and warm. 'Why don't you come in. I'm so happy you called.'

Twenty-One

OK, that was strange. But in a nice, fuzzy-slipper kind of way. The more I'd asked Mrs Liotta about my grandfather's medal, the more questions she asked about him.

I didn't find it unusual at first. Since her husband and Grandpa Kosmos had served together in Korea, it stood to reason that she would also know him.

But at some point simple, friendly curiosity had crept over into 'hunh' land and her happy expression whenever she spoke of him set off a quiet alert.

How well had Grandpa Kosmos known Mrs Liotta, whose full name was Iris Jensen Liotta?

Anyway, our conversation had ultimately boiled down to the understanding she was more than happy to return his medal ... on the condition that she be the one to give it to him.

Had to love it when a case was solved that easily. Now I had but to call my grandfather and tell him. Something I was waiting till later to do.

Right now I was making my way through the pile of documentation Rosie had put together for me, the information I'd asked for. I'd driven to Queens Center, a shopping mall I'd spent a great deal of time in as a teen, and was sitting in the food court sipping my frappé, figuring I could kill two birds by reviewing the data and finishing my Christmas shopping.

I'd been at it for an hour and my eyes were starting to smart from reading too much.

I'd always been a crammer. In high school, the night before quizzes, tests and exams, I could be found in my bedroom with a contraband frappé poring over textbooks and notes, absorbing anything and everything. The method had worked for me. No matter how tired I was during the test, I usually managed to pull at least a B out of the hat for my efforts.

Right now, though, the only items catching my attention were the fact that 'Bubba' Canton served a brief stint of time at an upstate prison for a gun-related crime. Shocker.

Oh, and that Rosie managed to scare up that Bruno's and Boris' last name was Kazimier, and that neither of them were officially listed anywhere as employees of Abramopoulos.

They were, however, well-known members of the Russian mafia.

Another shocker.

I stared at the background checks of Sara Canton's brother Robert 'Bubba' Canton and Elizabeth Winston's boyfriend, Daniel Butler, then marked my spot before putting everything into the backpack I'd brought along, thinking a little shopping might be just the break I needed.

My new cell phone rang, startling me since the tone was loud and featured a nasty song having to do with backing that ass up.

I quickly answered, offering an apologetic glance to a young mother who was wiping ketchup off her young son's face at a neighboring table.

'What's up?' I asked Rosie.

Only it wasn't Rosie who answered. Rather, a familiar male voice spoke ... one I would never have expected to hear, much less hear on my borrowed cell phone.

'Sofie? It's Dino. How are you?'

I sat for a solid minute in silence.

Dino? It couldn't be. He was in Greece.

I squashed the ridiculous thought, thinking about how close he sounded, as if calling from somewhere inside the mall instead of half a world away.

He was half a world away ... wasn't he?

And he was calling me on a phone no one had the number to.

'Me? I'm fine! How are you? How's the weather in Greece?'

Stupid, stupid, stupid.

'I'm OK. And the weather is good.'

'Good ... good.'

I wished I'd been given some kind of heads up, some kind of warning. I silently cursed Rosie, who must have put the call directly through. She could have told a girl what was coming. Given me a chance to prepare.

As it was, I sat dumbfounded, not a single word in my head worth sharing.

'My mom's working at your bakery,' I blurted.

God, did I really just go from stupid to ridiculous?

Yes, I was afraid I had.

'Yes. She told me.'

'Of course she did. Since, you know, you two talk...'

I squeezed my eyes closed.

'I'm sorry I have not called before now. For some reason I was not able to get through to your cell phone, or the agency. Now was the first time.'

'Oh. It's OK. I understand.'

Did I? Was it possible Jake had somehow not only booted out the competition but made it impossible for him to contact me?

Dumb question. When it came to Jake, everything was possible.

What did it mean that he had lifted the block now?

And what did it mean that Dino must have kept trying to call me until he finally got through?

And just what in the hell was I supposed to say to him now?

'Hey, sorry about your getting deported because someone I sometimes dated thought it might be fun. You really have to be careful nowadays, don't you?'

Somehow, I didn't think that would go over well.

'How are you doing?' I said. 'Sorry, I know I already asked that. What I mean is ... are you OK?'

'Yes. Yes, I am.' I heard slight static as if he'd

220

moved the phone from one ear to the other. 'A little difficult at first, but I'm adjusting. Even enjoying spending some time with my family. I missed them.'

I smiled and relaxed into what was otherwise an uncomfortable chair at the unmistakable sound of his smile. 'As I'm sure they missed you.'

Silence fell and I just sat there beaming into the phone, imagining him doing the same on the other end.

What was it about this one guy that made me smile from the inside out? Was it merely his smiling at me? I looked at myself through his eyes and saw myself in a flattering light. As someone who was not only lovable but worth loving, as well as loved.

And desired.

Oh, boy, did he make me feel desired.

'I miss you.'

His words were so faint I nearly didn't make them out.

And just like that I was snapped out of my brief sojourn into the land of all that was lovely ... if only because it was also posted with signs that read, 'Marriage Altar This Way. Good Luck and Good Fortune.'

'I'm not at the office so I can't talk long,' I blurted, wincing even as I said the words.

Here was this guy who had been deported because of me, who had probably been going crazy trying to get a call through, and I was being rude.

'I understand,' he said.

But I knew that he didn't.

I knew he didn't have clue one that whatever *this* was between us, I was nowhere near ready for it.

'I am awfully glad you called, though,' I said. 'It was good to hear your voice. To know you're doing OK.'

'Me, too. You know, about you.'

I allowed myself to smile absurdly into the phone for a few more moments then brought the conversation to a close.

'Have a nice Christmas,' I said. 'I hope to see you soon.'

'Yes. Same to you.'

I reluctantly disconnected then pressed the cell to my mouth for what seemed like a long time.

Until I realized the phone had come from Eugene and Lord only knew where it had been.

Ew.

I took a wet nap out of my purse and sanitized myself and the phone.

OK, where was I?

Oh, yeah.

Funny how a simple phone call had made me totally forget where I was, what I was doing.

In the back of my mind, I reviewed the many reasons why I wasn't ready for all that Dino so readily offered. I knew it was connected to my almost wedding eight months ago. Knew that I had wounds that had yet to completely heal, not to mention the scars that would remain for life.

I also knew that my runaway feelings for Jake

Porter factored in there somehow ... not to mention that hot kiss I shared with David Hunter outside that restaurant.

I scratched my head.

Just when I thought I had everything figured out.

What was I talking about? I never believed I had anything figured out.

What I did know was what I was supposed to be doing: shopping.

I got up from the chair, checked to make sure all the documents were carefully stowed inside the backpack, then hefted it to my shoulder.

I mentally reviewed who I had yet to buy for – pointedly ignoring all ideas related to the two men in my life, or, rather, the two men complicating my life – as I walked past the indoor storefronts, weaving my way around others with the same intention.

I spotted a cute baby jacket that would be perfect for Rosie's new nephew.

I stepped inside the specialized store ... and straight into my ex-best friend, Kati Dimos.

If it was cold outside, inside me the temperature had dropped by a good ten degrees below that.

On my list of those I'd least like to see, she rated the top spot. Well, OK, maybe the second; her groom and my ex-groom nabbed the first.

'Excuse me,' she said, apparently not realizing who I was.

Then she looked into my face and hers went five shades paler.

There was a time when seeing her brought joy and peace to my world. She'd been my best friend, the one I had on speed dial whenever I'd needed to share something funny, something sad, or just to say hello. She'd been my platonic soulmate, my twin, and the bond we shared transcended any romantic one.

That she so readily hacked those ties, much less stole my no-good groom ... well, I was beginning to believe that wound might never heal.

I had yet to forgive her. And I knew I'd never forget.

'Sofie!'

The last time I'd run into her was at a corner grocer and I'd come out of the accidental meeting with only the tiniest shred of pride left. It had been then I'd found out she and Thomas were engaged.

Now I knew they were not only getting married, but that it was to happen the day after Christmas.

Thank God my mother had told me the news. I can't imagine what impact learning that news from Kati might have had on me.

'Christmas shopping?' I asked.

She looked down at the two bags she held and her skin went from pale to beet red. 'Um, yeah.'

I squinted at her.

I knew Kati better than any other female on the face of the earth. I used to, anyway. But I was pretty sure I still knew when she was lying. And she was definitely lying.

Then it dawned on me ... the fact that she

wasn't just browsing through a baby store, but had made several purchases ... that she and Thomas were getting married so quickly ... that she suddenly couldn't look me in the eye...

'Oh my God ... you *are* pregnant.'

All things being equal, I probably really shouldn't have been triumphant over the news. One time, not so long ago, Kati had been my best friend, and now that a child would soon enter the mix...? Well, that changed everything.

And Lord knew she was certainly going to have her own cross to bear with my no-good, philandering ex.

Still, I couldn't help smiling.

I hadn't had to be preggers in order for him to marry me.

Of course, he hadn't exactly married me.

At any rate, I was bursting to share the news with somebody (if I thought it ironic that eight months ago she would have been that someone, I wasn't saying) and found myself finishing my shopping in record speed and driving into Astoria and parking next to Dino's bakery, thinking I was safe enough there since anyone who might be watching thought me still at the agency.

Thalia was less than impressed.

'That should have been my first grandchild.'

I gaped at her as if she'd just called me a name.

'Is that all you have to say?'

She looked at me as she wiped her hands on her apron. 'You were expecting something different?'

'The guy was a pig.'

'The guy was young. You could have turned him into a man.'

'I wasn't his mother. I was supposed to be his wife.'

'And your point is?'

'My point is I think you're certifiable.' Judging by the way one of the girls behind the counter looked our way, I presumed I'd raised my voice.

Trust my mother to leech the pleasure out of what was so far the bright spot in my otherwise gray day.

I thought about telling her I'd spoken to Dino, then decided against it. I could only guess what she'd have to say about that, and I'd just reached my quota of asinine commentary about a half a minute ago.

'Where are you going?' she asked.

'To sit in the back, have a frappé and work. Why?'

'Because I could use an extra pair of hands.'

Great. Now she was going to put me to work.

Probably I shouldn't have come here. Probably I should have gone back to the mall food court and reviewed the documents in peace.

Probably I should have *my* head examined.

She smiled as she watched me, then reached behind the counter and handed me an apron.

Grumbling, I stashed my papers in a cupboard behind the counter, washed my hands and asked her what she needed me to do.

226

Twenty-Two

After two grueling hours making *Christopsomo*, aka Christmas bread, and Greek holiday cookies, *melomakarana* and *kourebeithes*, I had gained a new appreciation for my mother, Dino and everyone who'd had a hand in making every sweet I'd ever put into my mouth. My back ached, my hands were sore, and I was convinced I'd need ten showers to get all the flour off of me.

I gratefully took my apron off, looked into the wall-length mirror behind the counter, wiped a bit of white from my cheek, then went back into the kitchen to say goodbye to my mother.

The place was filled with state of the art equipment, quality ingredients and the atmosphere was light and happy. I took in the tortes in various stages of completion along the left-hand counter, the cracker-like, freshly baked squares that would eventually be layered with custard and cream to make millefeuille, and was shocked – shocked I tell you! – I hadn't put a single thing into my mouth.

More than that? I didn't want anything other than an ice-cold frappé either.

I made a face. If making something meant I no

longer wanted to eat it, I was eating out from here on.

'Hey,' I said to my mom.

'Hey, *koukla mou*. Thanks so much for helping out. You did a great job.'

'No need for thanks. But you're welcome.'

I leaned against the marble-covered island where she worked, contemplating telling her about my earlier phone call.

'Yes, Dino already told me.'

'Told you what?' I hadn't said anything.

'That he talked to you.'

'And?'

She gave me a long look, then bent back to continue adding chocolate-mouse swirls to a chocolate torte. I stuck my finger under her squeeze bag, waited for her to give me some, then stuck the wicked sweet dollop into my mouth.

Pure heaven.

'So, what did he say?' I asked again.

'That he spoke to you.'

'That's all?'

She stared at me again. 'That's it.'

I squinted at her.

OK, I was confused. In a case like this, I would have expected Thalia to be all over linking the word marriage with my name and Dino's.

Instead, she appeared to be going out of her way to avoid it.

Another ploy? Like when she originally pretended she was matching up Dino with my sister

Efi in order to catch me unawares?

Strangely, I didn't think that was the case.

Hunh.

'I find that hard to believe,' I said.

My mother stood up. 'Do you know whose cakes I'm working on, Sofie?'

I looked again. 'No. Why?'

'Thomas and Kati's.'

I'd swiped another finger full of frosting that now dissolved like dirt against my tongue.

Thalia cursed in Greek under her breath and continued working.

'He's too good for you.'

I was positive I hadn't heard her correctly.

What did she mean? She couldn't possibly be talking about Thomas?

'No, I don't mean Thomas. I mean Dino.'

My heart pitched to somewhere in the vicinity of my toes.

Thalia pointed the tip of her decorating bag at me. 'He's a good boy. Ready to settle down. Good at what he does. Has a plan. He deserves somebody who knows what she wants. A girl who can be a good wife to him.'

The dirt in my mouth expanded to choke me.

'I want you to stay away from him.'

'What?' I pushed from the counter.

'You heard me.' She didn't look at me. She pretended to be wholly involved in creating those ludicrous swirls on Thomas' wedding cake.

'Look what you made me do,' she said, sighing heavily.

She put the bag down, picked up a frosting spreader, and carefully removed the last swirl, which was a little bigger than the others. She held it out to me. I took the spreader and threw it into the sink where it clanked loudly.

'What, you don't like what I'm saying?'

'No, I don't like it. At all.' I took a deep breath. 'As my mother you're supposed to be loyal to me.'

'Don't tell me what I'm supposed to do as your mother.'

I crossed my arms, trying to wrap my head around what she had said ... and the deeper meaning.

I'd never known her to so thoroughly adopt someone the way she had Dino. Oh, yes, she was loyal to no end. But I'd never in forever expect her to put an outsider above me.

'You thought Thomas was good enough for me.'

'I never thought Thomas was good enough for you. Thomas Chalikis was your choice, not mine.'

'So you wouldn't pick Dino for me?'

'I wouldn't pick you for Dino. Not now.' She returned to working. 'But you'll remember, I did. You would never have met if not for me.'

'I'm sure I would have met him at some point.'

'Maybe. Maybe not.'

'Definitely.'

'Anyway, until you work out whatever you've got in your system, quit that stupid job with your

230

uncle, I want you to stay away from Dino.'

'Because he deserves better?'

She paused and looked at me, the expression on her face rock solid. 'Yes.'

'Fine.'

'Good.'

'All right, then.'

'Kala.'

I pushed from the counter and stalked toward the swinging door, slapping it so it swung wide outward, then catching it when it swung just as quickly back at me.

Never had my mother turned against me in the way she just had.

The thing about it was?

She was entirely right.

Dino Antonopoulos deserved better than me. Far better.

Rosie called as I was getting into my sister's car. Night had fallen, bringing with it big, fat flakes. If I'd had to guess, I would have said it was too cold to snow. But obviously, I'd have been wrong.

'Where in the hell are you?' she blasted me, her voice so loud I had to move the cell slightly away from my ear to prevent drum breakage. 'I've been trying to call you all day!'

I'd had the cell on me, so the best I could figure is I must not have had a good signal inside the bakery. The ovens? That didn't make any sense. Then again, the cell model was an old one ... and I had no idea who the carrier was, so coverage might be spotty.

Then it occurred to me the problem might not be on my side at all. I pulled the cell away and looked at the display. Right there in black against a blue screen was Spyros Metropolis Agency.

Damn.

Damn, damn, damn.

'You called me from the agency.'

'Of course I called you from the agency. That stupid phone you gave me quit after I tried calling twice.'

I closed my eyes and counted to ten.

'Why are you counting? And why do I care? Hey, the phone's been ringing off the hook here. Your guy Waters says he has something on that secretary you got him following. Your cousin Pete quit. Your sister says she needs her car back, now. Emphasis on now. And there's been some creepy government guys in here looking for you, along with a scary thug-looking motherfucker I wanted to shoot.'

Bruno's brother, Boris. I'd bet a hundred on it.

'I'm hanging up. Call me on your personal cell.'

I disconnected on her without waiting for a response.

She called back a moment later, again from the agency phone. 'I forgot my freakin' cell at home. Why do you think I called you from here to begin with?'

I rubbed my closed eyelids. 'I need Waters' number,' I said. She gave it to me and I entered it into the phone. 'Now Pete's.' She gave me

232

that, too.

'As for the rest...'

I scanned the street around me, trying to guesstimate how long it would take them to catch up with me.

Then an idea occurred to me.

'What? What about the rest?' Rosie wanted to know.

'The rest is going to take care of itself, I'm afraid. I don't think you'll have anything else to worry about. But if that scary thug-looking motherfucker comes in again, use Lenny's gun on him.'

'Lenny ain't got no gun.'

'Yes, he does.'

'Nuh uh.'

'Yuh uh. Top right-hand desk drawer. Key for it is in the middle drawer under the paper clips.'

I pictured Rosie trying to handle the .45 Magnum and gave a mental head shake. Probably it would knock her on her ass.

Probably she'd blow whomever she pointed it at to kingdom come before she went down.

Providing she could lift the thing to begin with.

'Fine. But just so you know, I'm thinking I need my own.'

'I'm thinking the same thing.'

'Should I call you if anything else comes up?'

'No. I'll call you. I'm dumping this phone.'

A heartbeat of a pause and then, 'What are you going to do?'

Honestly? I had no idea. But I was starting to

form an idea.

'Call you in twenty.'

'OK. You know I knock off soon, right?'

'I know you knock off soon.'

'But you can call me on my cell after I get home. You know, if it's an emergency.'

'Thanks.'

'No problem.'

I started the car.

'Oh, and Sofie?'

'Yeah?'

'Be careful.'

'Yeah. You, too.'

I disconnected and then popped the back off the cell phone, removing the battery. As I thought, it was old enough that it had one of those SIM cards inside. Take it out and it was virtually untraceable, solely because the phone was unidentifiable, all user information on the card and not in the phone itself.

Of course, it also meant I couldn't make or receive calls on it, either.

I popped the thumbnail-sized card out and put the battery back in. I'd need to access the phone to get Waters' and Pete's phone numbers.

Question was, would I have a chance to use them before the next snatch and grab?

Twenty-Three

Oh, holy night, the skies are cloudy and threatening...

I drove like a madwoman to my parents' house, parking around the block and nearly breaking my neck three times as I hopped fences and slid on ice trying to gain access to the back door. I pounded on it, looking through the window where Yiayia was tasting something from a pot at the stove. She appeared not to hear me.

Of course, not. She never heard me.

I pounded again.

Efi answered.

'Thank God. I need my car,' she said.

'I heard. What's the emergency?' I dropped the keys in her hand and rounded her, gaining access to the house.

'Sale at Sandra's.'

I blinked at her. 'Seriously? That's the emergency?'

'What? You prefer someone were dying?'

Someone was dying: me.

'Where is it?'

'It's parked around the block.'

'What? Why?'

I gave her a long look as I put my bags of gifts

235

on the floor next to the pantry. Thankfully I'd had them all wrapped at the mall, so I didn't have to worry about anyone seeing anything they shouldn't.

'I couldn't find a spot out front.'

'What's the matter with the driveway?'

I ignored her as I grabbed the cordless phone from the kitchen table and dialed Waters' number.

'Where you been, woman? I've been trying to get a hold of you all day.'

'I heard. What's up?'

Efi stood in front of me. 'Where, exactly, is it parked?'

I turned away, trying to listen to Waters.

Since he'd been made by Bubba, I switched him and Pete so he was now tailing Elizabeth Winston, and Pete Sara Canton.

I winced, recalling Rosie telling me earlier Pete had quit. I could only imagine what trouble he'd run into.

Waters was talking and I realized I wasn't listening.

'Anyway, that Winston lady, she left work early. Nearly missed her, 'cause she don't strike me as the type to do anything that breaks routine. You know, in at nine, out at five, that kind of thing. Fine piece of ass, she is by the way. Not to say you aren't—'

'You plan on getting to the point sometime this year?'

'Maybe. Hey, there's not much more time left of this year anyway, is there?'

236

I knew whatever he had must be good or else he wouldn't be so happy ... or distracted.

'Anyway, she usually takes the subway, just like us poor working stiffs...'

He didn't take the subway and he wasn't necessarily a working stiff. But I kept both thoughts to myself.

'But instead she got this sweet-ass Mercedes coupé out of parking a block up from the Abramopoulos building. I had Rosie run the plates. Belongs to her.'

'And?'

'And I followed her.'

The mother of all tension headaches was beginning to build behind my eyes.

'Where?' I asked between clenched teeth.

Efi stepped into my line of vision again. 'That's what I'm waiting to hear. Where my car is parked.'

'It's around the corner!' I snapped at her.

OK, I'd officially lost it. I never snapped at anyone. Much less my favorite younger sister. The fact that she was my only sister notwithstanding.

'Damn, woman! Break a brother's eardrum already,' Waters said.

'You, shut up and tell me where she went.'

'Which is it?'

'What?'

'Do you want me to shut up or tell you where she went?'

'Where?'

I felt a sharp snap against my backside. I

looked to find Yiayia had just whacked me with a spoon. I stared at her. She whacked me again. I slid the spoon from her branch-like fingers and tossed it across the room.

Then stood there, mouth agape, shocked at what I'd done.

'You'll never guess,' Waters said.

I rounded my sister who was as surprised as I was and walked into the other room, which is what I probably should have done in the first place.

Then again, maybe not.

As Waters told me Winston had gone to JFK Airport, switching on a light bulb in my head, and the kitchen door closed behind me and I saw what waited in the other room, I knew I was about to pay for every sin I'd ever committed.

All in one night.

OK, I was getting really tired of this snatch-and-grab bit. Probably I shouldn't have taken Yiayia's wooden spoon from her. Probably she could have showed them new things to do with it.

Of course, I was ignoring two facts: that this very well might be my last snatch and grab – literally; and neither my sister nor my grand-mother likely had clue one I'd been snatched and grabbed. It had happened so fast, I didn't get a chance to say goodbye to Waters or scream for help.

Not that I would have done either.

'You know, you guys are officially off my Christmas list,' I grumbled from where I sat in the back seat of the familiar black sedan, two thugs on either side of me, another two in the front seats.

'You're lucky you're still alive to have a list,' Bruno said from the front passenger's seat.

'Right. Kidnapping to murder. Good one.'

'It's not murder if they don't find the body.'

I disguised my neck-to-toe shudder by pulling my coat tighter around me. At least this time I had a coat and was wearing shoes.

Not that it mattered. Dead was dead, no matter what you were wearing.

And I had a very bad feeling about this.

'You know, the FBI pulled one of your numbers on me yesterday.'

That got Bruno's attention.

I smiled at him.

'You talked to the FBI?'

'More like they talked to me.'

Even as I said the words, I realized I hadn't done the one thing the agent had asked of me: I didn't have my cell phone on me.

'You're working with them, anyway, so what's it matter?' I asked.

His turn to smile at me.

'You know, Miss Metropolis, I might think I've underestimated you ... if not for the fact that you're sitting in the back of my car right now.'

'Yeah, going to my parents' house rates right up there with one of the worst ideas in the past decade. Right after accepting my ex's marriage proposal.'

'I'm curious. Why did you?'

'What? Say yes to my ex?'

He remained smiling.

'My sister needed her car. She had an ... emergency.'

He laughed. Then laughed harder. The others joined in.

What I found stranger yet, I found myself laughing, too.

It was pretty dumb, my going back there. Even without knowing she'd needed it to get to a sale. Probably I should have just told Efi to take a taxi. Probably I should have ignored her altogether.

But when she'd asked for her car, it hadn't even occurred to me not to take it back to her.

I really needed to work on my priorities.

Just think. I could be that minute sitting somewhere in Manhattan enjoying a nice, big frappé. Instead I was wrinkling my nose at the overwhelming stink of garlic from human pores in a too small car filled with four too big men.

Bruno hefted a briefcase over the seat and put it on my knees when I made no move to take it from him. He clicked it open.

'There's twenty million in bearer bonds in there—'

'Why not cash? And why does it always have to be in a briefcase?'

He closed the case and clicked the catches. 'Cash is traceable and it didn't seem right to put it in a duffel bag.'

'Twenty million? Thought it was two.'

I chalked one up in Rosie's column.

Although she'd been wrong about the rest.

And just where in the hell was the FBI? If they were really working with Bruno, where were they? I should think they would be the ones orchestrating the drop. Why weren't they?

Could it be that Abramopoulos had contacted them? But Bruno hadn't? And the Bruno was acting as a free agent? Was that why I'd been pulled in by the FBI yesterday? To be kept in the loop in some way?

I felt the absence of my cell phone even more acutely now than I had five minutes ago.

'Where's the drop being made?'

'You'll see soon enough.'

'Why not tell me? Not like I'm going anywhere. And we do have this time to fill.'

'Flushing Meadows Corona Park.'

'Big park.'

'By the Unisphere.'

I looked out the windows at the snow that continued to fall. 'Bad night for a ransom drop, wouldn't you say?'

'Good night for getting rid of people who bother you.'

It was only the second time I'd heard Bruno's brother, Boris, speak. And his heavily accented voice sliced like a grater against my already frayed nerves.

I was pretty sure my rough swallow was audible in the suddenly silent car.

'What about the girl?' I asked.

'Let us worry about that.'

'And the kidnappers? Are you guys trying to

241

catch them?'

I wondered if the park was crawling with Bruno's people, including half the city-wide PIs he had working the case.

'Let us worry about that.'

Fine. If that's the way he wanted to play it, I'd keep my information to myself.

Ten minutes later we'd pulled to a stop on the far end of Flushing Meadows Corona Park.

'OK, this is what you're to do...'

Bruno spoke and I listened.

Then I was pushed out on to the sidewalk.

The sedan pulled away.

OK.

The snow was coming down harder now. Big, thick flakes that stung my eyes and clung to my hair. I tightly clutched the briefcase, knowing that if I lost it, it would mean my life.

What was I talking about? No one else was crazy enough to be out here in this weather after dark.

A pack of five teens speaking Spanish passed close by.

OK, I was wrong.

I clutched the briefcase even tighter and started walking.

Let's see if I remembered correctly: I was supposed to walk to the other side of the large metal globe that had been erected in honor of the 1964 World's Fair and featured in countless movies. Then I was to deposit the briefcase full of bearer bonds into a trash can there and then walk away.

Nothing more.

Nothing less.

Seemed simple enough.

Problem was, simple didn't appear to be a part of my vocabulary. At least not the Webster's version of it. I cringed whenever I heard it if only because I understood complicated – probably dangerously so – would end up hitting closer to the truth.

Off to my left I could make out the lights of the Terrace on the Park, a rental hall, which was funny because right now there was no real park. Only seemingly endless sheets of white.

My boots crunched against the snow-covered salt that had been spread to melt the ice on the walkway, but, after the teens moved on, even that sound emerged quiet.

Eerily so.

What I didn't get was, how were the kidnappers going to get the money? And when would I get the girl?

I reached the twelve-story-high stainless steel Unisphere that looked like a snow globe that had just been turned over and righted again, flakes swirling in the empty middle.

I paused, looking up at it. As often as I'd driven by it, I'd never seen it this close. I was impressed. Especially with the freshly fallen snow coating it, falling around it and inside it.

I began to walk around it, keeping an eye out. All I had to do was drop the briefcase inside the garbage can and then walk back to the street where Bruno and his men would pick me up.

I spotted the can.

OK...

I looked around, for what exactly I was unsure. Another can, maybe?

I thought about kicking this one with my foot, to test whether or not it stood on top of one of those sewer outlets like I'd seen in a movie or three. But where would that get me?

I reluctantly moved toward it, lifted the lid to stare at what appeared to be nothing more than balled-up newspaper inside, then placed the briefcase inside. I refitted the lid then took a step back, looking around.

Hunh.

No one ran to tackle me.

No guns were drawn.

No one shouted for me to step away from the can.

All was as it had been a minute before. Except I was minus the weight of one heavy briefcase.

Somehow I'd expected the drop to be more interesting, momentous, somehow.

Instead, I felt like I'd just thrown out my trash.

I had an urge to scratch my head.

What did this mean for the kidnapped girl? Was little Jolie Abramopoulos being set free somewhere even as I dawdled?

Ignoring every last survival instinct I possessed, I lifted the lid and looked inside again. There sat the briefcase right where I'd left it.

Double hunh.

I put the lid back on then reluctantly started to make my way back toward the street, disappointed.

And that's when I spotted the last thing I expected to see.

I stopped dead in my tracks ten feet from the street ... and prayed the turn of phrase wouldn't become literal.

Twenty-Four

There, within touching distance, stood Rudy.

At this point, I think we both pretty much resembled deer caught in the headlights.

What were the chances? There I was on a ransom drop and here he was as if hoof-hitching a ride home.

What was that red light?

Was that his nose?

I caught the ridiculous notion. Probably it was just a reflection of something, maybe a vehicle's brake lights on the nearby road. Of course, it couldn't be coming from his nose.

Could it?

I ignored that there were no vehicles on the nearby road.

'Here, Rudy, Rudy, Rudy,' I said softly, holding my hand out, palm up.

What, was he a dog? Still, I was hoping the soothing sound of my voice would draw him near. Or, at the very least, not scare him away.

He blew a steamy breath through his nose and shook his head, looking prepared to bolt.

I paused. 'It's OK. I'm not going to hurt you.' I smiled, looking at his antlers. He really was a reindeer. I mean, of course he was. I'd known that. I just had never seen one with my own two eyes up this close and personal outside a photograph before.

Beautiful...

There was somehow something quite magical about seeing him on this snowy night, alone in the park.

And I was alone, wasn't I?

I glanced around. The dark sedan holding Bruno and his thugs was nowhere to be seen. No one had made a move on the garbage can that I could see. And there was no sign of little Jolie being dropped off.

I focused on Rudy again.

'Your mama misses you,' I told him. 'Uh huh. Yes, she does.'

With each word, I moved infinitesimally closer, until I was within touching distance.

And touch him, I did.

His coat was soft, probably because it was thicker to protect him against the winter cold. I slowly stroked the top of his head, then smoothed my hand down over his snout, surprised when he licked my hand. I wished I had something to give him.

Then, without warning, he threw his head back and stepped away.

'What? What's the matter, boy?'

I spotted something in the wall of snow some fifty or so feet behind him. I squinted. It looked like a man. I squinted harder. Yes, it was very definitely a man, a bearded one wearing a blue parka, a red hat and ... was that a pickaxe he was carrying?

I shook my head and turned my attention back to Rudy, who, if he knew the figure was there, wasn't overly concerned with him.

If that was the case, what was he concerned about?

I found out way too soon as I was grabbed from behind and carried to a familiar black SUV that had pulled up without my noticing, the sound of their approach likely buffeted by the falling snow. I watched helplessly as Rudy backed a few more steps away, then turned and ran farther into the park.

I was stuffed into the back of the SUV.

Damn! I was long beyond tired of this.

An hour later I was dumped in front of the agency, the FBI getting no more than I was willing to give them ... which was nothing.

After all, they had nothing to barter with, mostly because I'd already figured out who set Dino up; partly because I knew they had nothing on me outside tampering with a federal case, something I hadn't actually done, because, as near as I could tell, there was no federal case. Which made me all the more curious.

While I knew it probably wasn't a good idea to piss off the FBI, if I'd been in a foul mood earlier, the one they inspired was doubly dark when they'd snatched me for what I hoped was the last time.

I went inside the agency, checked for messages, saw nothing that couldn't wait, then went out to Lucille where I'd stashed my cell phone.

I checked and found messages from just about everyone.

Yeah, well, they were all going to have to wait; I had one piece of business I was compelled to complete tonight.

I started Lucille's engine, grateful she was one thing in my life that hadn't let me down lately despite the frigid weather, and then dialed the woman connected to the one case I actually wasn't supposed to be working on.

Snow was coming down even harder when I met Mrs Claus – I mean, Mrs Nicholas – at the same drop-off point I'd been at almost two hours earlier. She pulled up behind my Mustang in an old, battered Ford truck with crate-like sides built up in the back bed. Both of our vehicles looked like bondo specials just this side of the dump, which made me feel a certain kinswomanship with her. She got out wearing much the same thing as I'd seen her in before, glasses included, which she now pushed up her nose.

Was it just me, or did it seem that while I was getting coated with snow, not a flake landed on her?

'I'm so glad you called, dear,' she said, coming to stand before me holding a small paper sack.

I breathed in. Licorice. She smelled like cherry licorice.

'Don't thank me yet. I'm not sure if he's still around or if he was scared away and is even now twenty miles inland.'

She stood for a moment, staring into the wall of white. I wondered what she was doing, but decided it best not to interrupt. I glanced at my cell phone and the time. I had tons yet to do; the sooner we got on with this, the better.

She turned her head to smile at me. 'He's here.'

How could she know that? 'How do you know that?'

'Trust me. I know.' She began walking forward. 'Come on.'

I didn't question her further for fear that I'd hear something I didn't want to. I merely followed her into the park, taking the same path I had when I made the ransom drop. I eyed the garbage bin, half hoping our trek would take us past there so I could take a peek inside. But Mrs Claus veered to the right, moving off the semi-cleared walkway on to the snow-covered grass.

I glanced down at my high-heeled suede boots and sighed before following. What was one more pair of ruined shoes? We were talking Rudolph here. And he was needed to lead Santa's reindeer.

I laughed.

Mrs Claus looked at me with a closed-mouth smile. I almost believed she knew what I was thinking.

Almost.

About fifty feet in, she suddenly stopped.

'What? What is it?'

'Shhh,' she quietly hushed me.

I pulled my leather coat tighter around myself

and pulled up my gloves.

'And stop fidgeting. You're making him nervous.'

I was making who nervous?

I followed her line of sight, squinting against the flakes falling into my eyes. My hair was soaked and I was standing in snow up to my knees.

And still not a single flake seemed to land on her.

'There.'

Where?

Then I made it out. The faint, red glow.

Mrs Claus gave out a whistle that didn't raise the hair on the back of my neck so much as electrify every hair on my body.

The red glow got brighter.

OK, I must have been more stressed than I thought; now I *was* seeing things.

The glowing stopped. I couldn't make out anything else in the white-out.

Mrs Claus reached into her bag and pulled out a shiny red apple.

The snow parted like a soft curtain and the reindeer I'd seen earlier stepped through it, raising and dipping his head as he walked, his breath puffing out before him.

Was my mouth open? I was pretty sure my mouth was open. And it was accumulating snowflakes.

Rudy went straight to Mrs Claus, tucking his nose against her chest before raising his head to lick her chin. She giggled like a little girl and smoothed her free hand over his coat.

'We missed you, Rudolph,' she said so quietly I almost didn't hear her.

Who was 'we'?

Probably her and the kids that visited her holiday display, I told myself.

'Oh, did you want this?' Mrs Claus laughed when Rudy nudged the hand holding the apple. She held it out and he bit into it, crunching away.

She glanced at me. 'You look like you've seen a ghost.'

I shook my head in amazement. 'Not so much a ghost...' More like a piece of fiction come to life.

Which was ridiculous, of course.

But awesome nonetheless.

'Go ahead. Pet him.'

I reached out a tentative hand, remembering the last time I dared touch him, recalling how he felt. My fingers met with his soft coat. So soft ... so warm.

His eyes met mine and I smiled, feeling something burgeon inside of me.

'The kids love petting him. He's always the star attraction,' Mrs Claus said.

'I can see why,' I whispered, wondering if he made them all feel this incredible sense of wonder. 'Why do you think he ran away?'

Mrs Claus finished feeding him the apple then reached into the bag again where she took out sugar cubes. She allowed him to smell them, but didn't feed them to him. Instead she put them back in the bag and gave him a final pat before fastening a lead on his harness and turning toward where we were parked.

'Oh, I don't think he so much ran away as got lost. He's such a playful one, you know. Always getting into trouble...'

Go figure.

A calm, peaceful silence fell as we walked back to her truck. I noticed she didn't have to pull on the lead once, and, even if she had, I wondered how this one little woman could hold power over this magnificent creature that was easily four times her size.

I helped her open the back of her truck and secure the ramp, and up Rudolph went on his own, seemingly as glad to be found as we were.

We closed the back and then stood facing each other.

Caramel. Scads of it. That's what she smelled like now.

'I will contact your wonderful Rosie tomorrow about payment,' she said.

I shook my head. 'No need. I never officially took the case so there is no official billing.'

'I insist.'

'No, I insist.' I smiled. 'Look at it as my gift to the kids.'

She hugged me, nearly surprising me out of my soggy boots. 'Thank you, Sofie Metropolis. You helped when everyone else turned me away.'

My eyes stung, but whether it was because of the snow getting in them, or her generous display of affection, I wasn't sure.

I walked her to the truck door and helped her inside.

'Merry Christmas,' she said, a smile as wide as Long Island splitting her sweet, pink-tinged face.

'Merry Christmas to you.'

She slowly began pulling away.

Apple pie. I smiled and inhaled deeply. Definitely apple pie.

I stood waving as I watched her disappear into the snowy night..

If I spotted a bright-red glow coming from the back of the truck ... well, I wasn't saying.

Twenty-Five

I thought about going home to my apartment, to get out of my wet clothes and into a hot shower, but while I was driving back to Astoria, I felt ... I don't know, energized somehow. And, as strange as it seemed, I was also dry. So I drove to the agency instead to see to the next item on my list.

I let myself inside and checked to verify that not only was I dry, but it appeared I'd never gone out trekking in three-foot snowdrifts in a storm at all. My suede boots looked as if they'd come straight from the box. Even my hair appeared freshly blown out. And a glance in the bathroom mirror verified that everything about me looked not only presentable but ... nice?

And I smelled like – I sniffed my coat – cinnamon.

Hunh.

In recent months, I'd come to understand it was best not to look at certain things too closely. But when it came to items of this nature ... well, I'd take Mrs Claus' missing reindeer over neighborhood vampire covens any day.

I went into my uncle's office, shrugged off my coat, switched on the rarely used TV to a local station and got to work, connecting the dots in a way not even a green prosecutor on his first case would be able to screw up.

A few minutes into my work, the words 'breaking news' caught my attention.

I glanced up at the television, watching as a popular female anchor readied herself before the cameras. She smiled. 'Seems all is well tonight in Manhattan as little Jolie Abramopoulos, daughter of real estate mogul George Abramopoulos, is recovered after a horrific kidnapping ordeal...'

The screen flipped to images of the seven-year-old girl being led by none other than my would-be arch nemesis Charles Chaney as he led her by the hand toward her father outside his famed apartment building, who scooped his daughter up in a hug reminiscent of a Jimmy Stewart film, snow swirling around them.

I shook my head, telling myself all that mattered was that Jolie was safe.

If I wished Chaney and whoever had given him the better job of collecting the girl, well, that was between me and my Glock, which I'd thankfully recovered from the FBI earlier.

The report went on to say the kidnappers were still at large and then the broadcast returned to the snowstorm that was burying the city.

I smiled.

Having gotten what I was looking for – I'd had a feeling little Jolie's recovery would hit the media, and, outside a crooked ponytail and wrinkled clothing, she looked well – I used the remote to switch off the television and picked up the office phone, making the first of several phone calls.

An hour later, I'd done most of what I wanted to do with few complications. Seeing as tomorrow was Christmas Eve, I'd expected some more resistance or at least a few groans. I was happy to say I got none outside my cousin Pete, who I wasn't able to get through to.

A sound out front.

Of course, I was frequently known to speak too soon.

I craned my neck to see out through the crack in the door into the reception area, which I'd left dark. I couldn't make anything out. Probably because it *was* dark.

Damn.

I wheeled my uncle's office chair back and went to have a look. I'd locked the front door, but even if someone had managed to pick the locks, I'd have heard the cowbell.

I hoped.

I slowly opened the office door, resisting the urge to say, 'Hello?' or something equally lame like, 'I've called the police. They're on their way.'

The light panel was near the front door, so I had little choice but to cross the area in the dark. A flick of two switches and the room was awash with light, sweet light...

Revealing two guys with whom I'd grown all too familiar.

Well, what did they want?

'What in the hell are you doing here?' I asked Boris and his forever sidekick.

He grinned at me and began to lurch forward.

I slid my Glock out of the holster and pointed it at him. 'Unh unh. I've long since surpassed my patience for your meeting methods.'

I was relieved I'd at least had the presence of mind to have the FBI return my firearm during our earlier meeting ... and more than a little grateful.

'You ain't gonna use that,' Boris said taking another step.

I took aim and shot. I'd meant for the bullet to pass between his legs somewhere in the vicinity of his knees, but it instead it whizzed a little higher and took a little inner thigh with it. I watched as the fabric of his pants billowed out and then winced at the sound of the round hitting the second from the bottom drawer of the filing cabinet behind him. Well, at least I knew there were enough files in there to prevent it from traveling into the next office.

Boris yelped and both hands went straight for his crotch.

'Don't worry, I don't think I hit anything vital.'

Unless, of course, he was one of those malformed men whose penis hung to his knees.

I cocked my head, keeping my Glock aimed at him. Nah...

His pal was bent over looking at the flesh wound and both of them were speaking in rapid-fire Russian. Or what I thought was Russian, anyway. For all I knew, they could be speaking Swahili. Although I think the chances of that were slim considering their background report.

'Let me rephrase the question: what do you want?' I asked.

Boris stared at the smear of blood on his hand – certainly not enough to write home about – and glared at me. 'Where is the money?'

'Right where you had me put it,' I said. 'Or in the hands of the kidnappers.'

He made the same tsking sound Rosie was partial to, although hers was much cuter. 'I get report you went back to park.'

'Ah, yes. I did. To find Rudolph.'

The two men stared at me.

'Anything else?'

They looked at each other, Boris still holding his thigh as if afraid something might fall out if he didn't.

'Well, then, I'll wish you a good night, gentlemen.' Keeping my Glock trained on them, I opened the door, stepping far enough back so I was out of arm range.

They didn't move for a long moment ... then finally Boris lead the way out, mumbling no doubt profanity under his breath.

Hey, I did it all the time in Greek.

Well, maybe not all the time, but it did come in handy to be able to cuss in a foreign language from time to time. There was a certain beauty in no one around understanding what you were saying; no need for apologies later.

I closed and locked the door after them,

watching as they got into the sedan parked at the curb, one in the driver's side, the other the passenger's, and then drove off.

OK, that was interesting. I hurried to my uncle's office, thinking it would be a good idea if I got out of there. Not only because I was sure Boris was going to come back with reinforcements just as soon as he made sure I'd done no major damage, but because I didn't want to take the chance someone had heard the shot and called the police.

Or, more specifically, Pino.

Yes.

It was time to finally wrap this up.

As I entered the doors to Kennedy Airport, I glanced at the monitors flashing DELAYED on all flights and smiled. I'd known the instant Waters had called me with the news of his subject's whereabouts that the person he'd been following wouldn't be going anywhere for a good, long while. In fact, I knew from previous experience that the worsening storm outside meant that DELAYED would soon flash to CANCELLED and weary travelers and runaway kidnappers were going to be left stranded for the night.

It had happened to me once when I was a teen and gone to Greece for the holidays with my parents (we'd been made to sit at the airport for six hours, then went home, only to turn back when we were rebooked, and waited for another five hours for that plane to leave because of the bottleneck of flights trying to take off), and had watched as it happened at least one other time since. A quick phone call had also verified that no flights would be leaving for the foreseeable future, and the continuing snowfall pretty much guaranteed that would hold.

Not much was capable of shutting down New York City, but a good snowstorm did the trick every now and again.

'Hey,' I said to Waters, who was leaning against a store doorway flipping through a magazine and watching three black women walk by.

'Hey, yourself, hot mama.' He flashed his gold tooth at me as he smiled, looking none the worse for wear.

Well, relatively speaking.

'She come back out?'

He shook his head. 'Nah. Think she hoping they going get planes back up in the air again soon. Girl must be blind, 'cause it's still coming down like a motherfucker out there.'

'Yeah. Thanks for sticking it out.'

'No problem.' He ran his tongue around his teeth. 'That's just the way I roll.'

Indeed.

Probably he was mentally counting his bonus money.

Even eight months into the job, I found it interesting how these things worked. One change in a subject's routine, combined with one bit of information, and a picture materialized as quickly as colorized metal pixels attracted by a powerful magnet. Miss one, and the other didn't matter. Put them together and, voila, a case was solved.

I wondered if the process would ever cease to fascinate me. Did my uncle Spyros still experience the same rush?

It was better than sex.

My brain momentarily froze and three men emerged in my mind.

Three?

Yes. Jake ... Dino ... and, much to my surprise, David Hunter.

OK, maybe it was almost as good as sex.

Almost.

Of course, I didn't know what sex with David Hunter was like.

Yet, a small voice in my head whispered.

No. No way I was going there. Not with all the man trouble I had landed in lately.

Still, it was nice knowing the option was available...

'Where's the suspect?' Waters and I looked at where Pino had come up behind me.

'Still inside, probably checking her watch and sweating a puddle,' I said.

Then again, I wondered if people like her actually sweated. Did they possess some sort of deviant gene that made them think they were above the law? Entitled to do as they pleased without thought to the consequences?

Pino nodded at Waters who nodded back, then he moved aside to introduce two TSA agents.

'We ready to move?' he asked, putting his hands on his hips.

'Ain't gotta ask a nigga twice,' Waters said, smiling at the black female TSA agent who merely rolled her eyes.

'He gotta come with us?' I heard her ask Pino.

Pino looked at me.

I nodded.

'Let's go.'

We were on...

Funny how I forgot how large JFK and its various terminals were until I was forced to walk the length. It took us a good fifteen minutes to get to the right departure gate. And since the area was so large, we decided to split up as we entered the final concourse in case we were spotted instead of being the ones doing the spotting.

Which turned out not to be a worry.

Miss Elizabeth Winston, Abramopoulos' well-coifed and composed executive personal assistant, was sitting calmly in one of the coffee shops, legs crossed, her nose in a glossy fashion magazine.

I alerted the others and, taking different routes, we approached her.

'Elizabeth Winston, you're under arrest for conspiracy to kidnap Jolie Abramopoulos,' Pino said and then read her her Miranda rights while the two TSA agents stood at the ready.

I had to give Winston credit; she looked as calm as they came, barely batting an artfully lashed eye at the accusation.

'I have no idea what you're talking about.' She closed her magazine and put it on the table in front of her as easy as you please.

Waters pulled up his pants in the way Pino once had, causing me to wince and avoid looking directly at his crotch. At least his pants weren't in danger of revealing his socks; first because they were bell bottoms, second because they were long enough to cover most of his seven-inch platform shoes.

'Oh, yeah? Then whatcha doin' flying the coup to Brazil then, huh? Tell me that? I don't care how fine you are – and you are fine, super fine – you are busted.'

'I'm going to Brazil to visit my sister,' she said with a cool smile. 'The trip's been planned for over a month.'

Pino looked at me and I looked at Waters.

'Sounds like a crock of bull to me,' he said.

I agreed. But not because of his reasons. Because I had proof of my own.

'Tell me, Miss Winston,' I said, turning on a smile of my own I hoped held a fraction of the wry coolness hers did. 'Will Mr Daniel Butler be joining you there? Or are you meeting up with him somewhere else?'

While she may have had her trip planned in advance, I was also certain she was the one who'd enticed little Jolie Abramopoulos into that car after school on the day she was taken.

That was one piece of information gleaned from listening to nanny Geraldine Garcia's recorded interview time and again. Given her father's prominence and wealth, it had been drummed into the little girl never to get into a car with a stranger. Beyond that, she'd gone through two self-defense courses where mock kidnapping situations had been staged to make sure she couldn't be tricked or coerced.

Mrs Garcia had been adamant. 'Oh, no, little Jolie would never go with any stranger.'

So that day after school she had known the person who had come to pick her up, or else the well-trained little girl would never have gotten in.

And that person had been her daddy's executive personal assistant, Elizabeth Winston, whom she would have seen often since Winston appeared to accompany him wherever he went.

Oh, I was sure Winston and her accomplices had likely arranged for a faux 'kidnapping' shortly after the pickup, you know, a storming of the car by masked men. Something that would hopefully eclipse the memory of Winston's picking her up – or at least knock it down in importance – and eliminate her as a suspect.

In fact, I was fairly certain that unless asked directly about Winston's involvement, Jolie wouldn't even mention she had been the one to pick her up after school.

I'd bet on it.

Of course, nabbing Winston was one thing. Now the authorities needed to convince her to turn on her accomplices: her not-so-ex live-in boyfriend, Danny Butler, and his one-time cell mate Bubba Canton.

While there was a flicker of fear in her eyes, I had the feeling that wasn't going to be as easy as

I'd hoped.

Then again, who knew?

In the dog-eat-dog world of Manhattan, one's own tail was always more important than the other guy's.

I remember my uncle telling me that most cases weren't solved as a result of large events or confessions, but as a result of good research. That proved true in this case. When I'd discovered that Elizabeth's presumably ex-boyfriend had served a stint at an upstate New York prison, it hadn't really registered. Then I'd read that Bubba had been at the same prison at the same time...

Well, that, combined with Danny's connection to Elizabeth, connected those pixels that had been floating around in my head.

'Sorry I'm late,' Wendy Wyckoff said, out of breath, a camera around her neck. 'Stupid TSA didn't want to let me through.' She looked at the two agents with us. 'No offense.'

'None taken,' the black woman said, although she was clearly lying.

Wendy snapped a pic of Pino handcuffing Elizabeth who tried to hide her face by turning it away. She kept clicking as Pino led her away, Waters strutting on one side, the agents on the other. I hung back, having no need to be in the shots.

As we walked down the concourse, I checked my cell phone. Three messages. One from Rosie (who I'm sure had caught wind of the little girl's recovery); my mom (who was probably inspired by the Fates to knock me back down a few pegs); and the third was my grandfather.

I looked up and Wendy snapped my pic. She rested her camera around her neck and smiled, dropping back to walk with me.

'What did you do that for?' I asked.

'I can't very well run a story without the woman of the hour, can I?'

I gave her a long look. 'The woman of the hour deserves more than two sentences on her requested piece.'

'Oh. That.' She grimaced as she snapped a few photos of the group in front of us. 'Sorry.' She leaned in toward me. 'But when I land that job at a genuine city-wide paper? I promise to give you as much space as you need.' She raised a finger. 'Within reason.'

'What's the matter with *The Ledger-Times*?'

'The truth? I would have given your story the cover rather than Rudolph. And not just because I like you, either.'

I laughed. 'What's like got to do with it?'

She smiled. 'What, indeed...'

Twenty-Six

The following morning, I decided 'like' had a lot to do with a lot of things...

What a difference a week makes. Instead of scowling at Rosie's Christmas Carols, I was now humming them.

It was nine o'clock and we'd both come in a little early so we could leave early, Christmas Eve beckoning. I sat behind my uncle's desk, feet up on the desk, staring at the white board I'd moved against the far wall, *The Ledger-Times* resting against my legs.

I heard Rosie gasp and leaned to the side to see her through the doorway. 'What?'

She got up from her chair, pointing toward the filing cabinets. 'Quick, call the cops ... somebody ... is that a gunshot?'

Oops. I'd forgotten about the incident with Boris the night before.

'Um, no need for the police.'

She came to stand in the doorway, still pointing toward the cabinets. 'Are you crazy? Have you seen this? There's, like, a canon hole in my files!'

I took my feet down off the desk. 'Not only have I seen it ... I did it.'

She looked at me. Then looked again. 'What? You did what?'

'Long story. Suffice it to say it was my only option at the time.'

She tsked and waggled her finger at me. 'Nuh uh. You could have shot the sucker who made you get your gun out in the first place.' She crossed her arms under her breasts. 'Did you at least get the bullet out?'

I slowly shook my head.

She gave me an eye roll. 'Probably it went through all of my files. Probably it's lodged in the middle of the most important one.'

'Probably.'

'Well, I hope you don't expect me to get it out.'

'I'll remove it after Christmas.'

She frowned in a way that made her dimples pop. 'Yeah, well. Just so's you don't forget.'

'You seen this?' I asked, holding up the newspaper.

She came to the desk and looked over the Rudolph story. 'Yeah. I saw it. Did you see the other one?'

'What other one?'

She went to her desk and brought in a copy of the *Daily News* bearing a primo shot of Elizabeth Winston being taking away in handcuffs by Pino. Story was by Wendy Wyckoff.

I smiled. Go, Wendy. She'd taken her photos and her story and had leveraged herself a better job with a bigger paper.

'Got a picture of you inside there, too,' Rosie

said, popping her gum. 'Good publicity. Probably you'll be getting more kidnapping cases.'

I tilted the paper bearing the Rudy story. 'Yeah, kidnapped pets, maybe.'

She gave another eye roll. 'Whatever.'

She walked back out to her desk.

'If you hear anything on the other two, let me know,' I told her.

She didn't answer but I imagined she was showing me the palm of her hand.

I smiled and put my feet back up on the desk. That's OK. She'd get a whole lot happier when I gave her her bonus.

I'd already worked out what the agency could afford to give everyone. And while it wasn't exactly a paltry amount, it wasn't what I'd wanted to give, either. Then I'd come in this morning to find an envelope sitting in the middle of the desk. I'd opened it to discover a considerable amount of cash along with a note that read: *Merry Christmas, Sofie. Make sure it's jolly for everyone. Love, Uncle Spyros.*

Oh, yeah. It was going to be much jollier now. Especially since I decided not to look this particular gift horse in the mouth.

I didn't plan on taking any for myself. I didn't need it. Since going in on percentage with my uncle and his silent partner, Lenny Nash (who I was guessing was behind the Spyros letter), I was doing pretty well.

Receiving a phone call late last night from George Abramopoulos himself, thanking me for finding his daughter and telling me I'd be well compensated for my efforts to bring her kidnappers to justice? Bonus enough.

Maybe I'd get Lucille the makeover she'd been wanting.

Maybe I'd get myself one, too. Chuck all the suede I bought and exchange it for weatherproof leather.

Still, there were some elements of this case that made me itch. While little Jolie might be safe, I had yet to get word on the two main suspects. And forget the scores I had yet to settle...

My gaze snagged on something on the white board as I vaguely heard the cowbell above the outer door clang.

A brief rap on the jamb. I looked up to see Rosie standing there.

'Mrs Kent is here.'

I blinked at her. 'Did we have a meeting?'

'Yeah. Didn't you check the messages I gave you?'

When? I'd been there for all of five seconds. 'I take it the pictures came out?'

'You think I'd have scheduled the appointment if they hadn't?'

'Couldn't it have waited until after Christmas?'

She aimed a glance over her shoulder and lowered her voice. 'What with her calling every five minutes?'

Fine. 'Fine.'

'I'll tell her you'll be right there.'

'You do that.'

Honestly, I didn't know why I was reluctant to

take the meeting. Producing photos other PIs had failed to should have been the cherry on top of a successful twenty-four hours.

Why, then, did I wish I could sneak out back?

I pushed from my desk, pasted a smile on my face, and went out to meet her, Rosie holding out an envelope as I neared.

'Merry Christmas, Mrs Kent,' I said.

'Lois, please,' she said, her gaze stuck to the envelope while she licked her lips. You'd have thought I was about to offer a roasted turkey the way she practically salivated. 'And I hope that's my present.'

I held out the shots, almost half hoping they hadn't come out or had been deleted by my Latino pen-borrower. Problem was? I knew Rosie would never have ordered hard prints and set the meeting if they hadn't.

I looked at her. Or would she have?

Mrs Kent quickly opened the envelope. I didn't even look at the photos as she sorted through them. Rather, I watched her face.

Normally, I guessed she was a pretty woman. Depending on what normal meant, I suppose. But just then, she looked so ... calculating somehow.

Her satisfied smile should have made me happy. Instead it made me sick to my stomach.

'Bingo.'

She held up a shot of her husband draping Pamela Coe's coat over her shoulders. Pamela had leaned back as if to whisper something into his ear, her eyes half closed. The innocent move emerged somehow intimate.

'We didn't catch him in the act,' Rosie said.

We both looked at her: me, in question, Lois in triumph.

'Doesn't matter. This is all I need.' She put the shots back into the envelope. 'He was never messing around to begin with. In fact, I have no idea how you got these shots, but I can't thank you enough. I was afraid I'd have to stay married to the idiot forever.'

Rosie and I shared a glance.

'What do you mean you knew he wasn't messing around?' Rosie asked.

'Just that. Clark is as true blue as they come. He wouldn't have sniffed a pussy if you put in front of him. Hell, one of the PIs did exactly that. Nothing.'

'I'm not following you,' I said.

Then it dawned on me: she'd never intended for us to get proof; she'd wanted us to manufacture it.

And we'd done exactly that.

'But that don't prove nothing,' Rosie said the words I was thinking.

'It proves enough. And, I'm guessing, he didn't know the woman in the shots, right? Which means he'll deny knowing her because, well, he doesn't. Which will in turn make him look all the guiltier.' She gave a happy laugh that might have made her look attractive if only I hadn't known the cause.

She put her coat on. An expensive white fur.

'Look, I've been married to the guy for nine

years. Bore him two kids. And all the while I was bored. Bored, bored, bored.'

'So why not just divorce him?' Rosie crossed her arms under her considerable chest.

'And what? Walk away with nothing?' She shook her head. 'No way.' She lifted the envelope. 'This right here nets me half. Which is substantial. And might even get me half his pension. Which means I'm set for life. I'll never have to marry another halfwit like him again. I can't thank you enough,' she said. 'I'll make sure to add a little something extra when I pay my bill.'

She wished us both happy holidays and then turned on her expensive heels, leaving a trail of perfume behind her.

I stood staring after her long after the cowbell went silent.

'I feel like we just got a visit from the Wicked Witch of the South,' Rosie said next to me, her gum popping.

'West.'

'Whatever.' She uncrossed her arms and gave a visible shiver. 'Poor schmuck. He's never gonna know what hit him.'

No, he wasn't.

And I felt dirty somehow knowing I'd essentially supplied the two-by-four that was going to hit him upside the head.

Happy holidays, indeed.

Then whatever stop action lifted and the world began turning again.

I registered the Christmas carols playing.

The phone rang and Rosie answered.

I made out the sound of my cell chirping.

I walked to the office and answered it.

'*Kalimera*, Pappou,' I greeted my grandfather in Greek as I sat down. 'So can you make it?'

Where once I'd have been annoyed, now I was happy for the distraction.

'I don't know...' he said quietly. 'I'm not sure it's a good idea ... It is Christmas Eve ... Surely she has family...'

I squinted at the white board again, an idea ducking in and out that kept slipping through my fingers that had nothing to do with the matter at hand.

I'd called the widow, Mrs Liotta, to arrange a good time for Grandpa Kosmos to pick up the medal and she had suggested this morning. I'd left a message on his answering machine passing on her invitation. 'She's the one who invited us, so I'm sure it's fine. But if you don't want to...'

'No, no. That's not what I meant at all...'

The cowbell again. I looked to see Pino standing with his hat in his hands greeting Rosie. I took my feet back off the desk so I could lean farther to see her. Yep, she was showing him the bullet hole in the filing cabinet. Great.

'Well, what do you mean then, Pappou?'

Pino looked in my direction with a raised brow. I shrugged and waved him in.

'I'm thinking maybe I should go by myself.'

I squinted again.

'I mean, if you think it'll will be OK with

Iris?'

The intimate way he said her name made me wonder again just how well these two knew each other.

'If it's all the same to you, I'd like to drive you. You're obviously ... distracted. I wouldn't want you to get into an accident.'

'I could take a taxi.'

That settled it. 'I'll be over to pick you up in fifteen minutes.'

I disconnected the call, wondering just what the heck was going on with my grandfather.

If I didn't know him better, I'd say he was in love.

'What did the filing cabinet do?' Pino asked, coming to stand in the doorway.

I took him in and laughed. 'Attempted snatch and grab ... again.'

'Ah. I'd have shot it, too, then.'

I got up from my chair. 'So what's the good word?'

'How do you know there is one?'

'Oh, I don't know? Because you never stop in here?' I began to erase the white board.

'Maybe I should stop in more often.'

We shared a look.

'Maybe not,' he said.

I flipped the board and began taking the pins out.

'I just wanted to pass on Danny Butler's been picked up.'

I smiled. 'Good. And Bubba?'

'Still at large. Which is the second reason for

my visit.'

I stopped what I was doing to look at him.

'I want you to lie low until they pick him up.'

'Oh?'

'Checking his records this morning ... well, let's just say he has a penchant for revenge.'

'What could he possibly have against me? What did I do?'

He stared at me.

'Oh.' I grasped the items in my hands a little too tightly and one of the pushpins pricked me. 'Ow.' I emptied the contents on to the desk and then sucked the blood from my finger.

'You shouldn't do that. Do you know how many germs are in your mouth?'

'I'm more concerned with how many are on my finger. Do you know where it's been?'

Pino blushed.

I smiled. I liked that about him, that a simple comment was capable of making him blush.

'Anyway, I just wanted to give you fair warning.'

'Warned. Thanks.'

'You're welcome.'

I grabbed my coat and purse. 'Here, let me walk out with you.'

Moments later we were outside, wishing each other Merry Christmas and remarking on how the weather forecast called for warmer temperatures and rain – rain! – then he was pulling away in his cruiser and I found myself looking at two other familiar vehicles parked on the street.

Hunh.

Why in the hell was Chaney following me again? I reconsidered Pino's warning. Maybe it wasn't Bubba Canton I had to worry about. Maybe it was the pudgy old PI.

The other...

Before I knew it, my boots were carrying me across the street to rap on Jake's driver's side window. It was already rolled down a couple of inches and blue smoke curled out so I knew he was inside even though I couldn't see him through the tinted glass. I was trying to come up with something witty to say when it rolled down the rest of the way and I found myself looking at him, rendered instantly witless.

'Good show yesterday,' he said.

'That's why you're here?'

He didn't say anything for a long moment. Then he pitched his smoke to the street. 'No.'

'Meaning there's a different reason?'

He squinted, looking at me so thoroughly I almost felt like he was undressing me. Only it really wasn't that kind of look. Instead, he seemed to be seeing something that lay beneath the surface, something that maybe not even I knew was there.

'I'm not going to be around for a while.'

My kidneys contracted. 'Define a while.'

'Maybe forever.'

'Oh.'

'Yeah.'

Neither of us spoke for long moments. I knew why I couldn't – shock played a large role in there somewhere – but him?

'Anyway, I just thought you should know.'

I didn't know what to say. 'Thanks?' More of a question than a comment.

He gave me one of his sexy, lopsided grins and I found myself wanting to kiss him. Just one more time.

'Take care, kid.'

'Yeah. You, too.'

I didn't realize I'd put my arm on his truck until I had to remove it so he could roll up his window. Then I had to step back in order for him to pull away from the curb. He gave the horn a brief honk and away he went.

And there I stood in the middle of the street, watching him go, wondering if I should have said something more.

Jake had become such a fixture in my life, I had never stopped to consider how I would feel if he wasn't. Then again, why should I have?

The long and the short of it was I didn't feel good about it at all. It was almost as if someone had told me a close relative had suddenly died.

Speaking of relatives, Grandpa Kosmos was waiting for me.

A horn honked behind me and I realized I was blocking traffic.

'I'm moving already!' I said.

Then I crossed the street to Lucille and climbed inside, feeling oddly as if I'd woken up to find someone had changed a one-way street to move in the other direction ... and left me considering what the fine was for breaking the law.

Twenty-Seven

If my wanting a good frappé had anything to do
with my wanting to pick up Grandpa Kosmos at
the café rather than his side apartment entrance,
I wasn't saying.

I took a long sip from my travel cup straw. Ah,
yes. There were few things better than a nice,
freshly made frappé.

Well, OK, maybe there were more than a few.
But not many.

We were five minutes into our trip to Brooklyn
and my grandfather had barely said two words.
In fact, I wondered if he was truly in the car with
me at all.

'Fidget one more time and I'll boot you out
and make you catch a taxi,' I told him.

He looked at me blankly where we sat at a red
light. *'Ti?'*

I smiled at his Greek 'what?'. 'Nothing. Just
trying to get your attention.' The light changed
and I moved forward along with the other
Christmas Eve morning traffic. 'Now that I have
it, you mind telling me what the history is between you and the recently widowed Mrs
Liotta?'

He fidgeted again. 'She was the wife of my

best friend.'

'Uh huh. That, I know.' I gave him a long look as I sipped my frappé. 'What I want to know is what you're not telling me.'

He made a sound of annoyance. 'I think you're letting this PI stuff go to your head. Seeing mysteries where there are none.'

'Uh huh,' I said again. 'Give. How did you meet?'

'Iris and I?'

There it was again, his use of her first name in that way that seemed almost too intimate. Maybe it was the way his face transformed. Suddenly he appeared twenty years younger.

'Coney Island.'

He went silent.

'And?' I prompted.

'And what?'

It wasn't like Grandpa Kosmos to be so tight-lipped about anything. Usually he was chomping at the bit to tell a good story, usually with a beginning, a middle and an end ... and including, of course, a moral to the story.

I liked to think it was what made Greeks – ancient or otherwise – such great storytellers.

He finally seemed to relax into the seat. 'I was seventeen ... She was sixteen...' He drifted off briefly. 'I was there with my friends, she was there with her family. Strict father. He didn't like me on sight.'

I remembered the pictures of my grandfather I'd seen from those years. One, in particular, had been of him and a few pals at the Brooklyn park.

He'd been a handsome, grinning young man who looked full of 'piss and vinegar' as my mother liked to say.

'She wanted a hot dog and I bought her one...'

His smile told me he was keeping more details to himself than he was sharing.

'And you snuck off together?' I offered.

'What?' He looked at me as if just realizing I was there. 'No, no. Not that first night. Never. That's not how things worked back then.'

But they had snuck off.

I smiled.

'And your best friend, Al?'

His expression clouded up.

'He liked her, too.'

'But she liked you.'

He nodded. 'She liked me...'

His words drifted off along with his attention as he stared through the window, though I doubt he saw anything other than the memories floating through his mind.

'What happened?'

'What?'

'Back then. What happened that Al ended up with her and you didn't?'

He looked down at the folded hands in his lap, messing with one of his cuticles. 'I was introduced to your grandmother...'

Of course.

We drove in silence for a while, he contemplating a girl he'd once known, I what life might have been like for him had he understood there were other choices.

Had he considered bucking family? Tradition? Going for the girl he'd met at Coney Island so long ago?

Successive images floated like ghosts of relationships past, unconnected but so tightly bound you couldn't have cut them apart with pastry sheers.

My almost marriage to Thomas...

Dino...

Rosie and Seth...

I could only imagine those familial pressures and expectations had fifty years ago been triple what they were now. And while I'd never thought Grandpa Kosmos the cowardly kind ... well, he was also very traditional.

And there was the whole friendship angle to consider.

What had he given up?

Or, rather, what had he fantasized he'd given up?

Could Iris have been the love of his life? Denied until now?

'I don't regret a moment of my life,' he said.

I might have suspected he could read my thoughts, only he was deeply entrenched in his own, I didn't think he registered where he was, much less what color shirt I had on.

I reached over and took his hand. 'I know.'

We arrived quicker than I was ready for.

I really didn't want to go in with him. Sometimes the way he spoke Iris' name made me feel like I was somewhere I didn't belong.

But I did have one more question: 'And the

medal?'

He was staring at the place I'd pointed out as hers. 'I saw her one last time. Al and I were back stateside on leave. She was engaged to him ... I was promised to your grandmother. It was then I gave her the medal.'

This surprised me, considering he'd already made the decision not to pursue her by then. 'Why?'

He searched my face. 'Because it had been her I'd been thinking about when I earned it.'

His words touched me in a way for which I was unprepared.

I leaned toward him and gave him a tight hug, holding him there for a long moment.

Sometimes it was easy to forget that family members were people, too. With stories and joys and pains all their own that had nothing to do with you.

I drew back and looked at him through the film of my tears. 'Enjoy your visit,' I said. 'If it's all the same to you, I don't think I'm going to stick around.'

He nodded, as if the thought had occurred to him, as well. 'I'll catch a taxi home.'

I touched the side of his face. 'I love you.'

'K'ego, s'agapo, koukla mou. Thank you.'

'No, thank you, Pappou.'

I spotted the curtains move in Iris' apartment.

'Now go on, get. You have that, um, medal to reclaim.'

His answering smile was so bright it could have melted the snow. 'Yes. Yes, I do...'

I drove back to Astoria smiling with more than my lips. The day stretched before me filled with nothing but a little clean-up work and playing Santa. I stopped by my parents' to pick up the gifts I'd left there, then went to my place for more. I hadn't given Mrs Nebitz her Chanukah gift yet, either, so maybe I'd stop across the hall before going back to the office.

That's funny, I thought, as I opened my apartment door: no Muffy.

I glanced at where I'd left the window open for him and shrugged, figuring he was seeing to business. He'd be in soon enough. Anyway, I didn't have much time before Rosie left for the day, and I wanted to give her her bonus, as well as leave envelopes for the others getting one.

I crossed to my bedroom and reached in to switch on the light.

Only to realize there wasn't going to be anything quick about this visit.

'I knew you were going to be trouble from the instant I first laid eyes on you, bitch. Now hand me your fucking gun and get on the fucking floor.'

Twenty-Eight

Damn...

Bubba Canton stood in the corner of my bedroom aiming his favorite shotgun at me.

Pino's words from a while ago echoed in my ears. Why hadn't I heeded his warning? Oh, wait, I remember: because I was too busy gloating.

Double damn...

I held up my hands, wondering as I did why everyone always felt compelled to do that. Was it to say, 'Look, see? I'm not holding'? Or, 'Whoa, wait on a minute. Let's not be so hasty'? Or, 'See my hands? They're yours to do with what you will'?

In my case, I decided I didn't have anything better to do outside shooting him with my own gun, and somehow I got the impression he wouldn't approve of that.

'Bubba,' I said simply.

'Do as I fucking say now!'

Honestly, I was so busy getting over the shock of seeing him in my bedroom, I hadn't really heard what he'd said.

I made out Muffy's muffled bark and then furious scratching. I realized he must be locked in my closet. I glanced at Bubba, finding his right wrist dripping blood on to my expensive area rug and I noticed a tear in his left jeans leg.

He might have gotten one over on Muffy, but not without a fight.

I could only hope Muffy wasn't bleeding...

'Look, half the city is searching for you, Bubba. I figured you would have been halfway around the world by now.'

'You did, did you?' he adjusted his hands on the gun. 'With what money, bitch?'

I blinked at him. 'With the ransom money.'

'There ain't no motherfucking ransom money. That Abramopoulos bastard fucked me over; there was nothing in the garbage can.'

I didn't understand. I'd seen the bearer bonds. Delivered the briefcase myself, as instructed. What happened between then and the point where he'd visited the bin?

And what would have been the consequences had Bubba and his accomplices not released the girl before finding that same bin empty?

I stared at the man holding me at gunpoint and decided that whole Jimmy Stewart reunion bit yesterday might never have happened.

Bubba gripped his weapon, looking more than prepared to use it.

Yeah, I'd say little Jolie would be history right about now...

Muffy scratched like crazy then howled. I don't think I'd ever heard him howl before. The soulful sound made my stomach lining melt.

'It's OK boy,' I told him, sincerely hoping that

was the case, that he was just really determined to get out and not hurt.

Bubba looked toward the closet.

And I took full advantage of the momentary distraction and dove for cover into the living room, keeping low, moving fast.

The shotgun blast penetrated the wall, sending plaster spitting inches from my face.

I scrambled farther away and behind the far edge of the couch, freeing my Glock from my holster, and my cell phone from my pocket, as I went.

'Get back here, you fucking bitch! I need to make you pay for all the trouble you caused!'

My throat choked off air. Why was I thinking there wasn't enough money in the world to pay the kind of debt he was talking about?

I scooted a little farther along the floor, my ear against the wood trying to make myself the smallest target I could, my eye and gun trained on the bottom of my bedroom doorway: the former under it, the latter around it.

'And your sister, Sara?' I shouted, trying to right the cell phone so I could call Pino. I figured not only was he the right one to contact, but experience held he'd be the fastest to get there. Probably he was up the block, waiting for something to happen to me. At least sometimes it seemed that way. 'Does she want to make me pay, too?'

'Sara?' His laugh was more of a bark. 'That fucking idiot has no idea what it takes to make it in this world. If I'd have let her in on this, she probably would have gone straight to the fucking police. Or that fucking worthless ex of hers who cut her off without a dime.'

I briefly closed my eyes, thankful that Jolie's mom had more sense than her gun-crazy uncle. At least when it came to matters of kidnapping.

I scrolled through my numbers...

Feet.

I refocused my attention on the door, taking aim for Bubba's boots and firing.

I watched as leather and denim exploded outward.

The man who was wearing them groaned and collapsed to his knees.

Uh oh...

I hadn't planned that my shooting him would bring him down to my level.

And he was getting blood on a second area rug.

OK, I'd bought this one at the Chelsea Flea Market, so I hadn't spent that much on it. But seeing as it had literally been infested with fleas, and had taken me a good month to clean it, I had time invested.

It had also nearly gotten me arrested for murder. But that was another story I didn't have time to think about right now.

Long story short, the rug meant more to me than the expensive one in my bedroom.

I gauged distance and the open spaces between me and the front door and me and the window.

Shit! He'd get me either way for sure, no

matter how much pain he was in.

'Motherfucking motherfucker!' The shotgun cocked, nearly scaring my heart right out of my chest. 'Where in the fuck are you?'

My cell phone rang as if on cue.

I was convinced my heart had landed on the rug somewhere near his blood stains.

I hurried to answer it.

'Sofie?'

My cousin, Pete.

'Whatever you do, don't go into your place. I think that madman Canton is in there.'

'Too late,' I whispered as much to him as myself.

Another shotgun blast. I scrambled backward on my hands and knees, praying as I went, my cell phone sliding across the floor out of reach. The legs of my side table spat splinters at me, nearly catching me in the eye, the stinging of my cheeks telling me I'd eaten a few.

'You're not going to get away with this, you know,' I shouted. 'Everyone and his brother is on their way here now. You're going to end up back in prison for the rest of your unnatural life.'

Another blast, this time farther away.

I figured either he was trying to bait me out of my hiding place, or pain was blurring his focus.

I really wasn't all that interested in finding out which it was.

'I ain't going back to no motherfucking prison cell. Ever!'

'Well, you should have thought about that

before kidnapping Abramopoulos' daughter.'

'She's my niece, goddam it! Rich mother-fucker took her away from her own mother, wouldn't even let my sister visit with her. The way I see it, that bastard's the one who should be in prison.'

Call me crazy? But I didn't have a problem with that logic.

Movement outside the apartment door. I glanced hopefully in that direction. Until I realized it could just as easily be Mrs Nebitz as Pino or Pete.

The barrier swung violently inward and there stood none other than Charles Chaney.

'Put the gun down! Now!' he shouted, bursting into the room, the apartment door slamming shut behind him. He looked like my aunt's old, stained sofa with a perspiration problem and glasses. But he was holding a gun. A definite plus.

My hero.

Bubba aimed his shotgun at him.

'Shit!' Chaney swung back toward the door and took a blast straight to his overstuffed ass.

He made a sickening sound as he dropped to the floor.

I winced. That had to hurt. But at least I was reasonably sure he would survive his injuries.

What in the hell was he thinking? While a part of me wanted to applaud him for his almost heroic efforts, another wanted to bat him about the ears.

At least he could have left me a clear path to

the door when he'd created the diversion.

Now he completely blocked it.

I heard Bubba moving around. I chanced a peek around the bottom of the couch to find him tying off his ankle wound with a chocolate-colored neck scarf my mother had knitted for me. My favorite. Also ruined with his blood.

The asinine direction of my thoughts helped distract me from the fact that fear was ballooning in me at the realization he was regaining his bearings.

Tick-tock.

I closed my eyes, trying to empty my mind so something useful could fill it. All I could hear was Chaney's pitiful moans from the other side of the room, where I'm sure he was also bleeding on something I liked.

Another shotgun cock.

OK, maybe emptying my mind wasn't an option.

Instead I put my feet under me, took a deep breath, and slowly rose to my full height, my Glock held out in front of me, my right arm locked, my left hand supporting the gun's weight.

Bubba did the same thing on the other side of the couch. Only the shotgun was heavier and he didn't have a chance to raise it before I squeezed off one round, then two, then three.

The first shot hit him in his gun shoulder, causing him to drop it. The second, the neck, causing his head to lean at an awkward angle. And the third hit him right in the forehead.

Bullseye.

'Rule Number Three.' I heard my uncle Spyros' voice as clearly as if he were speaking right next to me. 'If someone's gunning for you? Don't aim to injure: shoot to kill.'

I stood frozen to the spot, watching as Robert 'Bubba' Canton collapsed on to my brand new sofa, his eyes wide open. In a ridiculous part of my brain that still worked, I imagined even in death he was saying, 'Yeah, bitch, I got blood on your couch. What the fuck are you going to do about it?'

The door swung inward again, windows shattered and, within a blink, my apartment was filled with SWAT members and FBI agents.

I didn't realize I was still standing with my gun held out in front of me, although my target had long since been eliminated, until the agent responsible for two of my snatch and grabs came up and put his hand over mine.

'Whoa. It's over. Why don't you give that to me now?'

I blinked at him, but couldn't seem to bring myself to move otherwise.

'First kill?' he asked, waving to the others to stand down where they trained their firearms on me.

I nodded.

I was vaguely aware of another agent verifying Bubba's death, and someone letting Muffy out of my bedroom closet; he ran to me, positioning himself next to my leg and growling and barking at anyone within nipping distance.

My sidekick.

I looked at him briefly to make sure he was OK, then stared at the FBI agent, just now realizing I didn't know what to call him.

'What's your name?' I asked stupidly.

He smiled. 'James. My name is James.'

Not Agent Smith ... or Jones ... or Davis, just James.

I finally released my grip on my gun, allowing him to take it.

'Just so you know, Jimmy, I'll need that back.'

'James is my surname.'

'Of course it is.'

'Michael is my first.'

I found myself smiling at him stupidly.

Then my legs gave out.

'Whoa.' He helped move me to a chair where I dissolved into little more than a liquid puddle of spent adrenalin.

My first kill...

A sledgehammer would fail to dislodge the words from my brain at that moment.

Or my question of whether or not there would be a second.

'What are you doing?' I heard a familiar female voice demand and imagined Mrs Nebitz taking aim at the officers with her cane, despite their superior firepower. 'Why so many men to do the job of one? For shame! Look what you've done to the place! You're tracking mud all over the apartment. And is somebody going to take care of this nice man lying in his own blood over here? He looks to be in a lot of pain.'

God love Mrs Nebitz.

She stepped over a moaning Chaney and headed in my direction.

'Sofie? Sofie, are you OK, dear? These men haven't hurt you?'

I nodded, then shook my head, trying to reassure her as she bent over to peer into my face.

'Not to rush you, dear, but when you're feeling up to it? I'm still having that problem with the plumbing.'

'Thank God,' my cousin Pete said as he entered the place, stepping straight over Chaney, as well. 'I thought I was too late.'

The SWAT members and FBI didn't seem to know what to do about those coming inside the open door.

'Shit,' Pete said, spotting where Bubba lay motionless on the sofa. Funny, Mrs Nebitz didn't seem to give him a second glance. 'Is he dead?'

Pino's voice: 'Hey, hey! Step away from the crime scene. Police area starts here.' He indicated the door. 'Anyone not authorized needs to be outside. Now.'

I was thinking that with SWAT and FBI here he probably also fell into that category. But I wasn't saying anything. I just wanted someone to show me how to get off this crazy ride.

I was dizzy.

I was afraid I was about to be sick.

But mostly I was terrified there was no exit to be had.

Twenty-Nine

Christmas Day was equally crazy, but in a far preferable way.

Well, for the most part.

Somehow I'd managed to return to moderate functionality directly after yesterday's events. Michael – I mean, Agent James – had kept the questioning to a minimum, going easy on me so long as I promised to come back after the holiday. Which I found was only right, considering he'd used me as bait. Like Pino, he'd suspected Bubba would be making a beeline straight for me, and had been shadowing my movements, waiting for the gun-loving madman to show himself. The monitoring of my phone had led to them hearing Pete's call and – bam! – they'd been there at the fourth shot of my gun.

Too bad they couldn't have been there at the first or that I hadn't known they were so close. Maybe now I wouldn't be haunted by Bubba's dead eyes staring at me accusingly, his voice echoing unsaid words into my ear:

'Now you've gone and done it, bitch. Don't even fucking think this is anywhere near over.'

I couldn't imagine what life had been like for his sister, Sara. I only hoped that, now she was free of him, she no longer felt he was the only one on whom she could rely. She could gather her wits about her and perhaps regain visiting rights to her daughter.

In my bid to help her in that regard, I'd contacted my cousin, Nia, the first lawyer in the family, and laid the groundwork for putting her together with Sara, to see what could be done legally to help her.

While Nia wasn't that experienced, I knew she wouldn't give in until she won. And right now I was thinking Sara needed someone like that in her corner.

Well, someone like that who didn't have a gun attached to his arm and thought kidnapping was the only way to go about it.

What I found more curious? My post-killing interview with Michael revealed that the ransom monies hadn't been recovered.

Had Elizabeth somehow manage to access it? Her boyfriend, Danny, before he was picked up? Was it even now stashed somewhere, waiting for them to claim it when they got out of prison?

Who knew? Wherever it was, it was one mystery I wasn't interested in solving.

Right now, I had bigger fish to fry.

Or, rather, cabbage salad to make.

I was in the kitchen with my mother and Yiayia, finishing up Christmas dinner preparations. Yiayia had poured the three of us glasses of wine in short, double shot-like glasses, which was Greek custom, signaling that after three hours of non-stop activity, our work was almost

297

done, and this was to help us relax.

Me? I liked sharing the quiet moment with them and could have easily enjoyed cod liver oil just as much.

'*Sten eyeia mas.*' My mother toasted our health, raising her glass.

'*Kala Christougenna.*' I wished them a Merry Christmas.

Yiayia just grinned and clinked her glass with ours.

The three of us drank the contents down straight, which was also custom, then stood smiling at each other.

The doorbell rang. I finished squeezing lemon on top of the finely chopped cabbage and carrot shavings and volunteered to answer it.

I hadn't told my mother what had happened yesterday. And, with any luck, she wouldn't find out. Not just today, on Christmas, but ever. I knew she was concerned about me, about the choices I was making in my life.

As far as that went, so was I.

I took my apron off and laid it on the counter before pushing open the kitchen door. Efi was busy setting the table. I paused and gave her a brief hug from behind and kissed the back of her neck before moving on past where my father read the newspaper in his recliner.

'Hey, where's mine?' he asked.

I smiled as I backtracked and kissed him on the cheek.

'Thanks, *koukla mou*,' he said. '*Kala Christougenna.*'

The emotional warmth of the day helped chase back some of yesterday's shadows ... but not far. I knew they were there, lurking, ready to seep back in and threaten to consume me. But I was glad the experience helped me better appreciate today. Not just because of Christmas, although I'd always liked the quiet peace and family togetherness of the holiday. No, the darkness helped me better see the light. And it seemed to glow around those I loved.

I opened the door to find Grandpa Kosmos standing on the porch.

'What are you doing knocking?' I asked, opening the door farther. 'You never knock.'

Then he stepped aside and I saw why.

'*Kala*, um, is it *Christougenna*?' Iris Liotta said, holding out an apple pie that looked to be made from scratch. 'I hope you don't mind my coming.'

'No, no! Of course, not. Come in, come in,' I said. 'And you said it perfectly. Merry Christmas to you, too.'

I kissed her on both cheeks and allowed her to pass, then hugged my grandfather hard, leaning back to give him a big smile.

He winked at me. 'Not a word.'

'Did I say anything? I didn't say anything. Nope, not a word.'

He hugged me again. 'No ... not yet, anyway.' He came inside.

I was just about to close the door when I saw my cousin Pete coming up the walkway.

Hunh.

He never came to these things.

I was glad to see him.

'Hey, you,' I said, hugging him and exchanging Christmas wishes.

'I can't stay long,' he said. 'I just wanted to stop by to bring some of my mom's home-made cookies ... and to give you this...'

He placed a large briefcase on the floor between us.

I blinked hard. Then I reached behind him to close the door, suddenly feeling the need for extra safety.

'Is that ... I mean, what ... Don't tell me that's the ransom money...?'

He looked sheepish. 'Yeah.'

'You brought twenty million dollars in bearer bonds to my parents' house?'

I nearly shouted the words, earning a 'What's going on?' from my father, and the curiosity of my grandfather, his date and my sister.

'Hi, Uncle Pericles. Merry Christmas.'

'Merry Christmas, Pete. Come in and keep an old man company.'

I heard my grandfather snort. Seemed the love of a good woman could only change so much.

I lowered my voice. 'What are you doing with this?'

'Long story.'

'Shorten it.'

'Well, you know I was following Bubba the day before yesterday, right? Well, I tailed him straight to Flushing Meadows. I saw you make the drop. Waited for Bubba to go pick it up.

Only something spooked him and he ran ... and I got the money.'

I squinted at him, trying to make sense of his words. 'You ... got ... the ... money.'

He looked down at his shoes, his hands deep in the pockets of a nice, full-length camel coat.

'And you sat on it for two days?'

He gave me a small smile. 'Yeah.'

The old Pete? Well, the old Pete would have made off with that money. Would have raised a hand and waved goodbye and disappeared into the sunset forever.

And, it seemed, the new Pete had surrendered to the old one ... for a couple of days, anyway.

Christmas?

Or was the change more permanent?

The concept was too large for me to work my head around just then. Especially since it would have been oh so easy for him to have kept the money with no one any the wiser. He could have taken the bearer bonds to Greece – anywhere! – and lived out the rest of his life without having to worry about working another case: ever.

I couldn't say with any degree of certainty what I would have done had our roles been reversed.

I grimaced. Yeah, I could. The prospect of keeping it would have never entered my mind.

At least that's my story. And I'm sticking to it.

Of course, none of that had anything to do with the here and now and the fact that I was now in possession of twenty million dollars.

I leaned forward and whispered urgently,

'What you want me to do with it?' I wasn't sure I liked knowing I was going to be responsible for twenty million dollars.

No, scratch that; I definitely didn't like being responsible for twenty million dollars.

'Keep it away from me,' he said. 'Temptation's too damn great.'

I stared at the briefcase. 'I heard that.'

Well, I guess that explained what Chaney was doing following me around after the ransom drop. With the money still out there, he probably figured his best bet of finding it was through me.

Instead, he'd caught a shotgun blast to the ass.

I couldn't help a small laugh.

Pete pointed inside the house. 'I'm, um, just going to say hi to everyone, OK? And give these cookies to your mom.' He held up the plate in his hands.

'OK...'

I stood where I was for what seemed like forever before I guessed I needed to do something. I picked up the briefcase and moved it to sit next to my father, which I figured was the safest place in the house.

'What's this?' he asked.

'My life. Don't open it.'

He went back to reading his paper as I pulled out my cell phone and walked across the room to dial Agent Michael James' work number.

A receptionist answered. I asked that she have him contact me as soon as possible about an urgent matter.

He called back nearly as fast as I disconnected.

'Be right there,' he said when I told him.

I turned around to find my sister and father and grandfather had the case open and were looking at it.

I gasped and crossed the room to take it from them.

'That's not what I think it is?' Efi asked, mouth agape.

'No. It's part of a counterfeit scheme I'm working.'

'What are you doing bringing work to the house? On Christmas Day?' Grandpa Kosmos wanted to know.

My mother came into the room with Iris. 'What's going on?'

'Nothing,' I said quickly. 'Just some nosy-rosies who can't keep their hands to themselves.'

'How much is it?' Dad wanted to know.

'Would you guys stop? An FB ... a friend is coming by to pick it up now.' I stashed the case in the front closet, leaning against the door for good measure.

'FB ... as in I? FBI?' Efi asked.

'Is he staying for dinner?' Mom asked.

'No, he's a friend. And, no, he's not staying for dinner.'

Thalia shrugged and walked back to the kitchen with Iris.

Thankfully, everyone else also lost interest.

But I wasn't moving more than ten feet away

from that door lest that interest reignite.

Five minutes later, a knock sounded on the door. I stopped pacing and opened it.

'That was fast.'

Only it wasn't Michael's face I was staring into...

It was Dino's.

Thirty

'Oh my God!'

My instinct was to throw my arms around him, so I did.

Without reservation.

If you had asked me to list the people I least expected to see on the other side of the door, his would have topped it. Hadn't I just talked to him the other day? Hadn't he been in Greece?

'*Kala Christougenna*,' he murmured into my ear, holding me so tightly I could barely breathe.

Which was the way I was clinging to him.

He felt good...

He smelled good...

Mmm...

Words sprouted wings and fluttered from my mind.

My father cleared his throat loudly behind me.

I reluctantly released Dino, my cheeks hurting from smiling so wide.

'Welcome home, Konstantino,' my dad said, stepping forward to hug him.

I accepted the bottle of wine and a box with a ribbon tied around it from him along with his coat then put all where they needed to go while he greeted the rest of my family.

Dino was here...

I wasn't sure what surprised me more: that he was there or my reaction to his being there. Probably it was a tie.

I caught my mother's eye, seeing the warning on her face.

I looked quickly away.

I didn't want today to be about anything more than today. Surely, she could understand that? I didn't want to censor myself, think about hidden meanings or tomorrow or three months from now, much less a lifetime.

Dino was here. And I wanted to enjoy that. Enjoy my family. Enjoy Christmas.

I wasn't being selfish ... was I?

Dino came back to stand near me and I couldn't help beaming at him. Didn't want to stop myself from beaming at him.

Truth was? He was the best Christmas gift I could have received.

And if somewhere in the back of my mind I knew Jake was the one who had given him to me ... well, I wasn't going to think about that, either.

Another knock at the door.

I opened it to find Michael on the porch. He wore a casual pullover sweater, jeans and a leather jacket, looking so un-FBI-like I almost didn't recognize him.

'Hi,' I said. 'Thanks for coming so quickly. The last thing I wanted to do was keep this in the house.'

'I'm not even going to ask where you got it.'

I smiled. 'Thanks.'

'Not now, anyway, but...'

'Yeah, yeah ... after the holiday.'

I debated whether or not to tell him I had a thing or two to discuss with him, as well. An idea on how he might help me settle an outstanding debt. Then it occurred to me he wasn't the person to go to. I glanced at Dino who was obviously trying to figure out how Michael factored into my life, and decided that the man responsible for both Dino's deportation, and return, was more the person to go to.

Jake Porter.

The question remained whether or not I'd be able to find him.

'Who is it?' Efi called.

I resisted giving an eye roll as I got the case out of the closet and handed it to him, feeling a million times better already.

No ... twenty million times better.

'You'd better run, quick, or else you'll be sucked in by the family Metropolis,' I whispered.

'Merry Christmas,' Dino said, appearing next to me and extending his hand. 'I'm Dino.'

Michael looked surprised as he apparently recognized both the face and the name. He shook Dino's hand and said, 'Michael. I just stopped by on an official errand.'

'Official?'

He lifted the briefcase. 'As official as it gets. Have a nice Christmas.'

He turned to leave just as my mother came up to see who was there along with my sister.

I soundly closed the door, unfortunately on Michael's face. Hey, I not only didn't want that case in the house one moment longer, I didn't want anyone to know everything that had happened over the past couple of days. Especially since I had yet to process it all.

It was Christmas. Was it bad that I wanted to leave it that way?

'Sofie!' Thalia gasped. 'That was rude.'

I smiled at her. 'Yes, it was, wasn't it? Let's eat, shall we?'

I linked arms with Dino and headed in the direction of the dining room.

Epilogue

If I liked Christmas, I liked the day after Christmas equally as much. Especially when it fell on the weekend, like now. There was no rush to be anywhere. No gift giving or meal fussing. Oh, at some point, the family would end up gathered at my parents', and food would definitely be everywhere, but there was no stress or worry or clock watching or dressing up. Just a nice, laid back day where the glow continued to burn.

I did, however, have a couple of items on my agenda that morning. One was more of a mission that I happily carried out first thing ... in the rain, of all things.

Had to love New York weather. Blizzards one day; fifty degrees and rain the next. Outside a few black piles that hadn't melted yet, it was hard to believe it had snowed at all.

Perfect for Boxing Day.

I understood in Canada and the UK that's what the day after Christmas was referred to. I remember being curious some years back, thinking it couldn't possibly have to do with the sport, not so close to such a religious holiday, and when I looked it up I liked what it in actuality signified. Outside being dedicated to a saint, it was traditionally a day when employee bonuses were given, in boxes. And seeing as Christmas Eve morning's events had prevented me from distributing them, I decided I was going to hand-deliver the bonuses myself.

When I'd popped up at my cousin Pete's mom's, he had believed it was some sort of reward for having returned the money. I assured him that wasn't the case; doing the right thing was its own reward.

I'd received a give-me-a-break stare in return, which told me he might be regretting his good deed. Well, if I hadn't noticed the way the tips of his ears had gone pink.

Next on the list was Eugene.

His apartment building wasn't all that dissimilar to the one in which I'd originally found Sara Canton. I'd knocked on the door twice, to no response, even though I could hear him inside, presumably arguing again with his 'woman'. Both of them saying things about each other's privates I would have preferred not to hear – ever.

He'd opened the door with an exasperated, 'What?'

I merely handed him the envelope.

'What's this? Hell, the way this nigga's luck is running today, it's probably a summons. If it is, girl, I'ma have to—'

The rest of his sentence was forgotten as he gaped at his bonus.

He'd been caught so off guard he hugged me. Then jumped back and straightened his 'fro as if he'd somehow spoiled his image by showing genuine affection that didn't have a sexual connotation.

His wife's voice sounded somewhere behind him and he'd quickly put the money back in the envelope and tucked it inside the front of his pants. 'Shit, this is the one place she ain't about to look today.' He then leaned toward me. 'Between you and me, OK? I don't want the old lady knowing.'

'About what? Us? Or the money?'

'Us?' He'd flashed me his gold tooth.

I gave him an eye roll. 'Of course, the money. And you don't want her to know, I'm not telling...'

Us.

I shuddered just thinking about it.

Next I stopped by the office where I left a box in the middle of Lenny Nash's desk. Oh, it wasn't much. Just a silver bell with a note that read: 'So you're not so silent.'

The next couple of stops were uneventful, envelopes left in mailboxes because the recipients – including Pamela Coe – hadn't been home.

Then came Rosie...

Oh, yeah, the spunky Puerto Rican and I definitely had our differences. But truth be told, she was still one of my favorite people.

'Sofie!'

She'd thrown her arms around me when she saw me standing in the doorway. I'd beamed nearly as brightly as when Dino had popped up as my Christmas surprise.

Despite the early hour and the fact she didn't

311

have to work, she was dressed to the ghetto nines, all tight top, jeans, clinking jewelry, high heels and higher hair. In fact, there was only one time when I'd seen her not look her 'absolute best' as she liked to call it, and that's because she was doing what she needed to in order to achieve that lofty goal.

I didn't think I'd ever forget her in that green facial mask and curlers helping me look for a missing ferret in the middle of the night.

Wait, there was one other time: when Seth dumped her.

Oh, boy, had that been a sniffling mess. I hoped never to see her in that condition again. Not because she still hadn't been beautiful, but because it had broken *my* heart to see hers so achingly exposed.

She'd been so overjoyed with the bonus and the gifts, it had taken me forever to find a crack in her non-stop chatter about everything and anything so I could make my getaway. But I finally had, and was now back home, letting myself into my apartment where I expected to stay for a few hours doing nothing much more than indulging in the yummy leftovers from yesterday before going over to my parents to eat again and bring home even more leftovers.

I stepped inside, Muffy demonstrating how happy he was for the unexpected return, doing his spring-loaded bit as I tried to close the door behind me.

'Whoa! Tongue away from the mouth, please,' I told him, hanging up my coat and settling him down with a scratch behind the ears. 'Yes, you like that, don't you? Yes, yes, you do.'

Sometimes I didn't know this person who talked to a dog like he was a baby ... but most times I liked her.

Where was Tee?

I still wasn't clear on why the old Tom had chosen my apartment as his winter camping spot, but he kept Muffy company and didn't cause any trouble so I didn't mind.

'Tee?'

Muffy ran past me into my bedroom, then out again, his tongue lolling.

'What is it, boy?'

I thought it was a pretty safe bet he wasn't excited about an intruder, so I passed the empty spot where the sofa used to be, ignoring the boarded-up windows and shotgun-peppered walls, and the bare floors from where I'd stripped them of the bloodstained area rugs and drew to a stop in my bedroom doorway.

Well...

Just when I thought there were no more surprises to be had ...

Turned out the Tom? He wasn't a Tom at all. But rather a Harriet. And that big gut? Hadn't been from overindulgence but because *she* was pregnant.

Hunh.

There on he floor in the corner, on my favorite suede jacket she must have pulled from the doorknob, lay Mama Tee and ... one, two, three, four tiny kittens.

'Aww...' I bent over, slowly outstretched my hand to allow Tee to sniff, before running a finger over their tiny little bodies where they nursed. There seemed to be one of every color.

'My, you've been busy, haven't you ... girl?' I asked Tee.

She batted at my finger.

'OK ... I'll leave you be to recover. But you and I? We have to talk.'

I sat on the edge of my bed, watching as Muffy none too gently sniffed and nudged the kittens with Tee's if not approval, then permission.

How cute was that?

I looked around my room, thinking of something I could use as a better bed for them – although I was pretty sure my coat was ruined – and my gaze caught on the wedding gifts.

Wow. I'd completely forgotten.

I glanced at my clock radio, realizing that at St Demetrios, right about now, my ex-best-friend, Kati, was marrying my ex-groom, Thomas.

I waited for some significant emotion to take root ... but I honestly felt nothing.

I smiled, opened one of the larger wedding gifts from one member or another of Thomas' family, then stared down at the hideous pink and green comforter inside.

Perfect.

I placed the open box on the floor next to Tee, comforter and all, and methodically moved the kitties to lay inside, their immediate mewling sounding too loud to come from something so small.

Tee glared at me and followed.

I stood up and back, watching.

I half expected her to transfer the brood back to my coat. Instead, she finally lay down with what I imagined was a long-suffering sigh, and then began licking her kittens as if to tell them everything was OK and she was back.

How cute was that?

Deciding my presence was not only unneeded but unwanted, I grabbed the throw from the foot of my bed and decided I'd head up to the roof to take advantage of both the break in the rain and the warmer weather. Muffy agreed and followed on my heels, appearing more happy, proud feline father than unrelated canine.

I wasn't surprised to find my next-door neighbor, Sloane, had the same idea. He sat on a folding chair, his too thin body wrapped in a blanket.

'Hey, you,' I greeted him, sitting down on the low brick wall that separated his roof from mine. 'Merry Christmas.'

'Warm greetings yourself, neighbor.'

I took my cell phone out of my pocket and checked it. Two missed-call alerts from my mother, a text from Dino, and a voicemail from my sister who'd tried roping me into shopping today.

Nothing from the man I'd hoped to hear from.

'Keeping out of trouble?' Sloane asked.

I laughed, draping the throw over my shoulders and looking out over the city. 'Of course, not.'

I sighed, clutching my cell in my hand. I loved the view from up here. The lower buildings of Queens stretched to the East River and her fraternal bridges, then gave way to the jagged Manhattan skyline that looked like a complicated skeleton key in the cloudy light.

It was then it struck me what I could do with the rest of my wedding gifts: I could send them to the happy couple.

My smiled widened. Yes ... that's what I would do. Most of them were from Thomas' family, anyway, so it was only right that he should have them.

I made a mental note to arrange to have them delivered tomorrow.

'Uh oh,' Sloane said. 'That naughty smile can't mean anything good.'

'You're right.'

'So long as it doesn't have anything to do with me, I'm cool.'

I liked Sloane. The only time I saw him was on days like today when we both found ourselves on our respective roofs. Sometimes we talked. Often times we didn't.

He was good company.

A cool breeze blew, carrying on it the promise of more rain.

I shivered.

The past week emerged time outside of time somehow, filled with red-nosed reindeer, an old woman who smelled like chocolate chip cookies, a CIS agent that kissed like nobody's business, a hunky hot Aussie who deported

316

the competition and touched me in places others couldn't hope to reach, and yummy Greek bakers who deserved better than me, but who I wanted to eat whole nonetheless.

I don't know. There was something about what went down the other day that made me look at everything a little differently. Compelled me to look at my life a little more closely.

My cell vibrated.

I looked down at the screen, my heart feeling like it had been given a jolt of electricity as I read the familiar name on the screen.

Jake.

He'd sent me a message.

I ran the pad of my thumb over the phone face, not immediately opening the text.

I'd tried contacting him last night only to find my call forwarded to some sort of service that said the number was no longer in service. I'd left a message anyway, outlining what I'd wanted from him.

I'd had no idea if he'd ever get it.

But I'd hoped he might.

And not just because of my unusual request, either.

I clicked to access his text.

'Merry Christmas' was all it said.

Then a video began playing.

I cupped the screen. I heard a thick Russian accent say something along the lines of, 'I'm a naturalized American citizen, you know. You can't do this, you know...'

I squinted, watching as none other than CIS

Agent David Hunter led a cuffed Boris Kazimier to a car and shut him into the back of it.

I raised my brows. Was it me, or had Hunter just looked directly into the camera and winked, presumably at me?

The video stopped.

I held the cell phone tightly to my chest.

Was it wrong for me to think the act of deporting Boris romantic?

I sighed wistfully.

If my reaction had anything to do with Jake not being entirely out of my life ... I wasn't saying.

Not even to myself.

'Good news?' Sloane asked.

I nodded and slid my cell into my pocket. 'Very.'

I don't know. Maybe my mom was right. Maybe I was making the wrong choices. But they were my choices. And, increasingly, circumstances were making it harder and harder to turn back to the girl I used to be. Providing, of course, I was ever interested in doing that.

Which I wasn't.

No. The only path for me now lay ahead. And the more I thought about what I might find ... well, the more hope and promise expanded within me.

And, in the end, wasn't that what all that was about? The future?

I hugged my knees to my chest, closed my eyes and took a deep breath, two words forming in my head: bring it...